Against the Light

By Paula Yourell

Cover design by James P. Wall www.oliver-marketing.com

First published in 2014

This book is dedicated to my family...loving our story so far...

Chapter 1

DAY 1 – Monday

Adela lifted her head off the pillow. Her alcohol-soaked brain was yelling with contempt and her left eye had begun to twitch. The after-party continued in her mouth, her tongue dancing with the bitter taste of excess. She flopped back down against the soft pillow and groaned involuntarily. Swimming her way to the bottom of that vodka bottle had not been the solution it seemed at the time. What a naughty girl she was.

Naughty and hung-over.

She rolled over onto her back, an envelope crumpling between her sweaty fingers.

How long had she been here? The details leading up to this moment were lost inside her brain and in its overindulged capacity it had chosen well its moment to retaliate.

Where was her phone? Feeling around the bed for it, her weak fingers touched only the satin texture of the duvet cover. These were not her sheets. Where was she? Whose bed was she lying on?

Adela strained to lift her head once more, this time struggling to entice one eye fully open.

Come on, brain, I'm sorry, I'll never do that to you again. I promise!

How exactly had she arrived in this plush room, with its cream walls and cherry wood floors? Did any of her friends own such a room?

Nope.

1

Pushing her mind to remember was no good; her focus was fuzzy and her delicate stomach rumbled and complained like an undisciplined child. With only the one eye open, she spied a painting on the wall, next to patterned curtains belted open by thick satin ropes.

Rolling onto her right side was a trick from her younger days, designed to help avoid any unladylike displays of vomiting all over clean bedcovers. What time was it? Was this a hotel? Sure looked like it. But the hangover reprimanded her before her one good eye could investigate any further.

Instead, she lifted the envelope and pulled it apart, getting to the note inside. In fits and starts, her twitching eye read:

"Adela, my drunken friend, you will be safe here. Your host's name is Gregory. He's a bit of an acquired taste. Don't rush him. He's not a bad person, but is rather self-contained. The entire human race has a tendency to irritate the wholly living hell out of him. Being a sort of a hermit, he will tell you to leave, but DON'T GO ANYWHERE. Think of this week as a stay at the Ritz being served by a waiter who has discovered you ran over his dog. Tricky situation, but not bad enough that you're necessarily prepared to leave.

Your friend

James L Brown (JB)

p.s. the suitcase you had packed in such a hurry is at the foot of the bed. I'll come by tomorrow…if Gregory is still prepared to let me in."

Her eyes reunited in darkness. This hangover would thank her for a few more hours of rest and the world could continue to stay far away. Adela drifted off to sleep, the note slipping from her fingers.

#

2

Creases rippled along Gregory's wide forehead, his thick eyebrows slanting down towards his silver-blue eyes. 'What are you up to?'

'Who me?' JB said, smiling through gritted teeth. 'You're like a bored, suspicious housewife, Gregory. You need to get out more.'

He didn't think so. 'Look at the way your feet are jiggling. Know what that tells me?'

'What?'

'You're trying to run from this conversation.' Gregory rubbed at his thick beard.

'Is that so?' Feet now still, JB concentrated wholeheartedly on his shoe laces.

The back door flung open and in padded Gregory's house companion, a two-hundred-and-sixty-pound St Bernard, its bushy tail wagging like a busy cleaner's duster. Norman nudged the door closed by reversing his backside into it.

'Norman, I've saved you some cake.' Gregory laid a plate of cream and sponge on the marble floor beside him.

'Your closest relationship should not be with a *dog*.'

Greg's eyes narrowed. 'Never mind the *hermit* lecture, you're up to something. Now, spill.'

Smoothing back his dusty-brown hair, JB stood up and started to inch his way towards the back door. 'Well,…'

'Well, what?'

His friend inched a little further. 'Okay, here goes…'

Norman gave a cream-filled bark from the back of his throat, as if he understood something peculiar was occurring.

'You know your guest bedroom with the sunken bath large enough to fit an entire girl band in it?'

3

'I do, yes…'

JB reached for the handle. 'Well, I left something on the bed for you.'

'You left *what*?'

'There's a note on the desk; it will explain everything.' With that, he scarpered out the door.

'What the…?'

But his friend had already disappeared down the tree-lined driveway.

'Come on, Norman. Let's figure out why JB wishes to give me such a headache.'

Gregory marched, feet pounding, with Norman padding along behind him. The handle of the bedroom door pushed down easily. In an instant, the "gift" was revealed.

'Girl band my ass.' His eyes absorbed what JB had sneaked into his house and laid out upon one of his king-sized beds. Norman approached, growling gently.

'I think you'd better leave.'

But Norman sat, staring into the face of the sleeping creature before lying down, placing his nose on his paws, and growling.

'Out!'

Gregory pointed towards the door, forcing Norman to skulk away from the bed. Despite obeying his master, a low growl continued deep in Norman's throat.

'Pizza and beer I might understand.' Gregory's face was as flat as his tone. 'But you left me a *woman*.'

He blinked at the set of bronzed limbs, lying haphazardly across the bed. 'What am I supposed to do with *you*?'

The woman's face was embedded into the pillow, although air was making its way in somehow as he could hear the dulcet tones of her best Darth Vader impression heaving out from the back of her throat.

'*Flattering*,' he muttered.

The note was waiting for him at the edge of the desk, just as his traitorous friend had instructed.

"I *know* you're a recluse, Gregory, but I need your help. This woman is my friend and she needs somewhere to hide out for a week or so. A sensible man could think of nowhere more appropriate than the house of a hermit. Plus, I wouldn't walk for a month if I arrived home to my darling Julia with such a girl in tow. You're well aware of sweet Julia's jealousy issues and as the postman of this village, I require legs! You may not appreciate Adela's beauty at this exact moment in time, but I assure you, minus the hangover drool, she is indeed quite gorgeous."

Chapter 2

DAY 2 – Tuesday

'Good morning.' She glanced at the marble kitchen table, set for one. 'I'm Adela. Gregory, I presume?'

The man stared at her before taking a large bite out of an apple. He nodded, crunching slowly.

When JB said he would help, she'd hadn't realised his intention was to bring her into some rich guy's *home*. No wonder he got her drunk first. 'Thanks for putting me up. I—'

Gregory raised his hand. 'Let's get one thing straight; *I* didn't put you anywhere.'

A rush of scarlet stained her cheeks. 'Excuse me?'

'You're thanking me for allowing you to break into my house and hijack my bedroom. In case you were too drunk to notice, I don't go in for welcome mats at my front door. I hate hotels, in fact, and have *never* pretended to be one.'

That was no simple five o'clock shadow on this guy's face. Hadn't he ever heard of a razor? 'You're not very friendly, are you?'

'You think *I'm* the one with boundary issues?'

The man's large dog was eyeing her up, juicy bone style. His kitchen, beaming with light and rich with its beiges, teals and creams, was the size of her entire apartment.

'Well, this is a pleasant start to the day,' she muttered.

He crunched into another section of the apple. 'Why are you in my house?'

A plate of plump croissants tempted her. 'Don't mind if I sit?' she said, swiping one from the top. *What was one more humiliation in her life?* She thought about David, the man she had agreed to marry. What was he doing right now? Words from a recent speech she'd made sprung into her mind.

"There are no mistakes, only lessons."

She imagined David in the audience, watching as she choked on these words. Telling anyone that every mistake they'd ever made was actually a lesson in disguise simply wouldn't wash any more.

Not after what she'd done.

Adela reluctantly noticed the hermit's well-conditioned physique and strong, broad shoulders. Gregory may not have much tolerance for a sharp razor, he did however have some gym equipment knocking about this place and judging by those arms, he wasn't afraid to use it. 'What did JB tell you about me?'

'Nothing.' Gregory opened a sleek, cream, integrated fridge door and landed a milk carton on the table in front of her. 'There's tea in the pot. As you don't seem to be familiar with it—*that* was an invitation.'

'Look, Greg—'

'It's Gregory.'

Ripping a croissant in half had never felt so necessary. 'Look, *Gregory*, I don't make a habit of waking up in the houses of strange men.'

'That is *such* a weight off my mind.'

Damn this man and his shark blue eyes steeling into her. She poured a cup of tea from his designer teapot, trying to keep calm. 'I'll finish my breakfast and go.'

'Good idea. You couldn't possibly stay here.'

'JB told me you'd say that.' *Had he noticed the smirk steamroll across her face?*

'How is that funny?'

He'd noticed all right. 'Because he also instructed me not to leave, regardless of what you might say.'

Gregory poured himself a cup of tea. 'Why *are* you here?'

Her parched mouth welcomed the warm drink. *Why, indeed?* 'It's complicated.'

'It always is, with women like you.'

Judgement was oozing out of this man already. At least the others had judged her with good reason. Hermits were mean. 'What kind of woman do you suppose me to be?'

Shark eyes cleared his throat. 'Beautiful women have a certain view of life; a vain, almost lazy perspective that allows them to believe they can have or do anything they want with little or no moral obligation on their part. The example I would suggest in your case would be breaking and entering. I refer to my earlier comment; my house is not, nor has it ever been, a hotel.'

The second gulp of tea tasted even better than the first. Where was a greasy fry when a girl needed one? Hangover fighting talk was *hard.* 'You think I'm beautiful?'

'That wasn't meant as a compliment.'

Don't think you'll put me down without a fight, Hermit. 'Who gave you the right to condemn every good-looking woman? You've already admitted you don't know anything about me.'

'Nor do I have any inclination to.'

The dog gave a sudden howl.

'That's one jolly dog you've got there. Whatever do you feed it?' *Fat...the dog was fat, plain and simple.* After laying down the cup, she reached out her hand. 'Hello, boy. What's your name?'

'I wouldn't do that if I were you.'

'Why not?'

8

The dog's howl turned into a growl. He started to walk backwards.

'He has a thing about women.'

'What kind of a thing?'

Gregory rubbed the dog's head. 'He doesn't like them.'

'They say dogs are kindred spirits with their owners.' Her mouthy smirk made its return journey. *Control yourself, face!*

'*My* feelings are not reserved solely for women; they extend to people in general.'

'Ever the charmer, Gregory. Where did you learn your manners?'

'You're one to ask such a question.'

It was time to leave the table. Breakfast was over. If this man knew why she was here, he would despise her all the more. Why should she stay, against the wishes of a bearded freak with the mean dog? Wasn't she depressed enough? But her head was pounding and she wasn't ready to face the outside world. Why had JB brought her here, of all places? Her friend had been trying to help her, but it was a mistake to intrude on this man; she could feel it.

A deep loneliness rose up from inside of her. Rejected even by a *dog*.

Adela imagined the empty space in her bed where David would never again lie; remembering the look on his face when he'd confronted her. The moment everything had changed.

'And if I refuse to leave?' she said, trying to avoid eye contact with him, instead giving the dog her best evil-eyebrow.

Gregory's hurricane hands whipped the teapot from the table . 'If you refuse to leave?'

'Yes, if I refuse to leave…what then?'

Teapot abandoned in the sink, his next stop, the freezer. He turned to her, glaring. 'Then I had better take out a second portion of lasagne.'

Chapter 3

'Knock, knock.' JB's head appeared around the door. 'Anyone at home?'

Norman uncurled himself from his basket and padded over to JB, his tongue hanging out the side of his gooey mouth. The skin on Norman's head shook from side to side with the exuberance of JB's rub.

'Hello, big fella.'

'Ah, look, Norman, it's our favourite postman.' Gregory's gaze left his laptop, instead casting an intense glare in the direction of his friend. 'Letters and packages, fine, but what you delivered here yesterday is outside the terms and conditions of your employment.'

'Where is she?'

'Attending to her reflection, probably.'

'Look, I'm sorry about landing her on you.' The arm of the beige leather chair sagged under JB's weight. 'But she's totally adorable; worth the inconvenience, don't you think?'

'Truly,' he said, closing the lid on his laptop. 'You know how to spoil me.'

'You're *very* mad, then?'

'Yes, I believe I am.' The skin beneath his watch was making him itch. That woman kept twisting his words earlier, trying to make him feel bad for not being delighted with the intrusion. Well, *he* wouldn't play pretend like most people did. It wasn't in his nature to do so. 'Why did you leave a *woman* in my house?'

Adela appeared at the door, her formerly blonde hair now the colour of ebony.

11

Observing the change, Gregory frowned. 'Well, *this* isn't strange at all!'

A whistle escaped JB's rounded lips. 'Hey there, sexy boots, I like the new hair. Makes you look so *different*; from fun and frolicking surfer chick to dark and mysterious sex siren.'

'Do you want to tell Gregory or will I?' Her pool green eyes flickered.

'Didn't you recognise her…with the blonde hair, I mean?'

Recognise her? A pair of skinny jeans and a striped navy-and-white top skimmed her toned body. Gregory had only met her once but yes, he recognised her. 'Nope.'

'Adela's quite famous, actually.'

He noticed the blush rising in her cheeks. *Embarrassment.* 'Famous for what?'

'She's a bestselling author.'

'Wrote a nice story, did you? Delightful. Yet again, though, I find myself wondering what you're doing in my house.'

'Adela had a run-in with the media. You know how it is these days. They can find you anywhere.'

'Except here?'

JB clicked his fingers. 'Exactly!'

The bottom of Gregory's coffee mug left a wet brown ring on the wooden table. He attempted to mop it up with his finger. 'Does your girlfriend know about your need to rescue such successful women from themselves?'

'It's not like that. Adela and I are old friends…from college.' JB's usually clear cheeks began to glow pink.

Adela's nose wrinkled. 'Looking for a bit of drama where there is none?'

'Julia knows Adela too,' JB said, slipping his index finger inside his shirt collar, as if to fix it. 'I just haven't yet mentioned that Adela's staying in the village. To be honest, I don't want to further antagonise her. Harry's still

12

feeding three times a night and Julia's annoyed enough with me as it is because I'm too tired for sex, even though *she's* too tired for sex. She cries every time she has a shower because her hair keeps falling out.'

'Poor, Julia!' Adela's head nodded in sympathy.

'The doctor says that's normal after having a baby, but it's freaking Julia out.' JB's pout would have rivalled that of any top model. 'And as for the stretch marks, she talks incessantly about the attack of those silver snakes on her body. I don't know what to be saying to her.'

Gregory didn't care about Julia's body issues. He turned to Adela. 'For how long do you intend to vacate your life by intruding on mine?'

'Jeez, be nice, would you?' JB said, shaking his head. 'Give the girl a break.'

'A week or so,' she said, maintaining eye contact with him.

Extended gaze, no dilated pupils; *hostile little creature, aren't you?* 'Fine!' Gregory's nostrils widened. 'But let me make this clear to both of you. I want as little disruption to my life as possible. I'll give you the grand tour later, and afterwards, you do your thing and I'll do mine. It's a big house; I guess we'll survive it.'

'Fine,' she said, her lips barely moving, her arms and ankles crossed as she leaned against the doorway. 'Thanks for your hospitality.'

'You're welcome.' He took note of her defensive gestures before turning his attention to JB. 'And as for *you*, James L Brown; I don't care how much the village likes you as their postman, if you ever do this to me again, *I'll redirect my post!*'

A relieved grin spread all over JB's baby face. 'Sure, sure. *Excellent.* Glad that's sorted.'

Silver hat pulled down on her head, Adela strolled across the room and linked JB by the arm. 'Come on, friend. You're taking me for a walk into the village. I desperately need some air.'

JB's overexposed grin got even brighter, as if they'd all become old friends. A quick pat on Norman's head and away the traitorous postman went with his surprise guest.

The window held Gregory's gaze, even after the pair had gone, the empty field beyond the glass so out of place amongst the beautiful shrubs and trees surrounding it. His gardener, John, was clearing out the shed next to it. Gregory could never quite bring himself to set in motion his plans for the field. The old man was laying all the gardening tools out on the grass, busy with the tasks of spring.

He would kill JB properly when all this was over. His home required no lodger. Why had JB not left well enough alone? A good citizen, Gregory's taxes were always paid in full and his house was well maintained. Using a keyboard and a credit card, he did his bit for charity, but he'd made a choice a long time ago regarding the direction he wanted his life to go. He was entitled to live his life as he saw fit. So what if the rest of the world didn't understand? His choices were…his.

Chapter 4

JB nodded to the man emptying Gregory's shed.

'Who's he?' Adela asked.

'The name's John. Works for Gregory on and off.'

The tips of her shoes played with the stones scattered about the driveway. 'So Gregory *does* manage to speak to some of the people from the village?'

'Not if he can help it. John does his thing; Gregory leaves him to it.'

'Seems to be Gregory's way. I have to admit his house is unreal, but what were you thinking, bringing me here?' Adela said, fixing her hat. His house was magnificent but its beauty meant nothing to her, her eyes translating everything to grey. 'I know he's your friend, and I generally try to see the best in people, but that man's a *twig*.'

JB laughed, his feet pressing against the mounds of sodden leaves along the path. 'You didn't think so the first time you met him.'

'I *never* met that man before in my life. Believe me, I'd remember.'

'You really don't recognise him, do you?'

'No, I don't.'

'Remember the New Year's Eve party I had in that flat I shared with those three head bangers in Rathmines in Dublin? You couldn't forget it; one of those eejits smashed the toaster through the bathroom window and almost got us all arrested? Gregory made quite an impression on you, although he was a lot younger, thin as a stick, his hair was shorter, and he didn't have a beard.'

15

'You remember everything, you weirdo.' *That could not be him*! 'Are you kidding me? Why didn't you tell me?'

He nudged her. 'Because you *never* would have let me bring you here, and his house is too much of a treat to miss out on!'

'He was pretty cute back then.' That younger version of Gregory was from another lifetime. His eyes had held Adela's attention during the party. They had sparkled but with warmth instead of ice. No overgrown hair shaded his lower face. The intensity of those moments had come to nothing in the end. Poof! And now here she was. How the circles of time could weave their endless magic. Good magic. Bad magic.

'I'm sure some women would still call him cute,' JB said. 'Although the sensible ones would probably refer to him as unique and difficult. Have you seen the pool yet?'

Water poured into a big, fancy hole. Whatever. 'No.'

A grey-haired lady's reaction to seeing JB from across the other side of the road amused Adela. Her friend lived a postman's life filled with waving, open-mouthed smiles and idle conversations.

'The jacuzzi's a floating tub.' JB raised his precise blonde eyebrows. 'It looks out onto Gregory's landscaped mini garden. Plus, there's a fire built into the wall next to it, to keep your chillies warm on a cold, winter's day.'

'You've always enjoyed the good life, JB.'

'Whenever and wherever I can get it!'

They turned the corner and made their way onto the main street. 'But doesn't it seem a ridiculous size of a house for one man and his overweight dog?'

'Ah, but now he has *you*! Plenty of room for three!' JB said, wiping imaginary dirt off the cuffs of his sleeves and pulling a funny face at her.

Old paint was peeling from the walls of the buildings and bits of rubbish scattered both sides of the road. One shop had a letter missing from its name that the owner hadn't bothered to replace. Windows were clouded and grimy. Adela noticed a wooden sign, attached to a six-foot pole, buried into the overgrown grass along the edge of a garden. It read, "Away With You".

She pointed to it. 'What's that all about?'

'Oh, Mad Margaret's responsible. She and a few of the village ladies went to some fortune teller who told them this whole place was cursed! I ask you! Mad Margaret loves the drama; she took it to heart, as you can see by the sign!'

A giggle escaped Adela's lips. 'Crazy people!'

'Now, where shall I bring you? The village shop, pub or petrol station? Each is delightful in its own special way. It's a non-stop party in this place. After a week, I promise you won't want to leave.'

'Take me to the pub,' she said, marching on but her thoughts returning to JB's party and to Gregory, before life became complicated, when parties and fun connected one week to the next. She'd always dived into life head first. This attitude had filled her weeks with adventure. Now she longed to rewind time and let it play out differently. She thought again of David. How could she have been so foolish? What was running away from her life for a week going to achieve? And why had the Universe landed her in this depressing place? Penance, karma, bad fortune? Wasn't she supposed to be the one with all the answers? It was obvious she had none.

The door of the pub was stiff on opening. She blinked her eyes to adjust to the darkness of the room, her nose sniffing at the lingering smell of stale alcohol dried into old carpet.

'Vodka, please,' she said to the ruddy-faced woman behind the counter.

17

'Afternoon, Daisy,' JB said, wrapping his knuckles on the wood. 'How's the leg today?'

'I'm rubbing away at it, but this cold weather is killing me.' A large vodka was banged onto the bar, the clear liquid swirling like waves against the sides of the glass. No messing about with this bar woman. 'A pint for yourself, is it?'

'Just an orange juice for me, thanks. I've to drive home to Julia and the little man soon.'

Daisy nodded at Adela. 'Who's the one?'

The one? Cheeky.

'Meet my cousin.' He patted Adela on the head. 'Can't you see the family resemblance? We've the same chin.'

The older woman's eyes almost turned themselves inside out with efforts at squinting in Adela's direction. 'Yeah, sure. Nice to meet you.'

They brought their drinks over to the window booth, the only place where light was shining into the dingy room. 'Your *cousin*?'

'You know how small towns are,' JB said with a wink, 'unless you're family, they'll be convinced you're my bit on the side. And you know the bad reputation postmen have.'

'Ugh, I came here to get away from all that.'

He raised his glass. 'Don't you worry, cuz, you'll be perfectly safe in this sad and sorry place. Do they look the type to have read a book like yours? They wouldn't have a clue who you were, even if your name was stamped all over your face! Airy-fairy notions mean nothing to these people; they're all spuds and spades around here. Well, except Mad Margaret, but she's in a world of her own regardless.'

'Cheers to the most depressing village in Ireland,' she whispered, relaxing a little.

18

They clinked glasses. This was probably not the place a woman in crisis should come to escape her problems!

Gregory slammed the door shut as JB directed a wandering Adela towards the kitchen table. 'Did you have to bring her back here drunk...*again*?'

Tapping his lips, as if deep in thought, JB pondered for a moment. 'I'd say she's more merry than drunk.'

A large hiccup exploded from Adela's half-opened mouth. 'No, I'm drunk. I'm definitely drunk.'

'I'll make her a strong coffee.' Gregory used the task of filling up the kettle to calm down; it beat looking at that pair of eejits. 'And stop hiding behind her, JB. You're really pushing my patience.'

'Well, you're not the most relaxing of hosts. I didn't know she couldn't hold her drink. She's only had a few. She used to be able to drink her share. Not anymore apparently.'

'I'm here, guys.' Adela waved her hands in the air. Then she looked at her hands. 'Maybe I'm invisible.'

'Oh, for God's sake.' Gregory laced the cup with coffee. Instant would do her.

'Remove your beard, hermit,' she said, pointing at him. 'I want to see your face.'

JB's thin lips curved into a helpless smile.

'What happened to you, poster boy? Down a great big hill, you went. Swoosh.' Hiccups escaping again, she turned to JB. 'Did you know, cousin, I'm a great, big magnet?'

'I knew no such thing.'

'Cousin?' Gregory's forceful stirring caused hot drops of coffee to spill out and hit the back of his hand.

'Oh, yes. We're all magnets. We attract...*everything*. We tune into each other's frequencies. How in the hell did I tune into *his*?' Shaking her head solemnly, she made further finger gestures in Gregory's direction before the ceiling took her sudden interest. 'My magnet's broken. It must be broken.'

JB stopped smiling. 'Okay, maybe she *is* drunk.'

Gregory put the coffee on the table in front of her. 'Drink up.'

Her bleary eyes found him. 'Maybe your magnet's broken too. Is your magnet broken?'

So the woman's a lush. He turned to JB. 'I'm going into my office. I'll leave you to clean up the mess.'

#

Gregory looked up from his laptop and stared at the closed, solid oak door for the tenth time. Adela's presence in his house was infuriating, a silly girl playing childish games with her life at his expense. Nobody had yet given him a real explanation as to why she was even here. He clicked into the internet and typed her first name and the word "author". He was about to click search, when he stopped himself and clicked out of the internet altogether. All he needed to know was that she would soon be swishing her multi-coloured hair out of his house.

He left his black leather chair and put a match to the pre-set fire, watching the flames turn the rolled-up papers beneath the sticks and briquettes to cinders. He made himself comfortable over by the window seat and looked out at a robin red breast jumping its way along the wall towards the bird table. They always flocked to his garden, especially in the cold spring weather. The sky was blue but a tinge of frost remained on the tops of the sheltered bushes. He'd been rude to her. But she'd been rude too.

Coming home drunk.

Like his father used to.

Gregory's arm began to itch again. Usually the fire, the birds outside, his work, or a hundred other ideas running around inside his head were enough to make the

20

day vanish without him noticing the moments of time slipping away. Today, it was as if he was stuck inside the ticking of a clock, going nowhere.

He glanced at his wall, a daily ritual in his life, his eyes moving beyond the framed painting of a bountiful orchard, to the word mounted in large letters next to it.

"Freedom."

Same word every day. Same struggle.

'This is no use,' he said, pulling down his sleeve. He needed to get back control of his house. Sitting down once more at his computer, Gregory began to type.

Chapter 5

Adela imagined the tomatoes, mince and herbs bubbling together, covered by their thick roof of pasta and smothered in lashings of creamy cheese sauce as the smell of the lasagne floated out into the hall. An afternoon nap and a long, hot shower later, she was feeling much more sober. She braved entering the kitchen. Norman barked as if to announce her arrival.

Gregory was pouring homemade dressing onto a salad. 'Dinner will be ready in five minutes.'

'Thanks,' she said, desperately wishing she hadn't asked him to remove his beard. 'Look, I'm sorry about earlier. It won't happen again.'

'No, it won't,' he said shortly, continuing to mix his salad leaves.

Breathe, Adela, breathe. 'Anything I can do to help?'

'Get out the filter jug from the fridge; the glasses are in that corner cupboard.'

What was in this hermit's fridge, she wondered. Two homemade pies wrapped in cling film, sitting neatly on top of one another, a rainbow-style fruit salad of mixed berries, grapes and watermelon, a large dish of chicken curry, some sort of casserole, a chocolate gateaux, as well as half a fresh-cream sponge cake. Wow, the fridge of a depressed woman's dreams. 'Did you cook all this yourself?'

'You sound surprised.'

'Not surprised…stinking, rotten jealous. I can hardly find the motivation to ring the takeaway. Your fridge looks like something from a cookery book.'

'Thanks.'

For the first time since she'd arrived, he smiled. It defrosted his face, a little less ice around the eyes. She observed her surroundings. Gregory must have literally poured money into this L-shaped kitchen, which had three parts to it: the cooking area, the dining area, and an expensive cream leather suite of furniture over the other side, a place in which to relax with a good book or a glass of wine.

A few ideas teased inside her.

Gregory's taste was impeccable.

Cooking was more than a requirement to him, it was an art.

A copy of Oklahoma sat on the shelf next to his TV.

Perhaps Gregory's tastes didn't extend to women. Maybe he had a boyfriend tucked away upstairs in one of his many bedrooms, waiting to be fed grapes! She giggled at the image.

Gregory laid a plate of lasagne in front of her. 'Enjoy.'

'Thank you.' The first bite tasted so good, she could practically feel her arteries hardening. Her plate of food was devoured with not a word spoken until after the final mouthful. 'Delicious.'

'So you said.' He continued eating.

Awkward. What now? 'We've met before, you know.'

'Really?' He stopped eating and looked up at her, his fork leaning against the edge of his plate. 'When?'

She tried to see the man from before in him, but her imagination wasn't up to it. 'At one of JB's parties…years ago.'

He seemed to be enjoying himself, staring at her like a doctor examining a skin disease. Was that a sparkle in his eye, a fraction of something she recognised from before? She searched for a hint of recognition on his face, but it had closed up shop, remaining dead pan, the creases of his mouth hiding out behind his thick wall of facial hair.

'I don't remember.'

'Of course you don't.' How she wanted to escape the proximity of this heated silence. 'Shall I make tea?'

'Sure.'

What would this man spend his time thinking about, sitting at his kitchen table, surrounded by so much silence? Not his next trip to the barbers, that was for sure.

'I'll give you the grand tour of the house afterwards,' he said.

Was that a mildly softer tone in his voice? Maybe he was happy that she was now sober and not trying to undress his face. How embarrassing. She longed to talk to David. JB had given her a new phone and kept her one, so she wouldn't weaken, use it, and be traced to the hermit's mansion. Such was JB's over-the-top spy theory, but she decided to go with it. David would probably never speak to her again. She missed his voice and his all-encompassing hugs. A week ago she'd been thinking about wedding dresses. But a week ago, her life had also been on fire, full of wedding plans and secret pains.

Even before the lid was blown off her relationship, she had known something was about to change…it had to, a volcano bubbling beneath the surface, unstoppable against a violent eruption. She had not imagined sitting in some stranger's kitchen, eating his food, intruding on his odd routines. When had she become this person? Ducking and diving, gulping and hiding. The media wanted to expose her whole life to the light, pinning her up like an x-ray. She no longer felt like a player in a real life, taken out of the game for foul play.

They drank their tea in almost complete silence, a usual pastime for hermits, she supposed. Not for her, she generally had four or five different distractions on the go

24

at once: her mobile, her laptop, the TV, checking social media updates, the list went on and on. Here, she was forced to concentrate on nothing other than tea-drinking and her mind was rallying against it.

At least she was about to get a tour of the house, a masterpiece from what she'd seen so far. That would kill another ten whole minutes. What did one man want with so many rooms? Gregory was surrounded by so much space, reams of silence lying about everywhere. How could anyone be content with the demands of constant solitude? The ways of a hermit would never make sense to her.

#

Gregory led her down the hallway. Her feet sunk into the plush, beige carpet.

'My office is over there. The dining room is through here.' He opened a doorway on the right. The room was big enough to hold a dining table with the capacity to seat at least fourteen people. The artwork on the walls was co-ordinated with the teal and beige theme of many of his rooms. Why he had chosen an oversized table? *Who did hermits invite to dinner?*

'It's beautiful.'

Still, Adela felt like a fake, fussing and fawning over his home. Having spent the last year in hotels all around the world, she was sick of interiorly-designed spaces and luxurious yet unfamiliar places. Something was definitely wrong with her. The colour had faded from her life. She thought back to those people she used to notice on the buses, going in and out of Dublin every day; their faces etched with undisguised sadness, weighing upon them like layers of old, wet newspaper. How terrible it had seemed that life should carve people in this way. Yet here *she* was, stuck like glue inside such a mould. She felt as grey as clouds in winter, her heart all bent out of shape.

Hotel rooms, swimming pools, a different restaurant every night…it should have been wonderful, yet the dishes were tasteless, the rooms banal, the packing and moving and fussing enough to make her long to climb to the peak of the highest mountain and try to shine some sunlight back into her jaded heart. What happened to planning a wedding, dreaming of walking down the aisle, wondering about honeymoons and flower arrangements? She was young and some would say beautiful; she was supposed to be happy, not get stuck in this cesspool of darkness.

Gregory escorted her out into the pool area, contained within a courtyard in the centre of the house, a glass roof dazzling above it. 'There's no lifeguard on duty so try not to drown.'

'You must be some amazing kind of rich.' She spied the Jacuzzi across the courtyard, through two glass walls. 'Those depressed village people must *despise* you.'

'You're a blunt sort of a person,' he said, leading her back out into the hallway.

'Why did you choose to build a mansion in a place like this? It doesn't exactly blend in with the rest of the village.'

He shrugged. 'It seemed like a good idea at the time.'

'Thanks for letting me stay. I'm sorry JB brought me here in a cloak and dagger manner. I don't usually arrive to my destination with half a bottle of vodka in tow.'

'JB does like to think of himself as a bit of a secret agent, always planning his next covert mission; you being his latest.'

'He probably sleeps in his suit. He's a good friend, on that we can agree.' She yawned. 'Well, I guess it's time I hit the sack. Thanks for the tour.'

26

'Goodnight,' he said, before walking back towards the kitchen.

Adela watched him until he disappeared, wondering how she would cope with making small talk with a bearded hermit for an entire week.

Chapter 6

DAY 3 – Wednesday

'Do you need anything from the village?' she said, zipping up her jacket. 'I'm taking a walk.'

He turned on the dishwasher with the determined press of a button. 'Like a native already.'

'Someone has to be,' she replied. Her hat fit snugly over her ears. *Did everything he said have to sound like an insult?* 'Are there any nice places to walk around here?'

'Go across the bridge and turn right at the next pathway. This brings you along the river, through the forest and back out around into the village from the other side.'

'Thanks.'

Closing the front door, Adela wondered what it must be like to live in such a house. As bad as she was feeling, when she awoke earlier that morning, the spring sun, shining into her bedroom, rekindled something in her. Maybe her heart wasn't as hopeless as she'd presumed. Jeez, she was indeed a glass-half-full person this morning! She even had to admit how much she liked his teal-coloured front door.

Pity about its owner.

And now the ghost of vodka past felt like it was catching up with her; her head was hurting and she needed to get some air.

On the way down the lane, she tried to contact David. Yet again, the phone rang out.

Her sister was on the other side of the world on business, so instead she dialled her mother's number.

'Hi Mam. It's me. Yes, I'm okay.'

Her mother ranted about journalists badgering her.

'I'm sorry, I know it's upsetting.'

'Regardless of whether or not we go to Mass every week, we're a good Catholic family, Adela. Your father doesn't want to leave the house for the embarrassment of it. You've made a show of us all. Our whole neighbourhood bought that silly book of yours and now you're a laughing stock, we all are. Mrs Murphy overheard Mrs Johnston calling you a hypocrite of the worst kind. What were you *thinking*?'

Adela wiped away tears she couldn't prevent from rolling down her cheeks, stung by the deeper hypocrisy of the situation. 'It was stupid of me, Mam. I do know that. Sure, doesn't our family always give the neighbours plenty to accompany their cups of tea? Less calories in the bit of gossip, and them with their gobs good and bloated from all that bile.'

'Adela, stop!'

'Look, Mam, you know I'm sorry. I've told you a hundred times. I've got to go. I'll talk to you soon.'

Gregory no longer seemed the worst of her problems and she understood exactly why she had stayed here, despite his obvious attempts to get her to leave. Adela kept her hat pulled down and her coat pulled up. The last thing she needed was for the press to discover her hiding out in this sad, little village. She felt like one of those leaves, lying cold and flat in the gutter.

Please let David call.

That damned waiter, those ridiculous cocktails, the confusion, the desire to be free from the nagging pain, the hopelessness. She had boycotted her intuition for a truly forgettable series of drunken moments. David would never forgive her...*why should he?*

29

The woman from behind the bar was standing outside her pub. Adela quickly crossed the road so she wouldn't have to make polite conversation, but as she got closer, it was clear the woman was too pre-occupied with matters of her own to bother about some uninterested stranger. But Adela did not remain uninterested for long.

'Mother, it's *not* snowing outside. Come back inside with me...*please.*'

A slight, elderly woman, with a toothless grin on her face, continued dancing, lifting the sides of her long skirt and kicking the imaginary snow. 'Go get me a carrot, missus,' she yelled. 'A snowman needs a nose. But first, we dance!'

The little woman skipped and hopped, twirling in circles. 'Hee...hee. La, la, la...come on, missus.'

Daisy wiped her forehead in frustration, the other hand on her hip. 'We'll make snowmen later, Mam. Come back inside for a minute. I've a nice cheese sandwich and a cup of tea waiting for you.'

The woman bent down and started rolling an imaginary snowball. Adela had to admit this lady was flexible for a woman of her age. The dry ground was not ruining her fun. She continued rolling all the way up the street, until the ball was as big as an invisible snowman's head. Standing up, she dusted off her hands with satisfaction and turned to Daisy. 'Did you get that carrot, missus?'

Daisy glanced across the road, her eyes registering Adela. 'Morning.'

'Morning,' Adela said, embarrassed at being caught watching.

Daisy turned to her mother. 'The carrots are this way. Let's go on the hunt for a nice big one, eh?'

The old woman rolled her imaginary snowball to the edge of the wall. 'I'll leave his head here until we get back, okay, missus?'

'Okay, Mam.'

The woman held out her hand and Daisy grasped it, like a mother would a child's. The woman chattered all the way into the pub. What kind of venom was Daisy currently feeling towards carrots? Maybe a moaning mother on the other end of a phone wasn't so bad after all.

The bridge lay up ahead. It was probably the prettiest part of the whole village. Stone upon stone, each one nothing without the other. Adela stopped and looked over the side, watching the water rush downstream. To the left was the path Gregory had suggested she take. Three people were standing, two being reprimanded by a lanky, uniformed officer with an interest in waggling his long, bony finger. The girl's head was down, arms folded, knees held tight together. The boy, who couldn't have been more than fourteen or fifteen, kept glancing over his shoulder, shuffling his feet into the dirt.

Adela continued over the bridge and turned onto the path, earwigging into their conversation as she passed.

'Morning,' she said, making eye contact with the girl, who glared back at her.

'Good morning,' the officer replied, blinking a number of times, surveying Adela, before returning to his conversation. 'Get home with the pair of you and no more rubbish, you hear?'

Teenage grumbling followed, but Adela heard no more. She noticed a worn path down to the water. Deciding to follow it, the dry dirt along the path quickly coated her runners with dust. A makeshift sign stood beside a pile of stones.

"Throw a Stone into the River. Then Replace."

No doubt this was Mad Margaret's doing. But Adela could see from the pile of stones that the villagers took heed of Margaret's spooky talk. Curse, indeed!

Adela marched back up the path and deeper into the forest. The noise of the river filled her ears and the hard ground kneaded her feet. The air was warm on her tired skin, the sun shining down through the branches of the trees, like diamonds reflecting light into her troubled eyes. David re-entered her mind, a teasing memory of lying against him, her arms wrapped around his chest. Her future had dissolved into an unconfirmed mess.

She started to run, the trees coming at her, faster and faster. Her heart thumped in her chest. The beat of her breath rushed in her ears, sweat filling every pore of her body. Her feet thudded brutally into the dirt, drumming in rhythm with the madness of her world. Muscles aching. Mind racing. One question kept repeating in her mind.

'What have I done?'

Chapter 7

Still hot and bothered from her run, Adela made a trip into the village shop. She knew immediately she was looking at Mad Margaret.

This woman had an oriental look about her, but what most struck Adela was her hair. Coloured jet black, Mad Margaret's hair had a life all of its own. It stood high on top of her head, backcombed and away from her face, diamanté clips adding sparkle against the harsh shop lights. Her lipstick was berry red and her eyes covered with thick lines of harsh black eyeliner. Her blue dress was cut low enough to reveal a decent cleavage and her belt matched her lipstick. Adela could picture this woman painting away at her "curse" signs, carefully deciding which colour and font to use to capture the attention of her public.

Adela browsed through the magazines in the shop. Her heart stopped when she spied a picture of herself and David on the front cover of one of them, a jagged line between them, indicating their split.

'Oh, Jesus,' she cried, grabbing the three copies of the magazine and stuffing them behind the Irelands Only collection.

'You okay there, love?' Margaret said, appearing at her shoulder.

Adela jumped. 'Sure. Fine. Great. Couldn't be better.'

Margaret gave her a whopper of a smile. Behind the costume drama, Adela could tell she was a pretty lady.

'You must be JB's cousin! I hear you're staying up with that Gregory fellow. Daisy told me about you. There are not too many people in this village who come with a set of cheekbones like yours, that's for sure.'

Adela put out her hand to shake Margaret's and was horrified when Margaret saw her flinch.

But Margaret laughed. 'It's okay, hun. The missing digit freaks everyone out at first.'

'I'm sorry,' Adela said, grabbing a random packet of dish cloths. 'I'll take these.'

Mad Margaret raised one spectacularly pencilled eyebrow. 'Doing Gregory's cleaning? How disappointing. Daisy and I placed no bets on *that*!'

'What were you expecting? In fact, no, don't tell me.'

Margaret let out a funny little whoop. 'Never mind us, we'd bet on two flies rolling around a cobweb.'

Adela paid for the unnecessary dish clothes and a bunch of red roses that also caught her eye.

'Aah, that's more like it.' Margaret nodded at the roses and wiggled her three fingers and thumb in the air.

'I'll be sure to tell Gregory you said hi.'

Margaret beamed at her. She held out Adela's change, but then curled her fingers around the coins. 'Hold on a minute, dear. Could you turn your head sideways for me?'

'Why?'

'Hmmm, there's something about you. Something familiar.'

'You must be mistaking me for someone else. I've never met you before in my life. I'd remember.'

Pausing, Margaret handed her the coins. 'Come back and see me sometime, on the condition it's not cleaning products you're buying. You tell Gregory to cop himself on!'

Despite the bad mood created by the conversation with her mother, thinking of Mad Margaret left Adela grinning all the way back to the house.

The back door was unlocked and the house toasty warm when Adela arrived home. She strolled into the kitchen, again hit by the glory of its perfect design. There was no sign of Norman or Gregory, but the house was so big they could easily be occupied in any other amount of rooms.

Dish cloths and roses discarded on the countertop, Adela went to the cupboard for a glass. Midway through pouring water from the filter jug, she noticed a new feature on the wall next to the door. The jug half-dropped out of her hand, landing onto the counter with a thud. Gregory had posted a notice in her honour.

Rules for the Week:
1. No unnecessary pretence at friendship
2. No drunken dramatics, day or night
3. No prying or crying
4. No use of female charm offensives
5. No flowers or perfumes in the house - Norman has allergies
6. No trying to bond with Norman - women put him off his food

'You have to be kidding me,' she said, re-reading his list. 'Seriously, Universe, what *am* I doing here? You intend on punishing me, don't you? How else would I have attracted this gobshite into my life?'

'By gobshite, I presume you mean my son?'

Adela spun around to find a lady standing at the doorway, blonde hair all sleek and smooth, four-inch heels on her tiny feet and wearing a pretty, black and white swing coat.

'I know this is perhaps an obvious statement but you weren't meant to hear that.'

The woman smiled and Adela could see glimpses of Gregory in her, but with warmth in her soft, blue eyes that he did not possess.

'I'll say nothing if you tell me why you're in my son's kitchen? Not that I'm complaining. Gregory could do with someone like you to shake him out of his comfort zone.'

'I'm an old friend of JB's. Gregory's helping me out. I'm staying here for a few days.'

The woman's fingers played with the large black buttons on her coat. 'Press still hounding you then?'

Adela stiffened. 'You know who I am?'

She nodded, removing her coat and throwing it across the arm of the couch. 'I sure do, despite your change of hair colour. My facial recognition is excellent. You're even prettier in the flesh. My, my, I never thought I'd find *you* in my Gregory's house.'

'Sorry about insulting him.'

The woman laughed, displaying teeth whiter than her age would naturally entertain. 'I'll forgive you because you're famous.'

'In my defence, he doesn't like me very much either, although I have been highly intoxicated for a lot of our time together, which probably hasn't helped.'

The hint of a tattoo crept up above the collar of the woman's blouse. 'You've had a difficult couple of weeks.'

'You could say that,' Adela said with a sigh. 'Speaking of the need to drink, I was down in the village. Are you familiar with it?'

'I should be.' She kicked off her heels. 'Gregory grew up here. I still own a house across in Riverbank. I'm Nancy, by the way!'

She had perfectly manicured toenails. This Nancy was exceptionally well-maintained.

'Do you know the woman who works in the pub—Daisy?'

Nancy laughed. 'Everyone knows Daisy. She's the owner. Well, it's her mother's pub but Daisy as good as owns it.'

'How long has her mother been sick?'

'About six or seven years now. Although, Elenora was always a quirky old soul. She's a brat! Poor Daisy has a tough time with her.'

'She was trying to make a snowman today. She's a lively little woman.'

'Daisy handles her pretty well.'

'And as for Mad Margaret and her curse! I met her today too.'

Nancy rubbed the polished nail of her middle finger against the soft skin on the inside of her thumb. 'Yes, her signs spook everyone out, but nobody is prepared to take them down. She has the whole village convinced. You won't forget Margaret in a hurry.'

'No.'

Releasing the back zip of her handbag allowed Nancy the quick retrieval of a nail file. 'By the way, a word of advice when it comes to my son...'

Adela's mind returned to the irritable hermit. 'Leave?'

'Not quite,' she said, scraping the file in sharp motions along the nail of her middle finger. 'He's a bit of an expert when it comes to reading people. If you're having bad thoughts about him, he'll know it.'

'Oops.'

Nancy grinned.

'Does he have a girlfriend?'

His mother gave a slight shrug, blew on her nail and tidied away her nail file. 'Not that I've been recently introduced to.'

'Boyfriend?'

'Boyfriend?' A chuckle and a quick search for tea bags later, Nancy asked, 'was it the sewing thing?'

'Sewing? No. But have you seen his collection of musicals?'

Nancy's laugh turned to a gentle smile, as she puffed up her hair with the palms of her hands. 'He used to be a real charmer.'

'What happened?'

'He turned his attention to money and success. As you can tell, he's a very rich man. Wasn't always that way. Growing up, we had a little less than nothing. Greg probably won't ever tell you this, but his father was a drunkard with not too much intelligence swinging about between those oversized ears of his. Greg got his determination and his brains from me and his tolerance from dear old daddykins. Swings and roundabouts.'

Adela had to restrain herself from hugging this kind, open woman. 'I'd be grateful if you didn't tell anyone about me being here. I just need a few more days before I face the onslaught.'

Nancy handed her a cup of tea. 'Of course, dear. I read your book, you know. I like that sort of thing.'

Adela's head drooped, shame cornering her from every direction. 'Oh.'

Nancy lifted her chin with the tip of her index finger. 'Maybe you should read it yourself? You've never needed your own advice more.'

'Fools advice is what that book contains. Easy words to read but impossible to follow through on.' Adela looked into the comforting face of this woman. 'You have no idea how much I wish that book had never been written. It's ruined my life.'

'Ruined your life, indeed!' Nancy's warmth was infectious. 'Nothing is ruined. You're exactly where you're meant to be.'

'I'm not sure my fiancé would agree with you.'

38

'Ah, but this isn't *his* story, Adela. It's yours. Don't let one mistake make you doubt yourself. Even bestselling authors are understood to be human.'

'I don't expect the world to understand why I did what I did, when I don't understand it myself. I do love my fiancé.'

'David?'

She nodded. 'I somehow ruined it…for what?'

'Everything changes, Adela. This nightmare won't last forever.'

'Mother…' Gregory laid Norman's lead on the counter.

As graceful as a dancer, Nancy moved to hug her son. 'Darling, I've met your new house guest. She's simply charming.'

'So I'm told,' Gregory said, spying the red roses lying on the counter next to Norman's lead.

Unable to help a quick glance at his list of rules, and another at the roses, Adela continued to drink her tea in perfect silence.

Nancy, who didn't miss a trick, swiped the roses out from under his nose. 'It's time you had flowers in your house, Gregory. Now pass me down that jar, it'll do nicely as a vase.'

Chapter 8

Gregory retreated to his office for an hour after his mother had finally drunk the last drop of tea from her cup. He spent most of that hour mulling over his dissatisfaction at having Adela in his home. His mother's visit couldn't have come at a worse time. That look in her eye said, "Hmmm, interesting situation you've got here, son".

This situation called for crepes, with a double pouring of maple syrup. Adela had said nothing about his list of rules, instead she'd chatted away with his mother, like they were long lost friends. To his utter frustration, they were using some kind of secretive female code that he couldn't quite crack.

He opened the door to his kitchen and there, plain as mud, posted on the wall next to his own list of rules, was a second list. His jaw dropped as he read it.

ADELA'S RULES FOR THE WEEK
No judgement
No rudeness
No contempt
And for goodness sake, no more lists

Standing back, he compared the two lists. So this was her grand reply to him, telling him off for being so rude.

'Hey,' she said, strolling into the kitchen in a pair of leggings and a vest top. Not a sniff of vodka in sight.

He stepped away from the wall, not wanting her to catch him reading the list.

'Do you mind if I use your gym?' she asked, filling up her water bottle.

So the woman had no intentions of reacting to either list? Well, he would play her at her own game. He poured her a strong smile. 'Work away. I'm making crepes for tea. I'll save you some.'

She thanked him, an odd look passing across her annoyingly pretty face.

Whisking up the batter, he wondered about JB's motivations for bringing such a creature here. If Gregory wouldn't mix with the world, JB would have the world come to Gregory. He wished his friend could understand his life and the choices he'd made. Gregory dealt with people in the course of his work life, just not face to face. The world could get along fine without him.

Half an hour later, crepes sizzling in the pan, he found himself peeking through the clear glass panel into the gym to check whether Adela was yet finished. Her perfume lingered in the air around him. It had a sweetness of summer about it. He had a perfect view of her from where he stood. Adela was stretching one leg out behind her and reaching her hand down to her feet, in a smooth and elegant movement. The woman moved in a way he'd never seen, lost in the music against the slow turns of her body, her skin smooth and glowing. He continued to watch, feeling like he had intruded upon something intimate. The music was haunting, curling its way up into the rhythms of his heart, making it beat too fast, unearthing secret chambers and melting delicately into each dark passageway. Watching her, he was both intoxicated and conflicted. Yet he didn't look away as her body turned and curled, moved and searched. He understood why JB couldn't have brought this woman home to Julia.

Adela stopped and turned towards him, her hands automatically reaching up to her neck. 'Oh, I didn't see you there.'

'Sorry, I didn't mean to intrude.' He opened the door wider, the words falling from his mouth like broken teeth. 'I was wondering if you were ready for your toast.'

'My toast?' she asked, picking up a towel and patting it against her rosy neck.

'Your crepes,' he said. 'I meant your crepes.'

It was a good thing she hadn't the same abilities to read body language as he. His body was suddenly ridiculous, heart beating rapidly and mouth gone dry. His stereotypically male response to her overt femininity irritated him. Served him right for trying to force the rules.

'I'll grab a quick shower and be with you then.'

'No problem.' He closed out the door. Those kinds of feelings reminded him of a life gone by and he wanted no part of them. Why had JB brought Adela into his life? Gregory has long since disconnected from intolerable human emotion. Feeble attempts at a happily ever after were well beyond his control or desire.

#

'You make good crepes,' Adela said, squeezing a large dollop of maple syrup onto her third one.

'Apart from JB and making lists, that's something else we have in common,' he said, 'we both enjoy our food. Why are you eating your crepe like that?'

'Like what?' she mumbled through a large mouthful.

'Before you take each bite, you turn the crepe upside down.'

Swallow first, then answer…only polite. 'Because it makes the most sense to eat it like that.'

'I'm sure it does.'

42

She held out the crepe and pointed to the maple syrup. 'Eating my crepe upside down means a direct maple syrup hit to my tongue. If I eat it the other way, the taste gets lost. I am simply maximising the benefit of this sugary delight.'

'Does this rule apply solely to crepes?'

'Hell, no! Toast with jam or marmalade, or even butter. Try it some time; once you turn it over, you'll never go back.'

'The regular way does me fine.'

'Why am I not surprised?' His wall of rules seemed to glare down at her. 'How long have you nurtured such excessive amounts of hair?'

'Four years.'

'I'm good with a scissors and an open blade, if you're interested.' She licked her fingers. Was this an actual conversation? *Well done, Hermit.*

'No, thanks all the same.'

She spied Norman watching her. Lifting a sliver of crepe from her plate, she dangled it out in front of him. But Norman didn't take the bait. He continued to stare at her, then at the crepe, without moving from his basket.

'Don't you ever get lonely?' she said, giving up on the fat dog, aware that she was pushing the boundaries on yet one more of the hermit's "rules".

'Is that an invitation?' he said lightly.

'Is that an evasion?'

He stood up and lifted his empty plate. 'Coffee?'

'Hmmm, yes please.' The smell of the percolating coffee had kept her company all the way down the corridor. 'Did you decorate the house yourself?'

'I had some help.' He removed two large cups from the bottom cupboard. 'So you thought I was gay?'

'Blame your fridge and DVD collection for that. Plus, your mother tells me you sew? Anyway, so what? I was just asking.'

43

'Are you a lesbian?'

She frowned. 'No.'

'Well, there you have it.' He placed the hot coffee in front of her.

Breathing in its smell always added something to the taste. 'What do you work at, Gregory?'

'Let's just say, I'm good with computers.'

'Good? You must be frigging amazing.'

'Because I'm so rich, you mean?'

'Yeah.'

He sipped his coffee. 'Where did you learn to dance like that?'

'I've always loved music and dancing, yoga too. I like to combine them all together.'

'Hmmm.' His eyes travelled towards the wall of rules.

What had caused a thaw in the tunnel between the hermit's mouth and his brain? JB would be highly impressed.

'Tell me more about this business of you being a magnet,' he said.

Crimson flushed through her cheeks. 'I was under the influence when I said that. You can't throw drunken talk back at a girl—it's not fair play.'

'What did you do?'

'Excuse me?' She gulped, some of the coffee catching in her throat.

'For you to agree to stay in this house with me— what did you do?'

'Are you trying to make me say it or do you seriously not know?'

'Both.'

Another quick sip of coffee provided a moment to think. He was asking her a direct question. She was living in his house, it wasn't unreasonable to ask. But one half-normal conversation didn't make a friendship. She could hardly say it out loud to herself, never mind to some judgemental hermit.

'You really want to know?'

'Yes, I suppose I do.'

Pushing back her chair, she stood up. 'Then look me up online, like everyone else.'

'Adela, wait—'

Her finger directed him to his list of rules. 'I refer to rule number 3. No prying.'

'I was —'

She looked around the kitchen. 'Where are my roses?'

'I got a notion of rule number 5 and threw them out.'

'You dumped my flowers?'

'They drive Norman's nose crazy. He has allergies.'

Her fists clenched by her sides. 'You want to know why I was calling myself a magnet? Because of what I seem to attract into my life. My vodka-induced question to this bizarre Universe was why I happened to attract someone like *you.*'

'Let's get one thing straight - *you* arrived on *my* doorstep, not the other way around,' he said through gritted teeth. 'Maybe if you drank less vodka you might have a better sense of direction.'

'Ugh,' she said, marching towards the door. 'Despite your cooking ability, Hermit, you always manage to leave a sour taste in my mouth. Good evening to you.'

Chapter 9

Gregory typed her name into the search engine. Why shouldn't he learn more about the woman who was sleeping in his home? It was the right thing to do. Only a crazy person would refuse convenient knowledge of his lodger.

"Adela Winters, author."

But Gregory wasn't prepared for what he read next. Adela, the woman whose closest relationship was with a vodka bottle, was also known in certain circles as some type of exotic, insightful mystic.

But this "mystic" had recently been caught cheating on her fiancé—with a waiter. Gregory clicked into the attached photo. That was Adela all right, in all her blonde-haired glory. The headlines were full of one liners, dragging Adela down from her enlightened pedestal. So the poster girl for "zen" had been exposed for being as despairingly human as everyone else.

He clicked into another picture, one of Adela and her fiancé "David", an average-looking man. Gregory read his profile. David did voice overs for television. Poor, deluded bastard. The waiter with whom Adela had done the cheating looked like one of those Italian gods, all thick, dark hair, tanned skin and a toothpaste smile. *David* must have been face-down in humiliation after that fine revelation. No wonder Adela needed somewhere to hide.

From the stories on the internet, both Adela and the ideas in her book had been embraced by the trendy folk. She was extraordinarily beautiful, with her full lips and almond-shaped, bright green eyes. Gregory understood that one look at Adela for many people would simply not be enough, such were her enticing combination of features. She tugged at something in the average person's brain, an insatiable hunger for beautiful things. Mystery was a powerful tool, which her publisher had exploited when they realised Adela had something else to sell, apart from those striking looks.

Of course the media was interested in her. Even Gregory had to admit she was intoxicating in a way that did not feel healthy. He looked once more at the picture of her and David at some event, Adela dressed in a long, red gown, slit almost up to her thigh and cut in a V shape down her back. David was smiling at her and Adela at the camera. He noted their body language. When was this taken? Five months ago. Adela's eyes were smiling but something was not right about the way her body was facing away from David.

'Did you even realise you weren't happy?'

Norman began to whimper and paw at the office door.

'Come here, boy,' he said gently. Norman came over and Gregory stroked his back, but within seconds, Norman had returned to the door.

'You know how to open it, Norman. Off you go.'

With that, Norman pawed open the door and left Gregory on his own. He looked up at that word on his wall.

"Freedom."

His eyes returned to the picture of Adela. Gregory did next what his mother had been badgering him to do for years, something he said he would never in his whole life do: he downloaded a self-help book with the intention of actually reading it.

#

'Who wants another beer?' JB said, opening the fridge.

Adela shook her head. 'None for me, thanks.'

'Me, please,' Gregory said, listening to the soulful tones of Delorentos' "Bullet in a Gun", glad that JB's arrival had forced the pair of them to return to the same room.

'What?' Adela gestured her hands towards him.

'Nothing.' Gregory looked away.

'Seriously, why do you keep staring at me? What have I done to annoy you this time?'

'Nothing,' he insisted.

'You sure?'

'I'm sure.'

JB handed him a cold beer. 'At least you haven't killed each other. That's good, I suppose.'

Gregory turned to Adela. 'The week's not over yet.'

Her stare was sharp. 'We're surviving.'

Gregory did not look away. 'So, who was the waiter?'

Adela almost spit out her mouthful of tea. 'You researched me?'

'You told me to!'

JB laughed nervously. 'You had to wait until *I* was here for this conversation. Great!'

Gregory noticed her unsmiling eyes as she tapped the tips of her fingers against her cup.

'He was nobody.'

'He's somebody now,' JB noted, raising up his shoulders and burying his head down between them.

'A bit of a thrill seeker, are you?'

'Well, yes, actually, but not in the way you mean.' She returned his gaze. 'I made a mistake. No judgement, remember?'

'And where does David feature in this whole scenario?' he said, his face softening.

'Not answering my phone calls, that's where.' She sighed. 'I suppose you also know about my book.'

'Someone who writes a book like that surely sets themselves up for a fall when the reality of life comes knocking at their door?'

JB nudged Adela. 'Greg's mother loves all that sort of airy fairy stuff too. She carries crystals in her handbag and always has some peculiar idea to try when trouble's brewing.'

Gregory thought again of the "Freedom" paintings framed on the walls of his home, the effects of his mother rubbing off on him over the years.

'Look, I'll admit I've made some money from a book that half the world is fascinated by and the other half thinks is bullshit. And I'm not even sure which category I fall into.'

He watched her squirm in her chair. Had one waiter really managed to pull her whole life out from under her? It seemed a high price to pay.

'You don't believe in your own product?'

She turned away from him.

'I'm not judging you; it's just a question.'

JB knocked his bottle against the table. 'Maybe we should talk about something else, eh? Like how Julia almost killed me when Daisy asked her how my cousin was enjoying the village.'

Adela's face brightened. 'Oh, JB, I hope you told Julia what's going on. Maybe I should ring her and explain.'

'It's probably best you don't.' JB patted her hand. 'She already hated you, and that was before the waiter. Julia's a suspicious creature. Women are bloody mad, Adela. And as I've explained to you before, you don't want to be on the wrong side of my one.'

Gregory watched Adela smile, but he could tell there was so much more going on behind it. For all its supposed advice, her book hadn't helped her much. What was he doing, even thinking about reading this woman's

49

ridiculous work of fiction? He'd be glad when she was finally gone from his home and order could once again be restored.

#

JB had returned to his girlfriend and baby, leaving Adela once more alone with the hermit. Gregory had been loosened up by a few beers and Norman kept inching a little closer to her all evening, while still maintaining a distance. He was now resting his face on his front paws and looking at her with his big, sad eyes.

'The title of your book,' Gregory said, moving his beer bottle from side to side, 'was a brave choice.'

'You mean a *stupid* choice.'

'So you *don't* think it contains the "Formula for Happiness" then?'

Did such a thing exist? All those people who had been prepared to snap up copies of her book in the hope that it held life-changing secrets. Was she a con artist? She shivered at the thought. 'I can understand why you may believe the formula needs a bit of tweaking. I'm not the most reliable witness, or so it would seem.'

His eyes revealed a slight thaw. 'I've started to read it.'

She tried to reach down to pet Norman, but he crawled backwards, away from the possibility of her touch. '*My* book?'

'Yep.'

'And what have you learned so far that has amazed the pants off you and will change your life forever?'

Gregory paused, taking a sip of his beer. 'I liked the statement about how every thought we think, every word we speak, and every choice we make is a building block in the construction of our lives.'

'Yes, that is a pretty amazing idea, I suppose.'

'Do you believe our thoughts really have that kind of power?'

She curled her legs up under her. 'I wrote about it, didn't I?'

'It's like that whole law of attraction business?'

'I guess so.'

'So, why hasn't this knowledge saved you from the saga of David and the horny waiter? Where did the formula go wrong?'

'You're kind of nosey…for a hermit,' she said. 'Understanding ideas and living by them are not always the same.'

'What thoughts were *you* thinking that led you to me?'

She shifted the other direction in the chair. 'You give me a shitty list of rules. You read a couple of chapters of my shitty book and you're now attempting to sift through my deepest thoughts? What's going on here?'

'Well, it seems to me that if you believe our thoughts do create our reality, then your thoughts about your relationship with David must have been pretty bad as they led you to cheat on him with the waiter. This leaves me wondering whether you actually love your fiancé.'

'Of course I love him! What about *your* thoughts and your life? Why have *you* created a life of solitary confinement?' she challenged.

'Hardly solitary confinement—I live in a mansion.'

'*Alone.*'

'Don't listen to her, Norman.'

'Okay, you tell me what led you to this life and I'll tell you about the waiter.'

Norman crawled a couple more inches back towards her.

'I don't like people.'

She held out her hands. 'That's it?'

'Simple as that.'

'Okay, if we're doing the short and sweet version, then I've always had a particular weakness for men in white shirts. Hence, *the waiter*.'

'But after doing what you did, how can you be so convinced you love the David guy?'

'What happened with the waiter was a stupid mistake. David was my *fiancé*. Of course I love him.' Why did she feel like a child who'd been caught with her hand in the cookie jar?

'Then you've answered your own question about why I live the way I do. Why would I *want* to live any other way? Love pretends to be pure. I'm not even sure any of us knows the first thing about love. It's a brilliant idea that we can't seem to cope with. Like handing a baby a china cup and expecting him not to break it.'

His answer intrigued her. 'What made *you* so cynical about love?'

Gregory ignored her question, instead glancing at their wall of rules. 'You think David is lost for good?'

'He won't answer my phone calls. He's had his private business splattered all over the newspapers, all over the internet. Could *you* forgive what I've done?'

'Probably not. But I also think everyone's formula for happiness is different. My idea of happiness and yours are poles apart.'

'I like to jump out of planes and climb mountains and you like to make lots of money and teach your dog weird tricks, how to ignore women, open doors and get really fat.'

'Hey, leave poor Norman out of it.' His dog received a consoling pat on the back. 'If you are part of David's formula, he'll forgive you.'

'You really think so?'

'Ah, but as your book would suggest, it's not what *I* think that matters. It's what *you* think. If you have no faith in that as the outcome, how will this Universe of yours find a way to bring it to you?'

'Yeah, I guess you're right.' She pointed to the picture of the orchard on the wall. 'You have that same painting in the bedroom; what's your obsession with apples?'

'You don't like apples?'

It was hard to read his expression from behind all that hair. 'I do, but not the way you do. You even eat them for breakfast; I mean, who eats apples in the morning? Yuck.'

'Maybe they're part of *my* formula for happiness.'

She laughed. 'Maybe, Gregory. Maybe I should start eating apples in the morning and the rest of my life will fall perfectly into place.'

He observed the painting.

Time to stand up and stretch out her legs. 'I should take myself to bed.'

'Yes, indeed.' He lifted himself out of his own chair. 'Goodnight, Adela.'

Would she ever get to see the face behind that four-year-old beard? 'Goodnight, Gregory.'

Adela dumped the remainder of her cup of cold tea down the sink, before strolling out of the kitchen and down the corridor, grateful for the moment of distraction that their conversation had provided her. The bedroom door closed behind her, she lifted up her phone to check its screen.

One message. JB most likely.

No, not JB.

The text was from David.

It read, "We need to talk."

Chapter 10

Adela could hear him breathing down the phone.

'I'm so sorry for hurting you.' She spoke in a whisper, her stomach aching with prickly nerves.

'I don't even know why I rang you back.' The tone of his voice was like cement. 'I always knew you'd let me down. My mother never thought you were good enough for me, even with all the fame. I tried to convince her otherwise; I tried to convince myself, but I should have listened to my gut.'

Is that how he'd really felt, all those times he'd been loving her, wooing her, adoring her? What was real inside the heart of another? Could any of it be trusted?

'David, I made a mistake. A really, ugly messy mistake, which if I could take back I would—'

'Where are you, anyway?'

'Down the country, in some Bed and Breakfast,' she lied. Declaring that she was living in a mansion with a hermit and his food-addicted dog would do nothing to help the situation. 'I had to get away for a while. It was all too intense.'

'You expect my sympathy? You got us into this mess and you're the one who gets to run away,' he shouted. 'You may have been many things in my mind, Adela, but a coward wasn't one of them.'

She closed her eyes, wishing she could run even further. His need for retaliation was understandable, albeit like a hot razor blade slicing through her insides. 'Is there any hope for us, David?'

Silence.

He was thinking…raging.

'Were there more?'

'More what?'

'More men, Adela! Was *he* the first or do you normally do a better job at not getting caught?'

'Of course he was the first! I'm not like that, David. As you're aware, I was having a bad day when it happened. I know that's no excuse. I don't know why I did it.'

'How am I supposed to believe that?' he said. 'You're a liar, that's what you are. A hypocrite.'

'My hypocrisy wasn't intentional.'

'No bonus points for that, I'm afraid.'

More silence.

'I'm sorry.'

He huffed. 'I don't want you to be sorry. Sorry doesn't help me. I trusted you. You've made a fool out of me. Jesus, Adela, we were engaged to be married! I thought what we had together was worth more than the tried-and-tested lines of some goddamn waiter. He made a fool out of you too. Hardly a consolation, but there you have it.'

Her feelings bubbled inside her. She needed a pause, a breath, a moment to find a way through this conversation. David had contacted her to declare his pain in as many combinations as he could vocalise. Their relationship was over. There was no way back from this.

'The public hate you now. You've spoiled everything.'

Please, stop. 'I know.'

'I thought talking to you might help but it makes me feel worse,' he said. 'I can't do this. Goodbye, Adela.'

'Bye.' She sat for the longest time, staring at the painting on the bedroom wall, the phone still in her hand. *Stupid red apples*. That painting didn't tell the whole picture, it didn't show the fallen ones, the worms, the rot, the decay. It showed apples as red dots, perfect in their false simplicity.

It showed nothing as it truly was.

Chapter 11

DAY 4 – Thursday

'I've cooked you some breakfast.' Gregory laid out two plates. 'Sausages, eggs and bacon.'

'Lovely, thanks.'

He'd been up until three in the morning reading her book. 'Sleep well?'

'Not really.' Adela scratched her neck. 'You?'

'Sure,' he lied, lifting two sausages off the grill. The neck scratching--she was uncertain about something. 'The bed not comfortable?'

'Oh, no, it's fine. David rang last night. My brain forgot it needed sleep after that.' Her fingers pressed against the dark circles under her eyes.

'Good news?'

'Afraid not. He wanted to vent.'

'Ah, but he rang you. That's something at least.' *Why was he trying to please her?* Gregory glanced at her hair, loosely thrown back into a bobbin.

'I'm sorry you've had to witness one of the lowest points of my life.'

'Eat up,' he said, placing the plate of food in front of her.

'And now you're being nice to me.' She lifted her knife and fork. 'I must be really pathetic.'

'You're not the first person who ever messed up,' he added, sitting down on the chair next to her. 'Maybe you need to move on.'

'You mean move on from David?' She stabbed a sausage with a fork.

'If there's no other way. You can't force him to forgive you. He'll have to do that all by himself.'

'Will you come for a walk with me? I don't want to face your cursed village alone.'

'I don't do village walks,' he said, placing a lump of soft butter onto a slice of thick white toast. 'Sorry.'

'What's wrong with them, anyway? Why do they feel so cursed?'

'Who, the villagers?'

She nodded.

'Not enough money, not enough jobs, not enough opportunities. People are angry, upset…lost even.'

She lifted her mug of tea. 'You don't ever feel bad, cut off from the misery, hidden away in luxury while the village starves for a mere coat of paint?'

'You think I should feel guilty because I made different choices to the rest of them?'

'I'm asking whether you do feel guilty, not suggesting you should.'

'People attach way too much emotion to money, that's why they remain so far away from having it. They want it all the time. They'll never get it by wanting it so badly. It makes them desperate.'

'It's hard not to be emotional about money when you don't have any,' she said.

'When I was a child, my mother understood what poverty meant, but she was careful not to turn poverty into a state of mind. She never quoted those famous lines such as "money doesn't grow on trees". She put no obstacles in my way.'

'Clever woman, your mother.'

'Yes, she is. I'm comfortable with wealth because I was never made to believe otherwise. Even when all we had to eat was a tin of beans, my mother told me they were magic beans. The people in that village *feel* poor, Adela. Lack is their belief, not mine. I have nothing to feel guilty about. I don't think that money is the root of all evil. I believe I deserve to have wealth, we all do. Those who judge this belief would do well to examine it.'

'So you're saying that you attract wealth because you have wealth?'

'Not quite, I attract wealth because I don't believe wealth is inherently bad,' he said, simply. 'It's your law of attraction at work again.'

'Then where does love fit into your life?'

'Love?'

She pursed her lips and nodded.

'You have no need to feel sorry for me, Adela. I need nobody's pity. You hear JB calling me a hermit and automatically you judge me for it.'

'How do you live with the emptiness? Having nobody…filling all your own spaces. Don't you get bored?'

'Bored?'

'Don't we need more than laptops and swimming pools?'

'I don't need to be saved.' Gregory looked at her squarely. 'I may be a hermit, Adela, but I never implied I was a monk.'

'Oh.' She blushed.

'I don't need what other people need. I don't mind if I'm the only one who understands that. It's time I went for a swim. Enjoy your walk.'

He left wondering what else apart from David was making Adela so unhappy. He was certain from her body language over the last couple of days that she was hiding something. Yes, secrets were whispering and dancing around that woman.

Chapter 12

Adela wandered into the newsagents. She was half-disappointed and half-relieved Mad Margaret was not waving her four fingers from behind the counter today. Adela's intention was to purchase a newspaper and a supply of her favourite, take-the-head-off-you, menthol gum.

Browsing the aisles for no particular reason other than she had the time, she spied that scrawny officer with the long, bony fingers. He happened to look across at her and make eye contact. He put his small packet of washing powder back on the shelf and dandered over to her, his shoulders back, his head up straight and his fly a little undone.

'You following me?' he said in a strong Kerry accent, tapping the toothbrush she had in her hand.

She giggled nervously. Being close to a member of the Garda Siochána always made her feel like her guilty fingers were about to be dipped in ink. 'Surely you're the one supposed to be following *me*?'

He took a step back. 'Why, are you a criminal?'

'Not last time I checked.' She placed the toothbrush back on the shelf.

A large grin displayed a horsey set of slightly buckled teeth. 'One less thing for me to do before I finish up for the day, so.'

'Except a real criminal would never admit to being a criminal, so really you're no further forward.'

'I do like your keen powers of deduction, young lady.' He put his hand out. 'I'm Nigel, local keeper of the peace.'

'I'm Adela. Nice to meet you, Nigel.' His palms were slightly sweaty.

'You were the one watching me in action from the bridge, yes?'

'What had those kids done to get you so riled up?'

'What have those kids *not* done, is more the question. The highlight of their day is to get up my nose! You're new to the village?'

Too many questions. 'I'm here for a few days, that's all, Nigel. I'd better let you get on with your quest to find some real criminals.'

'Tell Gregory I said hello. No eating donuts for this member of the force.' He displayed his haphazard smile once more. 'Small village…people talk. Nice meeting you, Adela.'

Adela grabbed a paper and headed straight for the counter. Nigel had a friendly way about him; she liked how he emphasised the "d" when he said her name. But she couldn't let herself get drawn into anything more than polite chitchat. She had to keep a low profile. These days, with camera phones, as well as a feast of social media avenues, it was almost impossible to go to ground. Changing the colour of her hair would have helped but she wasn't ready for the media to come knocking at her door, looking for juicy answers to their salacious questions.

To avoid heading back to Gregory's quite so soon, Adela decided to treat herself to a coffee in the pub and enjoy a leisurely read of her paper.

'Greetings, JB's cousin.' The smile on Daisy's face was bright today.

'Hi, Daisy.'

'There's a bite in the air this afternoon, although it's not quite cold enough for snow,' Daisy said wryly, rubbing her ruddy red hands together.

Placing her paper on the counter, Adela had two options: ignore Daisy's remark completely or follow it. 'Did your mother have any success in her search for the perfect carrot?'

Daisy leaned on the counter. 'She decided the snow had melted and it was time for tea.'

'How old is she?'

'Ask her yourself, she's behind you!'

Adela turned to find the toothless woman grinning with all her might.

'Now, who might you be?' the woman said.

She reached out her hand. 'I'm Adela. Nice to meet you.'

'Elenora, but you can call me Elly. Daisy, give this nice lady some googleberry juice, on the house!'

'Coming up.'

Elly took Adela by the hand and brought her over to a corner of the pub. 'This is my seat. I run this place from here. See?'

Books, dog-eared magazines, a half-knit scarf and three quarter-eaten bars of chocolate were scattered about two seats pulled together.

'Very nice.'

'You're pretty. Who's your husband? Mine's dead, and good riddance. He was a big prick, you know. Ain't never told that before to anyone, but he was. Isn't that what you young ones say now? A big prick. Don't ever get yourself one of those, you hear me? There's definitely such a thing as too much prick, let me tell you.'

Adela tried not to laugh. 'I'm sure he wasn't all that bad.'

'He's better dead, and that's all I'm saying.'

Daisy arrived over with an orange juice in a long glass, some ice cubes and a green umbrella hanging off the top. 'Googleberry juice special…on the house.'

'I was telling this nice lady that it's going to rain at half three today.'

'My mother is convinced she can control the weather.'

'Made it snow yesterday. Missus doesn't believe she can control anything.'

Daisy straightened her shoulders. 'Doesn't stop me from trying.'

The pub was empty and devoid of any warmth, except for Elly and her googleberry personality.

'And today is our *busy* day! Everything's a struggle to survive here in this village.' Daisy answered Adela's unasked question.

She saw sadness flash in Daisy's eyes. *There must be more to this place than fake snow, a litter problem, a curse and an empty pub?* 'What do you lot do for fun around here?'

Elly pointed to her glass. 'Drinking googleberry juice is nice.'

'Life's small in this place, Adela. Expect more than that and you'll find bitter disappointment alongside your cold beverage.'

'The tourist board will never give you a job if you continue chatting like that.'

'Yes, I suppose you're right. That was a terrible answer. You caught me at a bad time, that's all. But in fairness, we have had the worst luck.' Daisy picked up a glass and her tea towel. 'Did JB tell you the rumour about our little village?'

'He did mention something.'

Daisy leaned forward. 'It's true!'

'You can't be serious, Daisy!'

'Young people dying before their time, the factory ten miles away closing down, half the village losing their jobs, the only café burning to the ground and our doctor of twenty years having a heart attack right in the middle of an appointment with Mad Margaret. The village is falling asunder…cursed, so the gypsy woman with the weird eye told Margaret and Nigel's mother a mere month before the poor woman dropped stone dead.'

'You can package it any way you like, Daisy, but that's called life. What's the craic with Mad Margaret anyway, apart from the curse?'

'Let's just say, she's what a lot of people do for fun around here!' Daisy chuckled. 'She's my best friend…total lunatic. I'm sure you noticed she's half Chinese with a little finger missing on her left hand. You hear her before you see her. She may be fifty-five but she has never lost her crazy! It's no wonder Nigel and Margaret separated. She was too much woman for him, I dare say.'

'Officer Nigel?' Adela lifted her paper.

'You've met Nigel?'

'Just now in the shop.'

'Mad Margaret owns the shop. I think Nigel frequents it to make sure she's still breathing. He never fully trusted her to keep herself alive to the end of each day. Still doesn't. Marriage to Margaret gave poor Nigel blood pressure.'

'He's not forty if he's a day.'

'He's forty-nine, actually. One of those baby faces with that freakishly skinny frame on him. He does amuse me; Nigel is a gentle, caring soul. I'm sure he should have been a social worker or something, not Mr Lock-Up-All-Your-Sins. At fancy dress parties, he always arrives as a skinny, slightly off-putting version of Superman!'

'Daisy, can I tell you something?'

'What?'

'I'm not JB's cousin!'

Daisy patted her on the hand. 'I never thought you were, honey.'

Adela never got reading her newspaper; instead she and Daisy continued to chat as she polished off her googleberry juice. When she felt she had wasted enough of their time, she said her goodbyes to Daisy and Elly, trying not to let that look in Daisy's eyes haunt her.

Elly was a funny, gentle, interesting soul, but that was easy for Adela to say when she could open the door of the depressing pub and walk out. Daisy's surroundings were bitterly drab, a prison of seventies wallpaper, bad odours and bockety furniture. Daisy was a woman in her sixties, yet despite Elly's obvious mental interludes, she was a spritely, joyful being. But Daisy was the parent in their relationship and that had to be hard for a woman of Daisy's age, for a person of any age, she supposed.

Despite the distractions of the village, Adela was unable to stop thinking about her conversation with Gregory. She had judged him as a sad and lonely man when what she was beginning to see was that he was someone more than capable of understanding what being happy meant to him. In a peculiar twist of circumstance, he had instead begun highlighting the shadows stirring within her.

She thought again about David's reaction to the waiter. The look of disgust had seeped into every feature on his face, nestling comfortably. Why had she allowed herself to fall into such a trap? Did all humans go off-course so easily? If that was the case, what was the point of this so-called life? Being human was like a bad joke.

And nobody was laughing.

Adela remembered when life was simpler, when the world expected nothing of her, without all the pulling and dragging, the ripping and shredding of herself, and all for what? The choices she had made; becoming one of the "world's most attractive gurus"…how ridiculous. Women were drawn to her looks, and the words in her book, marketed alongside pictures of her face and the offer of answers to the mysteries of life, had captured the imagination of the people, thirsty for something more than what was visible to them.

She had never intended for all this to happen. Her sister, Lizzie, had uploaded Adela's book onto the internet. The intense whirlwind of destruction began pretty quickly after that. By then it was too late to raise her hand and admit that she wasn't able to live by those words. She had tried when the publishing company offered her a publishing deal. But they didn't care, they saw something that appealed to them and they ran with it. So while the world began to want a bit more of her, she began to want a bit less of the world. They wanted poetic answers to all their repetitive problems and they allowed themselves to believe that she was some great magician, with a trick up her sleeve just for them.

David had loved the public attention. He liked to admire photos of the two of them in magazines or on the internet. Adela felt smaller with every moment of pretence, each lie taking an angry bite out of her. She'd been dragged from place to place, rhyming off formulated answers, smiling in all the right places, yet all the time the voice inside her head reminding her of one very basic fact…whatever these mystical, magical rules of being human were, she didn't understand them.

Chapter 13

Fresh from his swim, Gregory made a call. Adela was walking up the driveway as he slipped the phone back into his pocket.

'How was your walk, dear?' he said, noticing the bright pinkness of her face.

'Had you come with me, you'd know.' She hit him playfully on the back with her gloves before walking past him and into the house.

Norman followed after her. Gregory followed Norman.

'How was your swim?' she asked, opening a kitchen cupboard to get out a glass.

'Wet.' He leaned against the wall.

'I bumped into that Daisy woman, from the pub. And Elly.'

'Did she offer you the juice?'

Adela pretended to look shocked. 'You mean she does that to *all* the customers? I thought I was special.'

'It's Elly's equivalent of a handshake. JB adores Elly. He brings her for a walk every Monday afternoon, once he's finished with the post. Elly turns into a teenager around him. She's as cute as a button, always was. Daisy got her capacity for gossiping from Elly.'

'She was calling a member of the deceased community a big prick.'

'Oh, that'll be the husband. She varies the choice of noun occasionally, by all reports, but the meaning remains the same!'

'I feel sorry for poor Daisy. That's a lot of responsibility for a woman of her age.'

'Don't let Daisy fool you. She's as tough as old boots, that one.' He coughed. 'I finished your book.'

'Oh, *that*.'

'What's the secret?'

'Excuse me?' she said, her front teeth grabbing hold of her bottom lip.

'You're hiding something. Every time I mention the book, you give yourself away.'

'What are you talking about?'

'I can read you, Adela.'

She moved behind the island, holding the glass of water in her hands. 'Then *stop*. I came here to get away from intrusive strangers. Hermits are not supposed to care.'

'I never said I cared.'

'Oh.'

'I'm just stating the facts as I see them. You're hiding from *what* exactly? I no longer believe it's from the David/waiter situation. I think it's something else. The fact that I don't care might make it easier to tell me…or you could call up that waiter, he seems like a friendly fellow.'

'A hermit with a sense of humour…who knew?'

His frosty eyes declared themselves to her.

'Stop trying to get into my head, Hermit! What's on the menu for tonight? Would you like *me* to make dinner?'

'Actually,' he said, moving toward the counter. 'I won't be eating with you tonight.'

'Oh?'

'There's plenty of stuff in the fridge or freezer. The microwave is down there. Help yourself.'

'Thanks.'

He saw that unsheltered look in her eye, defensiveness in her actions. 'But maybe tomorrow night

I'll make us something extra delicious? Crack open a nice bottle of wine. What do you think?'

She moved back and forth on the chair. 'Sure.'

A knock came to the kitchen door and he heard a voice call. 'Hello? Honey, I'm home.'

'The door's open,' Gregory called, glancing at Adela.

The strong, heavy scent of too much perfume greeted them. Next, a bustling blonde appeared, heels clicking through the doorway, all long eyelashes, wide lips, toasted skin and fuchsia-pink nails. She carried with her a brown paper bag inside a plastic one. 'Dinner, Gregory,' she purred, noticing Adela. 'And you are?'

Adela offered her hand. 'A friend of Gregory's. Sorry, I didn't catch your name?'

'Josie,' the woman half-shouted. 'I'm Josie.'

Hands slipping around Josie's upper arms, Gregory began to walk her gently towards the kitchen door. 'You can head over to the den. I opened a bottle of your favourite wine. I'll bring the plates.'

All Norman could do was sneeze and retreat to his basket.

Eyeballs dangerously close to popping, Josie looked Adela up and down from over her shoulder. 'Are you trying to get me drunk, Gregory?'

'Terribly.'

'Well now, that's okay.' Boobs pushed up, shoulders back, Josie's nerves were rattled. 'Don't be too long.'

'I won't.'

She disappeared, leaving Gregory and Adela alone.

He went to the cupboard to lift out two plates. 'You'll get some peace for the evening.'

'You never mentioned you had a girlfriend.'

'Josie's not my girlfriend.'

'Ah,' she said, running her fingers through her hair. 'She's what you meant by "a hermit not a monk."'

'You could say that.'

Adela's hands retreated to her pockets. 'Have a nice evening, so.'

Closing the kitchen door behind him, Gregory went in the direction of the overcooked blonde with all her promises and delights.

He looked back at the kitchen door only once.

Chapter 14

Adela wasn't in the mood to burn the bottoms out of Gregory's expensive pots, so instead she took a stroll in the garden with her mobile phone. Any hunger she might have felt vanished with the arrival of the blonde. Her sister's phone rang out. It would have been nice for Gregory to warn her of his impending dinner guest.

Josie.

Hermit, my ass.

Then again, a man with money like his could have whatever he wanted…whenever he wanted. The rules of his universe had an application all of their own.

'Evening!' The gardener tweaked his cap at her.

'John, I believe? I'm Adela. Nice to meet you.'

He took a surprisingly firm grasp of her hand. 'Nice to meet you too, Adela.'

It was not his age, his baggy jumper or his bottle-green wellies, but the warmth of John's eyes that struck her.

'Do you always work so late, John? You must be freezing.'

He hopped from one foot to another. 'I've got my dancing wellies on, see? Keeps me warm as much as keeps me young. I'm finishing up here now, any road.'

She laughed, noticing some calligraphy writing along the long wooden handle of his spade. Twisting her head slightly, she read:

'"Smiling is evidence of your inner sun. Who says you can't control the weather?"'

'Who's A.S.B?'

John rested his arms on the top of his pitchfork. 'Aidan S. Bryant. He was a philosopher.'

'Where on earth did you come across a spade moonlighting as a philosophy lesson?'

'Oh, it's not just the spade; the whole troop is in on it.' No longer leaning on the pitchfork, he handed it across to her. 'I made them.'

'"Love, displayed, is all."' She laughed. 'I never heard of him.'

'Mr Bryant didn't start off his life so well. He was a fat baby with a big head and delayed speech,' John said, taking the pitchfork from her. 'He did well enough for himself in the end. Had crazy hair though.'

She handed him the spade. 'Is there a Mrs John heating up the oven as we speak?'

'Oven gloves ain't no use where she is, pet. Graveyards don't serve the warmest dinners.'

'Oh, sorry,' she said, putting her hand to her mouth.

'Are you kidding me? She was lucky all her life, girlie. No need to be sorry for her or me. I'm going home to a nice stew I've been heating up on my slow cooker since this morning.'

'Do you live close by?'

He nodded. 'Aye, I do.'

Adela couldn't face going back inside. 'Can I walk you home?'

'I suppose you can…on one condition.' He lifted up his strimmer and placed it neatly back into the shed. 'You might have a bowl of my nice stew so I can enjoy the look of surprise on your face when you taste it. You think an old yoke like me would be surviving on burnt toast and cups of stewed tea. Ha!'

'That's a deal.' She picked up a rake and a hoe and helped him tidy away the rest of his philosophy tools. John seemed like a nice old man, even if he did allow himself to be employed by the rudest hermit in Ireland. A

72

bowl of homemade stew sounded like the best offer she'd
had all day. It beat the burnt toast and stewed tea she'd
likely have been making for herself. She tried not to
imagine what was happening in Gregory's mansion.
Josie's face had been a picture when the girl found Adela
sitting in Gregory's kitchen. Adela imagined peeking
around the door and calling Josie outside for a girlie chat.
'Have no fear, Josie, darling. Your rude, money-mad,
rule-making, bearded hermit is all yours. Relax, Josie,
even with the wads of cash, fancy house and designer
taste, he's still as enticing as a sand sandwich.'

'Come on, little missy,' John said cheerfully,
gathering pace. 'Keep up.'

Chapter 15

'I wasn't expecting to find a woman in your house.' Josie poured him a second glass of wine.

Gregory could tell she'd been waiting for the first glass to kick in before mentioning the elephant in the room.

Some elephant.

Her body language was screaming jealousy. JB had warned him about this. "You can't expect her not to get attached, Gregory. Josie's heart actually has a functioning thermometer; it gets warm, it gets cold. She doesn't believe you when you say yours is broken."

'Adela's a friend.' He sipped his wine.

'Well, she has poor taste in clothes,' Josie said, tugging at her own skirt. 'And don't get me started on the shoes.'

Gregory was already bored. Josie's jealousy did not appeal in any way to him. 'Maybe tonight wasn't such a good idea.'

She immediately moved across to the couch beside him, placing her glass of wine on the table. 'Now, don't say that; the night hasn't even begun yet.'

Double bored. Great boobs though. 'Look, I don't want you getting the wrong idea. You getting jealous of Adela means you think there's more going on here than a bit of fun.'

'Jealous of *her*? I don't think so. Hey, I'm the queen of fun, Mr Sheridan.' She leaned over and kissed him on the side of his neck, pressing her body against his.

Okay, this was better.

He could feel himself responding to her. But even the glass of wine hadn't settled him. He pulled away.

'Come back here,' she said. 'You're not getting away from me that easily.'

His mind was racing against his will. Damn JB and damn Adela. His house was not his own with her moving about in it. His habits and routines had all been knocked off track because of that woman. 'Look, Josie, I'm sorry. I'll call you a taxi.'

He looked into her face, trying not to read the desperation, pretending he couldn't see evidence of what he'd done to her. Josie, he clearly understood, was in love with him.

'I can't keep doing this,' he said slowly. 'It's not fair.'

She stood up, facing him. 'Of course it's fair. We both know where we stand in this, Greg. Stop being so dramatic.'

It would be so easy to keep drinking the wine and ignore all he knew to be true.

'I'm sorry, Josie. I'll ring for that taxi.' He walked out of the den, towards the kitchen, wondering about the purpose of the thermostat within a person's heart. Knowing Josie would go home feeling a miserable, lovesick failure made Gregory realise he was better without one that functioned. He didn't love Josie. He wasn't even sure whether he had any feelings at all for her. His thermostat wasn't functioning for one good reason.

He had pulled it apart, smashed it, stamped on it, bashed it, and left it for dead.

#

John's house was a beautiful thatched bungalow on the other side of the village, just off the main road, with its two red chimneys and interesting, pale yellow walls positioned within a stunning garden, lush with well-established perennials.

'Your house reminds me of Hansel and Gretel,' Adela told him, sitting on one of his four thyme-green, wooden kitchen chairs as John lit the pot-bellied stove. 'And your garden...so well-designed and cared for. You hold magic in those fingers of yours, John. How long have you worked for Gregory?'

'On and off for about three years now.' John shut the door of the stove, grunting involuntarily as he stood up again. 'What's your relationship to him?'

Nibbling at her index fingernail, she thought how best to describe it. 'I needed a quiet place to stay. He's helping me out.'

'Surprsing!' Slow cooker off, time for him to lift the lid. 'He doesn't usually like to get involved.'

'So I believe.' *He kindly makes exceptions for big-busted blondes with no aptitude for perfume application.*

'But that's okay.' One delicious-looking ladle of stew was gently poured into each white bowl. 'Not everybody sees the world the same way.'

'How do you see the world, John?' She liked saying his name; she liked the warm feel of his home, of his gravelly voice.

He placed the bowl in front of her. 'Are you merely filling the silence or do you *really* want to know?'

Although she hardly knew this man, he interested her. 'I really want to know...'

Steam swirled from the top of his own bowl of stew in the direction of his face. 'I see the world as I see my garden as I see my house as I see my life--a place of the grandest creation...a place of such eloquence and beauty that we hardly have the eyes for it, the imagination for it.'

'Now, there's an answer.'

He lifted his own spoon. 'Some people run from visions of the world unlike their own. Do you want to hear what else I think?'

'Go for it.'

'The more we choose to see of it, the more of the world's magnificence is revealed to us. Like magic.'

Oh, dear, Adela thought. John sounded like a paragraph from her book. But as she looked into his eyes, she saw belief. A dart of jealousy ripped through her. She could rationally read and interpret the words of her book, all the advice it offered, its poetic insights, but as if its meanings could not break through some part of her, she was unable to feel its truth, to acknowledge it to the core of her being.

Life felt worse to her now than it did in the days before that damned book. No magic spell, no secret potion. Yet, looking into John's face, he seemed to have unlocked that door. So why couldn't she?

The first mouthful of John's stew was glorious, the flavours partying on the taste buds of her tongue. 'Can I tell you a secret?'

'You can, of course.'

She thought about her book, the reason the world was so interested in her. Of course she couldn't feel the power of its words, for she was not its author.

'I'm a fraud, John.'

\#

Gregory watched the taxi drive away, relieved Josie was gone, yet irritated at how he'd let himself get so conflicted. Without people to complicate things, his life remained calm and controlled.

'Adela?'

No answer.

She could be anywhere in the house. Or perhaps she'd gone into the village. Made herself scarce. He checked his mobile. Another missed call from his father. *What now?*

'Yes, Dad?'

'Took you long enough to call me back. You avoiding me?'

Deep breaths were always required during these phone calls. 'Nope.'

'Ah, good. Listen, I was wondering...'

The request always began the same way. *I was wondering...*

'What were you wondering, Dad?'

'Two thousand would do it. Hard times, Greg. Hard times.'

'How's Irene?' Wrinkled before her time, his step-mother was gaunt from lack of food and too much drink, yet a sweet-natured woman when not being tickled by the sauce.

'She got some work in the local launderette, so that's good,' his father said. 'You'll have to come over soon...for a nice Sunday dinner maybe.'

Sundays were their supreme hangover days. Sunday dinner was an idea his father held onto in his head, as unreal as the Easter bunny. 'Sure, dad. That would be great.'

'How's your mother?'

'She's fine.' His father always asked about his mother, when all other topics had been exhausted. He always answered the same way. 'I'll transfer the money this afternoon.'

'Great, son. Get me out of a hole, that will. I'll go tell Irene now. She'll be whistling all day. Chat to you soon. And thanks.'

The darkness of the kitchen was welcoming, light filtering in through the conservatory windows from the almost-full moon. How had his father and mother ever been a couple? Worlds apart, in every sense. The only trace left in his mother that resembled her younger life was the large tattoo curving all the way up her back. She was so capable, so unprepared to let life cast its eerie shadow upon her.

His father, on the other hand, had allowed his addictions to nestle deep within him, to take the reins and drive his life in crazy circles of dark desire and deep, unfulfilled wanting. The man could simply not bring himself to believe he had the ability to take control of the bullies within him. He gently accepted his fate, understanding he would always have one eye half-focused on the inside of a bottle. He was a man that would live in the dark. Drink was his domineering wife, his controlling husband, his overbearing mother, his pillow, his blanket, his lifetime mate. Gregory had tried to get him into treatment centres, but while his father found Irene in one of them, he had never quite recovered himself.

Gregory's own wine rack was filled with expensive wines; from where he was sitting, through the shadows he could see their dark necks jutting out. He thanked the Universe for not laying the same lure for drink upon him. Everyone had their demons, but what was the difference between those who gained control over them and those who didn't? His father was a kind man in so many ways. It just wasn't enough.

It never had been.

Chapter 16

In John's dimly lit kitchen, over a bowl of stew, Adela told this stranger the secret she'd been carrying about like a bag of logs.

'I can't believe I'm telling you all this.'

'Only tell me if you want to,' John said, wrinkles gathering softly around his gentle eyes as he smiled at her.

Adela hesitated. 'My granny was the kind of woman who enjoyed making the parish priest blush. When she died, she left the contents of her attic to me. I thought nothing of it, presuming I'd hold onto a few dusty ornaments and memorabilia of some sort or another. But instead I discovered a box of diaries. The best way I could describe them is the glue that must have stuck her life together…

…I read a few pages; she was so insightful, John. I made a project out of them, arranging the contents of the diaries into a book. My intention was to have copies of the book printed for my mother, my sister and I.'

John poured her a cup of tea. 'I made it strong. Drink up.'

'Thanks.' She smiled at him, adding a drop of milk.

'Drink and talk…drink and talk,' he said, giving her a wink.

'My mother and sister loved the book. But my sister always had an entrepreneurial streak in her. At eight years of age, she was the proud owner of her first business. Our neighbours, even my granny's friends, were all given the heavy-duty sales pitch. Lizzie made a fortune from selling cardboard people. She sold them for ten pence each, carrying them around in a clear plastic folder, like they were the crown jewels.'

John chuckled lightly, listening to her every word.

'Fast forward a couple of decades and Lizzie decides to upload the book I made from Granny's diaries onto the internet and sell it for 99c a pop. Lizzie reckoned it was both funny and wise. Of course she told me none of this until one day I got a call from a publisher interested in publishing "my" book. The internet version was a runaway success and I was suddenly signing a publishing deal, with this book having supposedly been penned by *me*.'

'That must have been exciting?'

'My sister and mother were thrilled. They felt my grandmother had left me her diaries, so they were mine to do with as I pleased. But the publishers put us under strict orders to keep that part of the story to ourselves. They all said I had weaved original sections of it together with my "clever wit". I became the official author, not having the least idea how successful the book would become. My life snowballed out of my control and now I'm hiding in Gregory's house after humiliating my ex-fiancé, myself and my entire family.'

'You never felt good about masquerading your grandmother's diaries as your own?'

'They were never my words to use.'

'Are you always so hard on yourself?'

'What do you mean?'

'The way I see it, your grandmother left you her diaries for a reason. They're a piece of treasure, which you discovered and "enjoyed".' He took a quick slurp of his tea. 'Maybe your problem is that you took ownership of her words before you had the chance to make them feel like your words too.'

Adela had never looked at it like that before. 'But they were never *my* words. I have read them, I have even given speeches about them, but they don't feel true to me. Every time I speak them, my voice takes me further away from them. Does that make any sense, John?'

He nodded. 'It does. It does.'

'I'm a fake. I stole my grandmother's ideas, used them for my own personal gain and now I'm paying the price. I'm a horrible human being.'

John curved his mouth into a smile, the sides of his eyes creasing merrily. 'So you made a mistake? Everyone does.'

'Not always on such a large scale.'

'Be careful not to bathe in your own misery or self-depreciation, Adela. Humans do way too much of that. This very village does too.'

'I know, I know. My thoughts create my reality. That was part of what my grandmother wrote about.'

'Ah-ha.' He tipped her on the nose. 'You say you know about this. How easy it is to say, "I know, I know", but if you really understood what it meant, you might not steep yourself in miserable, self-defeating thoughts, as if these thoughts have no consequences. You have obviously been doing this to yourself ever since your book was published, and that's why you are now hiding out in this lonely, old village. You don't feel like you deserve your success and therefore you're sabotaging it, moment by moment, thought by thought, word by word, and action by action.'

'Okay, but how do I change it?'

His expression was serious. 'Get honest about how you feel. Pay attention to your thoughts. Don't give the bad ones any energy. Enjoy the good thoughts. Allow them to multiply.'

'I've read stuff like that in my book. It doesn't seem to work.'

'I can give you a place to start,' he said, 'if you think an old man like me might have anything useful to tell you.'

'Shoot.'

'Take your book, or your grandmother's book, whichever you wish to call it, and take some time to understand it.'

'I'm sick of the damn book, John. It's caused me nothing but problems.'

'That's how you are *choosing* to look at it. I know we've only just met, but I have a suggestion. I could download it onto my eReader—'

'Did you use the word *download*…as a *verb*?'

He rolled his eyes. 'It's all about you young ones, eh? As I was saying, I could read a couple of chapters. You could read the same couple of chapters. Then you might come by for a hot sup of tea some evening and we could chat about it. You should know this about me, Adela, I've always loved helping strays. I was one once myself.'

'Who did you steal all your wisdom from? A great aunt? An older brother? That philosopher you have quoted on your spade?'

John chuckled once again. 'I'll even bet that by the time we're finished, you might have figured out one of the greatest secrets about life.'

Optimism was within reach for the first time in months. 'John, you have yourself a deal.'

Chapter 17

Gregory heard the key turn the lock in the back door. Adela burst out laughing when she saw him nursing his cup of lukewarm tea. 'I'm not sure what I was expecting when I came back here, but it wasn't you sitting at the counter like a stale turkey sandwich.'

'Tea?'

'No, thanks.'

'What's so funny?' *She was acting weird*. 'Have you been drinking again?'

Sitting up on the stool next to him, she sniggered like a school girl at mass. 'I can imagine why you might think that, but no.'

'Irish coffee?'

'Em…'

'Josie's not here.'

Her mouth puckered. 'Then, yes please.'

'What has you in such good form?' The kettle was already half-full, easy to boil up. 'Did David decide to take you back?'

A quick check of her phone from the pocket of her handbag displayed a clear screen and no new messages. 'Apparently not.'

Gregory opened the lid of the coffee. 'Well, what then?'

'I met someone.'

'Where? Here?'

'Yep. And I've had the most amazing evening. You can't imagine how nice it was to have meaningful conversations by a gorgeous fire, sipping tea, talking and laughing. To give yourself up to something, without fear or judgement, without any rules. To just *be*.'

Where's the damn whiskey? 'Are you teasing me?'

'Would you like me to?' She laughed again, seemingly unable to stop.

'You sure this bloke didn't slip something into your tea? Vodka, maybe?'

'Is that how you see life all the time? Don't you get bored of your suspicions, Gregory?'

He put a long-stemmed teaspoon into each glass. 'Boredom is a symptom of a dulled mind.'

'Why did your visitor leave so early? No, let me guess—you could never allow her to spend the night; that would imply an intimacy you're not prepared to offer. Your golden ticket permits only a limited entry to your magical kingdom?'

'You're a cheeky thing when you're merry.' He poured a capful of whiskey.

'Or maybe *she* walked out on *you*? Come to think of it, where's your healthy glow and messed up hair? If a man looked as composed as you do after we'd "had dinner", I wouldn't be sticking around either.'

'Cheeky *and* nosey.' He spooned cream on top. 'Not that you deserve it, but here's your coffee.'

'Thanks.' She met his gaze as he handed her the warm glass.

'What's the name of this man you just met?'

'John.' She took a sip.

'This village is full of Johns. John who?'

Adela shrugged. 'Dunno. Didn't get his last name.'

He wasn't getting anywhere with this conversation. It was irritating him to think about her being so irrationally happy with Anonymous John.

'You really have a lot of hair. Does Josie like your beard? How does she manage to kiss you with that thing hanging around all the time?'

'I do have lips in there somewhere.'

'I mean without getting a rash.'

He shrugged. 'I'm not a big fan of kissing.'

'Ah, you just haven't been kissed right.' She pursed her lips provocatively. 'And that monster dangling from your face is one way to avoid a really good kiss.'

'Hey, stop laughing at me.'

Leaning over closer to him, she inspected his beard. 'Let me shave it.'

Rule number four on his list. *Stop trying to bombard me with those feminine wiles, Adela. Stop breaking my rules.* 'No.'

Her voice turned soft. She looked up at him, all perfectly female. 'What would it take for you to let me?'

What would it take? He let himself wonder for just a moment. 'Not a hope.'

Adela sat up straight, but the mischievous glint remained in her eyes. 'There's a handsome man underneath that hair. Don't you want to introduce us?'

'Not particularly.'

She sipped at the drink he'd made her. 'You really don't remember me from all those years ago?'

He remembered her. How could he forget one of the worst nights of his life? 'I guess you don't always make the kind of impact you thought you did.'

'You still think I'm vain?'

'As I've said before, beautiful women generally are. It's in their nature.'

'What do you know of beauty, locked up here in your castle?'

'I know all I need to. Again, you retreat to assumptions of my imprisonment. You women are so desperate to feel complete that you project your own desperations onto the rest of us. Why do you try so hard to make *me* the victim? You see me as a victim, but really, it is you who feels like one. You have a beautiful shell, but inside you're a mess and guess what? I'm not here to save you.'

'Bring a girl down, why don't you.'

'Yeah, well you can blame my mother for all that insightful rubbish. I'm the victim of *her* need to feel better.'

'Your mother would never use that "rubbish" in the way you do.' Adela climbed down from the stool and swept her handbag off the top of the counter. 'Thanks for the chat. Mood-changing, as usual. Goodnight, Gregory.'

He was hard and he knew it. Normally this fact didn't bother him, all part of his decision about how he chose to live. So why was it bothering him now? He never should have agreed to let Adela stay.

It could not end well.

Chapter 18

DAY 5 - Friday

Adela had always loved the feel of the early morning, with its bright and hopeful atmosphere. All possibilities existed in such a moment. She walked through the village, listening to the squawking of the crows trying to peck at the dustbins, the noise of the occasional car driving by, and the chattering of conversation by some of the locals. Draped in sunshine, this place didn't seem so bad. She discovered another Mad Margaret sign, attached to a lamp post that read, "No Cursing". Daisy and her notion of the village being cursed continued to amuse her. People needed something to attach their blame to, she supposed.

She ambled over the bridge and down the path into the forest. Not far from Margaret's pile of stones, she could see a man standing in the river, swinging his fishing rod over his shoulder. The world needed fishermen, yet she could think of nothing worse than being wet up to ones knees all day for the sake of a couple of slippery fish slapping about on the inside of the boat. The feel of raw fish gave her the creeps, although she did enjoy a cooked one well enough on the end of her fork.

Walking further into the forest, she thought about Gregory's argument with her the previous evening. Did she feel like a victim? It pained her that the answer was yes—the victim of a runaway train, speeding her life out of control in the wrong direction—that was *exactly* how she felt. What did being a victim say about her? Weak, foolish, stupid. She didn't want to be those things. She wasn't those things. Yet that train kept on coming, despite itself.

She could see someone in the distance, sitting up on a tree trunk, head tucked between bent knees. She glanced back over her shoulder, but there was nobody else around. The sound of the river flowed through the trees. Momentarily, it occurred to her to head off track, to avoid passing the person directly, but at the last minute she changed her mind.

The limbs of the teenager stretched open like the petals of a flower as Adela approached her. Adela recognised the individual as the girl with whom Nigel had been playing his finger-pointing game.

'Morning,' she said.

Arms folded, the girl's eyes were bloodshot, her face blotchy from crying.

Adela stopped. 'You okay?'

The young girl let out a laugh. 'Take a wild guess.'

Something told her to push a little further. 'Care to walk with me?'

Her uncombed hair blew in wisps across her freckly face. 'Sorry, do I even know you?'

'Nope.'

'Sure I don't know you?'

'I'm sure, but you look like you could use some company, and to be perfectly honest, so could I.'

'Don't you have no friends?' the girl asked, stretching one leg out.

'None useful to me right now.' Adela started to walk. 'You coming?'

'Na.'

'Suit yourself.' Moving past her, Adela deliberately looked forward. The girl could not be forced to go walking with some strange woman. Asking was all she could do. But as Adela continued her journey alone, a bit of company along this beautiful forest walk became appealing. What was happening in the mind of that young girl? Boy drama or something more?

Adela thought of her own particular boy drama. David was the man she'd believed she would marry. Could life be so fickle? Was she at the total whim of its twists and turns, despite her grandmother's suggestion to the contrary? This idea filled her with fear. She wanted to sail through life with confidence and strength, to be the person life didn't defeat. In all her imaginings, she never saw herself as a failure, yet she was failing spectacularly in so many ways. It didn't seem fair.

'Hey, wait up,' a voice called from behind her.

Adela turned to find the girl running to catch up with her.

'I'm Adela,' she said simply, giving her a fraction of a smile.

'Toni.' A moment of eye contact, before the girl dug her hands into her pockets and began kicking through a mound of leaves.

#

'What are you reading?' Gregory closed his book and turned to face her.

'Nothing much,' she said, changing the position of her eReader on her lap. From the corner of her eye, she could see him open back to the page held by his index finger, read a few words, look up at her, and then down again to continue reading another line.

'You're still annoyed with me, then?'

'I'm not annoyed with anyone.' She pressed onto the next page. 'I'm reading.'

Silence once more as she glimpsed his glazed eyes struggle through another line of words. It was obvious he had not the slightest interest in the book he was holding. What about Josie, the woman who couldn't say no to her perfume collection? What must have happened between them to have put Gregory into such a bad mood the previous night?

'Did you enjoy your walk?'

'Yep,' she said.

"Enjoyed" was probably overdoing it. Toni, all frowns and murmurs, was a young girl with a leaking heart.

Gregory laid his book down on the table next to his chair. 'I'm sorry for being such an ass.'

Trying Toni's trick from earlier, Adela gave him a look so fleeting it could pass by unnoticed. 'Fine.'

'You can't say, "fine" and continue to read.'

'Oh, so *now* you want to talk?'

'Yes.' His eyebrows arched like the open beaks of two young birds. 'Talking would be *nice*.'

'Okay, I'm reading the first two chapters of my book, as in the one *I* wrote.'

'You're reading your own book? Why?'

John's invitation, of course! 'Vanity.'

His eyes rolled like half-spun marbles. 'So you haven't forgiven me?'

'My vanity prevents me from doing so.'

'Okay, maybe I did judge you because of your looks. But you judged me because of my beard. What's the difference?'

She thought about this. 'Well, *I* was the one who had "no judgement" on my list of rules, not *you*.'

Gregory got up from his chair, walked across the floor and sat on the chair next to her. 'I'm sorry for making a list of rules. Okay, so I'm an ass.'

'Two apologies in the one conversation. Gregory, have you been *drinking*? Vodka perhaps?'

His grin was hard to escape. 'Damn, you're hard work.'

'Unlike the lovely Josie, I imagine? Once you get past the perfume.'

'You don't like her, do you?'

'She doesn't like *me*. There's a difference.'

'Jealousy is an emotion I presume you've encountered before? She felt threatened.'

'Is she your girlfriend?' *Could he hear the tightness in her voice?*

'I'd say she's not even my *friend* after last night.'

'Things didn't go so well, then?'

'No, I don't suppose they did.'

'She's in love with you, you know.'

The colour of his shark eyes gathered depth. 'I had guessed.'

'Won't you let anyone in? Not even the blonde with the exceptionally big boobies?'

'Relationships are overrated.' His voice was deep, like he was talking in a basement. 'The oversized beard is a great big hint.'

'I have a suggestion,' she said, touching his leg to get him to look at her. 'You might prefer to call it a *challenge*.'

'What type of *challenge*?'

'I propose you and I go into the village this evening and have a couple of drinks together. What do you think?'

His eyebrows stood to attention once more. 'You know I don't go into the village.'

'My point exactly,' she said. 'That's why it's a *challenge*.'

'What about you?'

'Well, here's the other part of the challenge; you called me vain, so I will go out this evening without a scrap of makeup, wearing the worst clothes I packed and without even brushing my hair.'

His face softened. 'And my challenge is to go into the village?'

'Yes and no,' she said, rubbing her two hands together. 'Your challenge is to go into the village…leaving all that excess hair behind.'

Chapter 19

Gregory lay back in the chair as she rubbed shaving foam on the remainder of his beard.

'You trust me, don't you?' she teased. 'With this exceptionally sharp blade.'

'This is supposed to be relaxing,' he said, watching her in the mirror. *How had she talked him into this?* Adela's perfume filled the air as she moved around him, her face coming up close against his, in concentration; her hand pressing on his skin.

'I *always* wear makeup, Gregory, so don't think I'm getting off lightly.'

She wouldn't expect a reply, for he had to keep still, her hand expertly scraping the blade against his face.

'And while I have you quiet, I'll have to meet you in the village later…let's say, eight o'clock in Daisy's. I'm meeting up with John for an hour beforehand.'

Gregory held still. Mentioning the mysterious John would drive him mad; unable to speak, to ask questions, having to accept what Adela was saying without a word. Who was this John? Wasn't she supposedly heartbroken about David the ex-fiancé mere hours before the introduction of John to her life? Was she so fickle? Physical beauty allowed her to be, as he'd originally suspected.

Why had he agreed to socialise in the village? Josie had asked him time and time again to join her for drinks, but he always refused. The village offered him nothing he didn't already have. He didn't want their small talk. Worse still, he knew he would become the object of their gossip. And was this really Adela's idea of keeping a low profile?

Finished with the blade, Adela ran a cloth under the warm tap and then laid it on his face. Closing his eyes was as good an option as any. JB would have a field day if he knew Gregory had said yes to her. Beautiful as Adela was, Gregory had no desire to change his habits and succumb to her charms; although as much as it pained him to admit it, she was mildly charming.

Mildly.

'Okay.' Cloth removed, she wiped any last traces of shaving foam from his skin. 'I think we're done here.'

The mirror was in front of him. He caught her eye through the reflection. Staring into time, remembering back to when they had seen one another at JB's party; a precious moment before it had turned to stone. His face now looked like it did then, when life had been enhanced to Technicolor, and without logic or reason, they had approached one another as if no other direction was possible. Magnets. Attraction. As quickly as that memory escaped, he confined it. It no longer belonged to this lifetime.

Still watching him through the mirror, her fingers reached out to touch his chin. 'You have a nice face, Gregory,' she said, before lifting the blade and rinsing it under the tap.

He came over to her and placed his hand on her right shoulder. He didn't want to remember those feelings from before, yet they played with him, teasing and flirting with him. 'Thank you.'

She nodded, not looking up.

'I'm going to go for a swim.' Moments like these...tricks of the mind. He needed to keep his focus. 'See you at eight.'

#

'Evening, John.'

'Adela!' He waved her into his home. 'The kettle has just whistled. Tea or coffee?'

'Tea, please.' His hall held the scent of a summer garden. 'Are you sure you don't mind me coming over like this?'

'It's a burden I'll have to bear.' John closed the door behind him. 'I got busy reading your book last night. I can see why people liked it. It may help some of them feel less afraid of their confusions.'

The first item out of her bag was her eReader. 'Do you really think books like this help? Don't people read them, throw them into a corner somewhere, and then continue on making the same mistakes regardless? That's what *I've* done and I'm supposed to be the *author*.'

'You feel guilty because you believe you're supposed to be the finished product?'

'Of course! People expect answers that I don't have any right to give them. I like to dance, to read, to go mountain climbing. I'm not some mystic who climbed down from some blessed mountain. Climbing down from my grandmother's attic was as far as it went. I keep dreaming that the people who bought my book are chasing me, demanding to know why their lives haven't changed.'

'You think any one of us is the finished product? Not even me, and I'm giving it a darn good shot! And you know what—that's perfectly okay.' John patted her hand. 'Chapter One talks about how your thoughts create your reality.'

'Yep.' She nodded. 'My grandmother believed thoughts translate into actions and actions create life. Yeah, yeah, I get that one.'

'So what did *you* change as a result of "getting" this idea?'

She touched her fingers against her chin. 'What do you mean?'

'You say you get it, but did the understanding of that idea *change* your life in any way?'

'Not really. The idea of thinking positively is really nothing new.'

'Are you so sure about that?' A dimple added texture to his cheek. 'Being told it's good to think positively doesn't tend to have much of an impact. It feels a bit like a lecture from your parents or a teacher. The real question is *why* it's so important to be positive.'

'Why, then?'

'Because your thoughts and feelings are the ingredients of your life. Alter the ingredients, you alter the taste. Your thoughts and your feelings are *that* important, Adela. They are powerful creators.'

'Creators?'

'Yes! Do you see the difference in the two messages? One tells you to be positive because it's a nice way to be, it's moral, it's right. The other tells you to be responsible for every single thought in your head, as these thoughts will affect *your* life. Positive thinking is much more than a catchphrase...positive thoughts are the seeds from which all good things can grow.'

She nodded. 'So, my life is a mess because I was conflicted about the book? My thoughts then created the havoc around me.'

'Perhaps. Let me ask you a question; would you call what is happening in your life "failure"?'

'Definitely.'

'And what would happen if you turned your life around? What would you then experience?'

'Success, I guess.'

'Do you see something special in that? You would never be able to understand the experience you define as "success" if you had never felt what it is like to "fail"?'

'So what, I need to have the down in order to experience the up?' she said, frowning at him.

'Something like that. It's one of life's cheeky little truths. Without the existence of dark, light would mean nothing. Without the existence of failure, success would mean nothing. Failure is a tool that can encourage us towards a different experience, if we choose it to. That's why our thoughts and feelings about everything in our lives are so important. Success to some is failure to others. Success and failure are points along the same line, like hot and cold, wet and dry, light and dark.'

'So what? The horrible experience I'm having now might make me appreciate the great stuff that's going to happen to me in the future?'

'Sort of, yes. Nothing has any importance except the meaning to which we give it. What's important to you could mean nothing to me. We choose what is important to us, both the good and the bad. We look at the world through our own individual telescope; we see only a fraction of what exists. We listen to the story of our world, as told by others, and cling to their beliefs as our own, even if they make us miserable.'

'How do you mean we *choose* what's important to us? Surely, it either is or it isn't?'

'Think about it, Adela! Decide for yourself what you believe, what is true for you. Your mind will be a lunatic if you let it. Thousands of crazy thoughts wander around it all day long. Some we consider good and others bad. It's no wonder we get mixed results. We think there are no consequences to negative thinking, so we make judgements, have a gossip, get angry, feel like we're victims, see ourselves as more successful, less successful.'

'So I shouldn't sit about in Gregory's house feeling sorry for myself? You're telling me my life will remain like this if I do?'

'It's likely! All our thoughts, which are made up of the same energy as we are, swirl into the magical mix of life and throw our own stuff back at us. Our inner reality creates our outer one. We all live in different versions of the world, Adela.'

'How do we have any proof of that? How was my grandmother able to write about that in her diaries, long before she could read about it on the internet?'

'Truth is nobody's hermit; it's available for anyone to discover. Humans have simply been wandering about in a fog for a very long time. Maybe we need to realise we might not yet have all the answers. Maybe we need to stop asking the same old, jaded questions and find some new ones to ask. The fog needs to clear, Adela; the fog needs to clear.'

She tried to take in all he was saying.

'Okay, chapter two. "You get what you give." What does this chapter mean to you?' he asked.

'My grandmother was saying, if you want love, then be loving. If you want money, then give money to those who need it more. If you want judgement, then judge others. What you put out there, you get back. I tend to think of this message as, "you reap what you sow". It is a message to be good, kind and generous, *or else*. Again, another idea as old as time.'

'Can I tell you *why* I believe the world works this way?'

'Of course.'

'The law of attraction says that like attracts like. Therefore, you can only attract love if you have enough love to be able to give love away. If you give love away, the Universe recognises you have enough love within you to give some of it away and through the energies of the law of attraction, it will attract more love to you. If you give judgement, through those same energies, you will be judged. The Universe reflects our thoughts and feelings back at us in physical form.' Despite the depth of his conversation, a cobweb in the corner of the room caught

John's eye. Sweeping brush in hand, he climbed up onto the closest kitchen chair.

'I'll do that, John. Get down!'

But he continued as if he were still sitting at his table, drinking tea. 'We should never underestimate the power of all that goes on behind the scenes. Our conscious thoughts direct our subconscious. Think of your subconscious as the one with the tremendous power and wisdom; it beats your heart, it pumps your lungs. It even heals you when you break, it knows how.'

'Yeah, I suppose so.'

'But for all its power, your subconscious needs direction.' He poked the end of the sweeping brush into the cobwebs, all sticky and dangling. 'This is where your conscious thoughts come into play. They instruct your subconscious. Think fearful, miserable thoughts full of failure and, through the law of attraction, these get channelled directly to your subconscious, which has all the Universal wisdom and ability to oblige. It is not concerned about which thought is good for you or bad for you. It is your humble, brilliant servant, but without understanding its power, as well as the power of your conscious thoughts, your life can tumble upside down and inside out.'

'So I can't constantly bathe in my misery and expect the Universe or what you may call "my subconscious" not to react?'

John laughed. 'Did you know that a good hypnotist can appeal to a person's subconscious, suggest any symptom upon that person, and he or she will develop it? Tell someone under hypnosis that her body is covered in hives and she will scratch her clear skin until it bleeds. The power of suggestion is more important than we realise."

'Ahh, I see!'

'I was blind but now I can see.' His eyes grew wide, wiping the cobwebs off the top of the brush with a piece of paper towel. 'Because we have thousands of thoughts and feelings every day, we often dismiss their importance. We think we can't see, feel or measure them, yet, in fact, we can. Look at a person's behaviour, relationships, wealth or body, and you can understand so much about the thoughts and feelings that flow through them. Our lives are our measuring stick of the quality of our thoughts and feelings. If the world truly understood what that meant, the world would change.'

Impressed by the agility of his body and mind, Adela watched and listened.

'Of course, another way of looking at why you get what you ask for is through the science of energy. We are all energy, Adela. But more importantly, we are all made up of the same energy. From the cosmos to your left toe, it's all made up of different expressions of the same stuff. Science has proven it. But do you understand what it actually means?'

'What?'

John moved his head closer, as if about to impart a valuable secret. 'Every single cell of your body joined together makes the solid mass you call "you". Each cell might not look like you, but every cell is part of you, every strand of hair, finger, eyeball, toe, they are all *you*. On a larger scale, it's no different to the parts of our bodies. We are all made of the same stuff, Adela. Can't you see?'

'I'm trying, John! I really am!'

'We are all inter-connected. We are all *one*. And that's why you get what you give…you're connected to everything and it to you; when you give to someone else, you give to yourself; when you take from someone else, you take from yourself—it's all part of the magic of our beautiful Universe.'

'This is not the sort of stuff they teach in schools, John! Where did you learn all this? Now, obviously your philosopher friend played his part, but seriously, did you spend years hiding out in some Ashram in India or what?'

The dimple took ten years off his beaming face. 'Ha! You think I have a guru on speed dial?'

She shrugged. 'Nothing would surprise me with you!'

'Actually, my life was nothing of the sort. Had you known me in my youth, you wouldn't recognise a single thing about me. We don't always begin the way we end.'

'What were you like?'

He leaned in closer to her. 'Let's just say, I would have stolen the tooth right out of your head.'

Chapter 20

'Pint please, Daisy,' Gregory said, resting on a bar stool, feeling the eyes of the pub-goers all over him.

'Well, well, if it isn't Mr Sheridan, come down from the top of his hill to delight us with his presence.' Daisy grinned as she poured. 'It's mighty good to see that face of yours again after all this time.'

'Good to see you too.' This was a bad idea, Daisy looking at him with reflections of the past in her eyes. As he was debating his exit, the door opened and in breezed Adela. She had sacrificed nothing in coming here with no make-up and tousled hair.

'I wasn't sure if you'd make it,' she said, offering his shoulder a quick squeeze. 'How fancy do you look?'

The tension within him tried to coax him back out the door. 'What will you have?'

'Vodka and tonic, please,' Adela said to Daisy, who was smirking and observing their exchange with great interest.

Daisy then exchanged a wink with plainclothes Nigel who was sitting at the far end of the bar. 'Well, lady, you must have some powers of persuasion to get *that* man into this place.'

Despite the dark feelings trying to scare him into defeat, Gregory accommodated a moment of humour for this whole ridiculous situation. 'You have no idea, Daisy.'

'Let's find a table.'

Daisy handed Gregory his change and went away looking most pleased for having acquired a valuable piece of village gossip.

Not to be forgotten, Elly was sitting in her chair in the corner of the room beside the fire, waving and shouting. 'I know you.'

Adela nudged Gregory in the old lady's direction. 'Hi Elly. What are you knitting?'

'A jumper, can't you see?' she said, swinging it in front of her, the length of knitted wool shaped more like a scarf. 'Will I let you into a secret?'

'Sure.'

'I'll be dead soon.'

'Oh, don't say that. Of course you won't.'

'Why does nobody want to discuss this with me?' Elly grabbed a square of chocolate. 'Missus is as bad.'

Leaning in close, Adela said, 'it's a bit morbid, that's all. People don't like to talk about things that make them sad.'

Elly munched on the chocolate as if she had the whole bar in her mouth. 'Death will be a grand aul business. Sure, don't I want to get organised before the big event. I'm knitting this jumper for my funeral. To keep me bones warm in the coffin.'

'That's one way of looking at it, I suppose.'

Elly's chocolaty fingers waved her away. 'Go have a drink with your husband. Come visit me again sometime.'

'He's not my husband...'

'Why not?'

Gregory moved out from behind Adela. 'Hi, Elly. It's me...Gregory.'

After a quick rub of her hands down the sides of the chair, Elly returned to her knitting. 'And I'm the Queen of Sheeba.'

They waited for twenty seconds but Elly acted like they were no longer there.

'Come on, husband,' Adela said, 'let's find us a table. We'll be all the chat after that.'

104

'Wait until they discover you have another man from the village on the go.' Gregory grabbed a couple of beer mats. 'They'll nearly wet themselves with that one.'

'At least it's giving Daisy something to smile about. Lord knows she needs it. This pub is crying out for a facelift. It's so depressing and dated. How does the brown and yellow flowered wallpaper not make them want to vomit? Elly's the only thing that gives the lounge area a bit of character. Does nobody try to change anything in this place?'

'You're seeing this village with fresh eyes; theirs have adjusted to what's around them.'

'Maybe we all need to try to look at our lives with a fresh pair of eyes.'

'Maybe.' The wooden chair he sat on rocked a little under his weight. 'Well, how's John?'

She poured her tonic into the glass of vodka and ice. 'Amazing.'

'Did you tell him you were going out with me tonight?'

'I did, actually.'

There was that look in her eyes again, giddy and bold. 'So, you're over David the voice-over guy already? You work fast.'

Laughing came too easily to her. 'Gregory, if I didn't know better I would think you were jealous.'

Gregory Sheridan didn't do jealousy. 'Well, it's a good thing you *do* know better.'

She reached out and touched his cheek. 'I'm glad you left the long hair and beard at home.'

'I've had that beard a long time. My face feels weird without it.' He was beginning to relax, to forget about the villagers and their eagle eyes. But he had so many childhood memories of this pub, of roaming the village streets, running through fields and getting up to mischief. Sitting here was very bittersweet for him.

105

'There's a jukebox!' Within seconds, her purse was open and the gathering of loose change had begun. 'It hasn't turned this place around in my estimations but it's a start.'

Feeling the smoothness of his lower face, he watched Adela lean against the glass as she decided what track to choose. She had the look of a contented holidaymaker.

'Daisy,' Adela shouted, moving a coin between her fingers. 'Another round for myself and that handsome man over there.'

'Sure thing.' Daisy almost skipped with delight in response.

Dancing her way back to the table came way too easy to her.

'Sorry,' she said, making a pretence at looking meek. 'I couldn't help myself.'

'We'd better stop messing about with these gossip mongers. You'll be gone and I'll be left with the interrogations.' Once spoken, his words struck him.

This was a temporary arrangement. She would soon be gone and the silence would return.

'Ah, Gregory, this town could use our help livening it up. It needs to forget about curses and concentrate on having some fun. Don't you see? It needs to remember it's alive.'

But don't *you* see, Adela, he thought, watching her. I'm beginning to remember I am too.

#

'Who was that man you were talking to?' Adela asked, after Gregory returned with a fourth round of drinks. 'You two looked very serious.' *Like you couldn't stand the sight of each other.*

'Someone I used to know.' He glanced back at the man who was already reaching for his coat.

106

Distracted by the change in his appearance, Adela tried to stay fully-focused on the conversation. Had he really let her cut not only the length from his hair but also the hairy monster hanging around his face? The beard had been hiding a strong, handsome jaw; Gregory's complexion now younger, fresher, his shark eyes turned wild blue. 'Do you want to talk about it?'

'Nope.' Gregory took a slug of his pint.

The pub had filled up a little. Adela needed to lighten the tension that had somehow slipped in. 'I have something to tell you about this new man of mine.'

'Oh?'

Leaning across the table, she intonated with her index finger that he should do the same. 'It's *your* John.'

'*My* John? You mean John the gardener? You can't be serious.'

'You dirty minded eejit, it was never like that. He took pity on me when Josie was trying to seduce you. He gave me a bowl of his stew.'

Creases gathered around his smiling eyes. 'You are an evil sort—pretending to be interested in an *old man*.'

'Oh, I wasn't pretending. John is *very* interesting.'

'Yeah, very funny.'

'That's the problem with being so cocooned in your home, Greg. You miss out on all the other good stuff. John's a gem. Don't be fooled by those wrinkles; he owns an eReader, he chats to his children online every second night, his house is like something from a fairy tale and he talks so much sense his words feel like silk to my soul; it's hard to explain. How can I put it? He makes understanding life seem possible. Do you realise how rare that is? He makes it all sound so *easy*.'

Gregory frowned.

'Don't be so critical. Have you ever even bothered to have a conversation with him?'

'Not really. Mostly, he works and I let him get on with it. I guess I always imagined it suited us both. I didn't realise he was a talker.'

'He's a really good listener too.'

'So then, as John is not a potential candidate in the meaningful sense, does that mean Mr Voiceover still stands a chance with you?'

'Don't you remember? It was David who broke up with me. *I'm* the one who doesn't stand a chance.'

'Why did you cheat on him?' Gregory stopped smiling. 'I don't see that kind of person in you, yet you've admitted you did it. Why?'

Her face lost its desire to smile. 'Why do you want to know? Your list of rules was very exact in its interpretation, Gregory. You don't want my friendship, remember?'

'I want to know.' His eyes met hers.

'Why?' she challenged. 'A sucker for the sordid details?'

'No,' he said, a little too loudly.

Daisy's knowing eyes darted in their direction as she dried a pint glass with a tea towel.

Unflinching, Adela held his stare. What was it about this man? He was moody, critical, challenging. Yet, sitting here with him shouldn't make her feel so alive. Was she trying to escape her life by pretending their week together was becoming something it wasn't? Gregory was a *hermit*. By definition, hermits didn't enjoy the company of other people. So why was he sitting, all freshly-shaven, in his local village pub with *her*? What was going on here?

'Why did I cheat on David?' *What was the answer to the question?* Because she got drunk out of her mind and left herself vulnerable? Because she didn't know when to stop? *Why?*

'I'm sorry,' he said, tapping her lightly on the hand. 'It's none of my business. I guess you were right about me; I am terribly nosy once I get started. Forget I mentioned it. I'll hit the jukebox again.'

'Sure.' She watched him leave their small wooden table for the charms of the old jukebox. What seemed like a week of escaping her problems might not be quite the escape she'd had in mind.

'You're going to love me for this one,' he said, returning to his seat.

'You do like your female pop singers! Mix that with your love of musicals…I worry for you, Gregory.'

He pretended to shoot her, blow away the smoke, and then twirl his imaginary gun around his index finger and back into its holster. 'Lady songs ain't so bad.'

'It's probably the videos you like! All those hotpants and shaking asses.'

'No comment!'

'Can I tell you something, Gregory?'

'Of course.'

She sat up dead straight in the rickety, old chair. 'It's part of the reason I'm in the mess that I'm in. This story involves a deceased grandmother, a dusty old attic and one enormously stupid decision.'

Chapter 21

DAY 6 – Saturday

Someone was shuffling about outside her bedroom door. Adela lifted her head and drank some bubble-filled water from the pint glass next to her bed. A rectangular piece of paper had been shoved under the door and was lying on the beige carpet.

Climbing out of bed, she thought about her night out with Gregory, confessing her secret to him. And to John before that. Gregory had reacted with unexpected kindness. They ended their evening over a nightcap sitting at the island in Gregory's kitchen. It had been…nice.

Adela scrambled back into bed, note in hand, and pulled the covers up before opening the piece of paper.

"Mistakes are the glue that binds us together."

She hugged the note to her chest and lay back down in the bed, touched by Gregory's attempt to bandage her wounds. Everyone was at it. John and his philosophising gardening tools obviously had more of an influence on Gregory than the hermit realised.

First, scratching; then the bedroom door opened and Norman, in all his might, appeared. He came up to the edge of the bed, lifted his nose to sniff her, before relaxing his large body on the floor beside her.

'Good boy, Norman,' she said, reaching down to pat his back. Even *he* was beginning to accept her. But her week was almost over; it would soon be time to leave. The panic whizzing around her mind had begun to settle. Having arrived here upset and depressed, John's hopeful conversations as well as Gregory's challenging company had begun to put a spark of colour back into her day. She had opened up to them about what she had done, without anyone suffocating her with judgement or criticism.

Perhaps JB's plan to bring her here wasn't the worst decision he'd ever made, after all. An image of Gregory cooking crepes popped into her head. She remembered his conversation with the man in the pub the previous night. His humour had soured for a short while afterwards. Gregory obviously had history, but what had been so terrible to drive him away from people altogether? The note he'd slipped under the door displayed a tender side he rarely admitted to. She was beginning to realise she might just miss him when she was gone.

Her mind shifted to Toni, the young girl from the forest. They hadn't spoken much on their walk together, minor conversation about nothing in particular. What was Toni's story? Why had the young girl been all alone and crying? Was everyone carrying around a secret pain, weighing them down like a prefect's schoolbag? Could nobody travel light? Did it always have to get complicated?

Adela's mobile buzzed with a message from her sister, hoping she was managing okay. No further contact from David. And what about Gregory's question to her the previous night? Why had she cheated on David? She'd been so overwhelmed by the tour, by the book itself, by too many questions, and, of course, by the lie. As if all that wasn't enough, one of her best friend's had revealed such a cruel secret that infamous night. A secret Adela's brain couldn't bear to process.

Why had Adela's father tried it on with this friend behind the back of Adela's parents' house during their last New Year's Eve party? However difficult Adela found her father's usual indiscretions, knowing his boundary had extended to include his daughter's friends wounded her deep inside, damaging a part of her meant only for love and protection. He'd compromised that sacred father-daughter connection. In her angst, Adela chose to drink herself into an abyss of forgetfulness, reaching a place with no desperate fathers or creepy lies. Unfortunately, the place to which her drinking brought her was not the tranquil escape she was seeking.

An interesting thought popped into her head. She had branded herself a liar and a cheat, maybe not out loud, but in her heart, and with each moment of flirtation with that god-like, Italian waiter, the universe had answered, "Your wish is my command."

Chapter 22

Adela adored John's house more every time she visited. Inside, it was simple, clean and homely.

'I still can't believe you were a gambler and a thief. Should I move my handbag?'

'I was a bold boy, all right.' John rubbed the back of his neck. 'I've been down so low that I don't get much scared by anything anymore. And here's the lesson I've learned about fear; when you stop feeling afraid, your life can begin. Fear ties a person down in so many destructive ways, knot by knot.'

'But how could your parents have thrown you out?'

'This country was a different place then. Families were big, and money scarce. With twelve other kids and a drink problem to feed, one less to be responsible for meant more rations for them. It can be hard to have the capacity to nurture yourself, never mind twelve young bodies and minds. They knew no better, poor souls.'

'You don't resent them?'

He touched the tips of his fingers together. 'I wish you could come inside my world, even for a moment, to understand how large the world is to me. In answer to your question, no, I don't resent them.'

'Did you ever get back in contact with your brothers and sisters?'

'I did. We occasionally meet up…some of them are nice, but we're different. I love them but I'm not very close to them. I've accepted that. We often feel so bound by blood. I've always found that strange.'

'Strange? Why? You're such a family man with your own kids and grandkids…'

113

'Yes, but like my gardens, I realise the need to nurture those relationships. Like a warm, fresh slice of bread left exposed on a countertop, any relationship can become utterly stale and unpalatable.'

His words reminded her of the difficulties with her own parents. 'It makes us uncomfortable to openly admit that.'

'I remember huddling up in a dirty blanket next to the shelter of a park bench, having gambled away my last penny and knowing I would be eating from restaurant leftovers…discomfort is all relative, Adela, a state of mind. Now, back to you and your book…'

'Okay…explain what you meant by "we're all acting"? I don't understand.'

'Your grandmother wrote about the need for balancing the three aspects of yourself: your body, your mind and your soul. The body aspect is quite obvious in this modern age. Eat according to the messages your body gives you, and exercise to keep it supple and strong,' he said, crossing his legs at his ankles. 'As for your mind, we've already been chatting about the importance of lassoing those negative thoughts. Allow negativity no air to breathe. Control your mind, allow it to know you intend to be its master and your life will change.'

Would he think her bizarre if she started recording his conversations? Yes, he would. Leave the phone in your handbag, Adela! Don't be a crazy woman.

'But there's also the soul, the deepest and wisest part of us, the part connected to magic beyond our human imaginings. I believe our soul feeds our feelings, our instinct; it shows us the way forward, if we open ourselves up to feeling it, to believing it.'

'Again, John, I do understand what you've said, but part of me is going, "yeah, yeah, heard it all before and it hasn't changed a thing.'

'That's why you met me!'

'Look at you, all full of yourself, the big ego on you, there,' she teased.

'Okay, picture this: a woman whose husband dies suddenly and leaves her all alone, with no money, no home and with three young, grieving and hungry children to feed. Plus one of the children is deaf. The woman depended on her husband, not only as a provider, but emotionally he was the stronger of the two. She doesn't know how she will cope with the responsibility she must now bear. The drink whispers but she's determined to deny it for the sake of her children. She's twisted up in knots, her stomach sick, and her heart broken, unable to imagine what will become of them all.'

'That's horrendous, John.' A drop of tea escaped the corner of her mouth before getting quickly mopped up by the back of her hand.

'Now imagine you're a brilliant actress, Adela. Your role is to play out the life of that woman. Picture yourself on stage, holding onto your children, creating enough tension in the theatre you could hear a pin drop.'

'*Imagine* I'm an actress? Shouldn't be too much of a stretch!'

He flashed a quick grin. 'Each night, as you slip into character, you slip into her; you feel her anguish, but part of you is aware you are not her, and therefore your anguish is not as intense as when I first told you of the woman, because you now understand you're acting out a role. That woman is a part of your life now, but you are so much more than just her. That's how I see life, Adela. We are actors in the most magnificent theatre of life. We simply can't see the stage door.'

Okay, she kind of got that. Kind of. A vague understanding of what John was trying to tell her.

'We are actors lost in our roles, constantly expressing ourselves. It is only when we can see our role

115

from a distance can we relax and know nothing is as it appears to be.'

Adela imagined looking at herself from outside of herself. 'If that were the case, John, then why would I bother lacing myself with guilt and shame over what I did to David? If I could see my behaviour as a mere part that I was playing, surely anybody could justify anything they do in this way and the world would turn upside when everyone realised they didn't have to take it all so seriously?'

'Life doesn't want you to take it seriously. That's the whole point. Your life is meant to be happy, you're just too caught up in the drama of your role to realise it. I'm not saying bad things don't happen, but again back to my example of the woman, depending on which perspective she takes will affect the path she chooses. If she decides her life is over, it will be over. If she decides her life will always be a struggle, then that is what she will experience. But perhaps she may choose to overcome her desire for the drink, perhaps she will choose to experience her own strength, to extend beyond anything of which she ever imagined herself capable.'

'Doesn't that only happen in films?'

'It happens in some form in every person's life, we just don't get to examine the full contents over a two-hour session with a bucket of popcorn on our laps! Why do you think such stories get written? Because we write about what we know. So, the woman begins by searching inside herself during this desperate time and remembering her talent for dressmaking. She starts up a small business in a freezing cold room, hemming clothes. Her children have some food to eat. She realises she is able to care for them after all. She is very careful in her work and her customers begin to value her. She can now afford to heat her home. Because she works from home, she has time to help her children with their homework.'

'Okay, it's sounding a bit more hopeful now!'

'She focuses on making them strong and independent and as the years pass by, they are full of love for their wonderful, caring mother. She never allows them to feel poor on the inside. Her children grow up to become strong, successful people, despite their setbacks. She is hemming a beautiful, green dress the morning her heart stops beating. Everyone remarks at what an outstanding person she was, and how she triumphed in the face of adversity, and all because of the clever choices she made. Now, does it sound like a bad life, when you can see it from a distance? '

Adela took a breath. 'No, I guess not.'

'It is important for you to realise all that I'm sharing with you is *my* truth, Adela. It doesn't have to be *yours*. Take of it what you want and leave the rest. Enjoy that feeling in your heart when you hear something your soul understands to be true. Let your feelings steer you, for they connect you to your soul, to your bigger wisdom. Ignore them and you'll still get to your destination, but not before getting stuck in rush-hour traffic first.'

'But everyone has a different version of the truth. Your truth, his truth, her truth…who are we to believe?'

'Again, you're listening but you haven't heard. Believe your *own* truth. Pick and choose your beliefs based on what your own instinct tells you. If it makes your heart sing, it's in! Allow your feelings to steer you towards your truths about your life. Don't be persuaded to follow someone else's path. Don't dismiss your own individuality. Instead, examine everything; put this whole magnificent, terrifying world up against the light and decide what is true for *you*.'

Chapter 23

Could anyone sense, from the expression on her face, the change she was beginning to feel inside? John had concluded that the worst thing she could do was to wallow and dwell pityingly on her own misfortune. Continuing to talk about the waiter, to think about the waiter, kept her consumed with regret and misery about what she had done. By separating herself from the recent events of her life, she was beginning to see she was fully responsible for hurting David, but not in the accidental way she had imagined.

The beliefs of her subconscious were merely taking physical form. External chaos was a sure sign of internal chaos. She had read similar words in her grandmother's book, words people around the world heard throughout the ages in different forms, but she was now beginning to understand them. She thought she knew what they meant, but she had used her granny's words like a tacky one night stand, never taking the time to link them to her own feelings, her own life, or her own truths.

This new understanding, instead of further depressing her, had broken through to another world inside of her, a world without restrictions, where no matter what she had done, it was possible to start again with a clean slate…all she had to do was choose. How did she choose? Spring clean her thoughts and change her perspective.

Wow.

She saw Daisy shuffling down the road on the opposite side. Adela crossed over. 'Daisy,' she called.

'Adela, dear. I didn't see you there. Where are you coming from?'

'I was having tea with John, Gregory's gardener.'

'Bessie's John?'

'Bessie's been gone ten years, Daisy. Is that what you still call him?'

'Another of my bad habits, dear. Add it to the list.'

Adela heard Daisy putting herself down and wanted to share the knowledge of what she was beginning to understand, but was stuck for the words. 'Nice morning.'

'It is, I suppose.' Daisy pulled up her tights a little at the knees. 'How's Gregory?'

'Fine.' *Be careful, Adela! Remember Daisy is the centre of village life!*

'I was ever so surprised to see him in my pub,' Daisy said. 'He stopped coming near us a long time ago.'

'Why?' Adela said, knowing she probably shouldn't have asked...

'I was his chief nappy-changer when I was younger, you know, for a while anyway.'

'I wasn't aware.' *Too strong an image for so early in the morning.*

Daisy's face softened. 'He was a fine, strong brute of a boy, even then.'

'I'm sure he was.' Adela could see real rejection on Daisy's face.

'I'm glad he has you, any road. I never thought he would—'

'Oh, no, we're not together. We were just messing about last night.'

A frown trampled through Daisy's ragged features. 'Then why are you here?'

'It's complicated.' Unable to repeat her request to know why Gregory had shunned the village, Adela shrugged.

'Josie heard about you two visiting the pub. She wasn't happy.'

Perfectly innocent this time, Adela was not prepared to blush. 'That's not really any of our business, don't you think, Daisy?'

Daisy's eyebrows acknowledged the reprimand. *What to talk about that wouldn't get her into trouble?* 'What's that building over there? I notice it every time I walk this way.'

'Oh, that's *the barn*. It was converted into a fancy centre with a restaurant, but the plans were shelved before it opened its doors.'

'Pity,' she said. However unique its style, the barn looked so empty, its gardens wild and neglected…almost sad. 'Like so many other businesses that went to the wall in the Recession.'

'Well, no, actually. Gregory owns it.' Daisy's voice hardened. 'Not that he cares a toss about it.'

Adela looked into Daisy's eyes, the hurt unveiling itself like a blind rolling up too quick. 'You two were close?'

'I suppose you could call it that. I can hardly remember now. Memories fade. Feelings too.'

'Well, it's a pure shame this village has an empty building where its heart should be.' Adela reached out and touched Daisy's arm. 'Let me carry that shopping bag for you.'

'Potential that isn't explored means nothing. Our village will win no prizes; that's just the way it is. The people are good, but somehow nothing quite comes together. That damn curse doesn't help us.'

'I hadn't taken you for a defeatist, Daisy.'

'Ah, I tried to make changes, and then I tried a bit less. I'm too old for all that now.' She shuffled from one foot to the next. 'Speaking of which, I haven't seen John for an age. How is the old codger?'

Despite her shortness and gossipy ways, Adela was beginning to like this funny little woman. 'I imagine, Daisy, he may be the happiest man in your village.'

#

'You actually went to Daisy's?' JB shook his head.

'It was a couple of pints. Stop making a big deal out of it.' Gregory threw a tea towel at his friend's face. 'The woman *forced* me out of my own home. I hope you're happy.'

'Forced you to cut your hair and shave your beard too, did she?' JB lifted the tea towel off his head and folded it twice. 'I told you she was enchanting.'

'Hmmm.' The image of her dancing her way back from the jukebox returned, as if his brain was amused by his interest in it. 'She's not quite as irritating as I'd first imagined, I'll give you that.'

The back door opened and Adela came breezing in. 'Good afternoon, gentlemen.'

JB sniggered. 'I leave you for a couple of days and you're like a changed woman.'

Laying a box of creams cakes on the table, Adela turned to Gregory. 'Has this interfering old fool been giving you a hard time, darling?'

Gregory blew her a kiss. 'Nothing I can't handle, honeybun.'

'Jeez,' JB said, fanning himself with his hand. 'Get a room, would you?'

They all laughed. Adela sat down and told them about her conversation with Daisy.

'Once you see through that tough exterior of hers, she's an old softie. She misses you, Greg.'

'Ah, Daisy's not the worst.'

'Greg?' JB wiped his spoon with a tissue before stirring his tea with it. 'Daisy's days are busy with Elly; I'd say she's fed up with her life and she gossips to get

121

herself through. She doesn't whinge about it, though. She's strong, like the trunk of a tree.'

'You have the cheek to call *her* a gossip! Now, that's funny,' Gregory said with a smirk. JB loved to gossip as much as any idle housewife. What he didn't know about the village wasn't worth mentioning. 'Were you not just imparting the latest update about Michelle from the petrol station and Dr Harry Morrison?'

'Yes,' JB said. 'But *where* do you think I got that bit of gossip?'

Adela laughed as JB retrieved a cream bun from the box. 'You know a girl called Toni…she's about fifteen? Short, cropped hair. Large, green eyes?'

'Yes, I know Toni.' JB lifted a knife to cut his bun in half. 'She's a right troublemaker, that one.'

'What kind of trouble?'

'A bit of thieving and drinking, maybe drugs too, I'm not sure. Toni's father was never on the scene. Her mother's a manic depressive. An unpredictable sort, she's more like a child than a mother.'

'I saw Nigel coming down hard on Toni. She must have really pissed him off, whatever she did.'

'I *know* exactly what she did! Jeez, I *am* good at this gossip stuff, even if I do say so myself.' That boyish grin suited JB's charming ways.

'Well, don't keep us in suspense,' Gregory said, removing a cake of his own from the white cardboard box.

'Nigel caught her climbing over the wall into John's back garden!'

'My John?' Adela said, fingers tickling the air, still deciding which cake to choose.

'Yep! Nigel was cursing her all the way up the road, so Sheila told me.'

'John never mentioned it!'

'John wouldn't want people to think badly of the girl. She got her telling off. To him, that was enough. She's a hard nut, that one.'

'Obviously!' Adela's eyes darted from bun to bun.

'She picked the right place to grow up,' JB said, licking the sugary top from his thumb. 'Perfect resident for a cursed village.'

'Well, if you ask me, you lot should get a kick up the arse for the way you complain about the curse of the village yet never do anything to help improve it,' Adela said, at last lifting out a coffee slice. 'The main street has been abandoned, except for Margaret and her mad messages. Daisy and I were only talking about that barn you own, Gregory. Why would you let such a building go to waste when you have the money to take care of it?'

A nervous cough tickled JB's throat. 'Well, anyway, never mind, never mind…wait until you hear what my child did last night…'

'No, JB. Adela wants to talk; we should let her.' Gregory put his cup down on the marble table. 'But let me add that I would appreciate if you chose *not* to discuss my business with the locals. I hadn't realised I needed to make that a rule too.' He knew his words would sting but what right did she have, waltzing in here and judging him, especially after he'd gone to the trouble to ensure she hadn't felt judged the previous night.

'*I* wasn't discussing you…' she replied. 'Daisy was, but only because she feels rejected by you. Maybe you've been lucky enough never to suffer rejection, Gregory, but the rest of us mere mortals have and it sucks. My point about the village remains. You simply don't want to hear it because it makes you uncomfortable.'

'Adela, stop,' JB said, reaching out to touch her arm.

Gregory watched this display of affection. He didn't like it.

'The world doesn't work in practical terms like your airy fairy book suggests, Adela. One person cannot fix all life around him. One person cannot control the lives of the people around him. If the villagers wish to throw litter and feel so unworthy they don't look after their homes or shops or whatever, well, that's not my problem to solve. If they want to believe their village is cursed, then let them. It's up to them to figure out that there should be more to their lives than self-pity, pain or black magic.'

'Oh, right, so the obvious solution is to hide out in your own little patch of the world, and screw everyone else.'

'Why not?'

'You drive me mad.' She grabbed her jacket off the back of the chair. 'I'm going for a swim.'

'There are no starving children to feed in my swimming pool, dearest.' He glared at her. *How dare Daisy tell Adela about the barn. It was none of her goddamn business.*

Adela turned to him. 'By the way, in accordance with your kind and generous nature, you won't mind that I've invited John for dinner tonight. I'm cooking steak.'

Gregory's eyes followed her as she marched out of the kitchen.

'Phew, you know how to rub each other up the wrong way,' JB said, calling Norman over to feed him a taste of his bun.

From where he was sitting, Gregory could see John planting bulbs of some kind, close to the empty field where the apple trees should be, yet where no apples grew. Part of him wanted to run after Adela so they could scream at each other some more. To scream and shout and roar. Stop it, Adela. Stop making me feel the burning hole inside of me. *Stop.*

124

Chapter 24

Gregory poured John a glass of wine. 'Adela's quite the chef, don't you think?'

John smiled, still chewing on a piece of steak. 'Indeed, yes.'

Wiping a strand of hair from her face, she stuck out her tongue at Gregory, still half-annoyed at his behaviour earlier. 'Gregory is quite the comedian. I like to refer to this meal as village steak.'

'Village steak?' Gregory asked, raising an eyebrow.

'Yes,' she said, 'steak with a little black magic of its own.'

John's face scrunched up like a used napkin. 'I burn mine too. That's the way I like it.'

'Not to worry, there's always dessert.' She shrugged her shoulders. 'As you can probably tell, I grew up tying the apron around my shoulders instead of my waist.'

Gregory leaned back in his chair. 'Supergirl...now there's an image!'

'You were more of a tomboy, then? Climbing trees, cut knees, that sort of thing?' John said.

Adela nodded, still echoing in her ears the sound of her mother's voice shouting to get out from under her feet. 'Although I was always fascinated by the hive of activity that was our kitchen. My mother was a great cook but she didn't have the tolerance for a sous-chef. I'm always intending to book myself onto a cookery course. Someday I'll find the time.'

'You've got time this week,' Gregory said. 'I could show you a few of my moves, if you like.'

Her nose wrinkled. 'As long as we're still talking about cooking?'

John burst out laughing. 'Wicked girl, that's what you are.'

'Well?'

A simple offer…why had her mother been incapable of even that? 'Is this your way of trying to make friends again, Gregory?'

Gregory leaned his two elbows on the table. 'It might be.'

'Okay then, you've got yourself a deal.'

They shook hands as John crunched on the slightly underdone vegetables.

Gregory turned to him. 'I believe I've been stealing your gardening tool quotes for my own personal gain. You're partial to a bit of philosophy?'

With unbridled relief, John laid down his fork, a half-cooked carrot embedded between the silver prongs. 'Sure. I've also developed a fascination for quantum physics. I would have made an excellent scientist…had I studied science.'

'He reads physics books for fun…can you imagine?'

'I would have looked great in a white coat,' John said.

Adela gave him a wink. 'There's definitely a smidge of mad scientist about you, John. Maybe it's the hair!'

Gregory lifted up his glass. 'I propose a toast…to new friends, the odd argument, a bit of cooking and the genius of philosophy and science.'

They clinked glasses and laughed together, enjoying their evening immensely, despite the bad taste of the food.

#

'What's the deal with that Toni girl?' Adela asked as they strolled along the walkway towards the bridge, Adela having insisted on walking John home.

'Young Toni, all fists and eyeliner?'

She nodded. 'That would be the one.'

'I suppose you heard about the incident?'

'Sort of. What happened?'

John bent down and lifted a wide, flat stone from the ground. 'Nigel caught her climbing over my back wall last week, a black plastic bag and a knife sticking out of her trouser pocket.'

'Why on earth was she doing that?'

He shrugged. 'They say she's a bit light-fingered.'

Adela thought about the version of Toni she'd seen crying on a rock. A shiver ran through her, thinking about what may have been hiding in Toni's pockets as they'd walked together in the forest that day. 'Nigel wasn't very happy with her.'

'I'm sure she was a beautiful baby,' John said, taking a detour down towards the river.

'Well, she'd better not come near *your* house again, the cheeky brat.' Inside Adela arose feelings of supreme protection towards John. Who did that girl think she was?

'Ah, never mind. Nothing was taken. It was all fine in the end.'

'That's not the point,' Adela said, huffing at the thought. 'I hear her mother is hard work.'

'Whose isn't? Come on; let's put the heart across Eamonn if he's at his usual fishing spot. He's always good for a laugh, is Eamonn!'

Adela followed John blindly. She would follow him anywhere; she already loved the bones of him. That Toni wretch would have *her* to deal with if she tried any more nonsense.

#

'Daisy, this is a surprise.' Gregory handed her a cup of tea. 'What can I do for you?'

Daisy toyed with the idea of lifting a biscuit from the plate. 'I was chatting to Adela earlier and we were discussing some of the misfortunes of our village, Gregory. We were talking about the curse.'

'The village isn't cursed, Daisy. I thought you'd have more sense than to believe in such nonsense.'

'The whole village believes in its own bad luck, not just me. People are trying so hard, but they're getting tired and fed up. They're good people, Gregory. They need some extra help, is all.'

'Did Adela put you up to this?'

'No, but she has led me to thinking and somebody needs to do something.'

Suspicions aroused, he tried to remain calm. 'You think I owe this village anything, Daisy? What has this village ever done for me?'

'Don't you think it's time to move on?'

'I *have* moved on. I just don't want the village to drag me down like it's dragged the rest of you.'

'Now you listen here, Gregory Sheridan, I don't care a toss about fancy kitchens or swimming pools. But I do care about people. They need help and I'm asking you to help them.'

'Why can't *you* help them? Tell Margaret to stop freaking everyone out—that would be a start.'

'I've an elderly mother, a gammy knee and a pub standing within an inch of its dowdy life. That's the irritating truth of it. I'm too old and I don't know how. I'll do what I can but I can't do it alone. Something needs to change in this village…and soon.'

Women were demanding creatures. 'I will not force myself to be what you want me to be. I'm sorry, Daisy.'

'Well, I'm sorry too, Gregory. I didn't want it to be like this.'

He cursed himself for having gone near Daisy's pub the other night, letting her think she had a right to come waltzing in here.

'What do you mean?'

She leaned closer to him. 'I know who Adela is.'

'What?'

'Actually, it was Elly who recognised her from one of her magazines.'

Unable to speak, all he could do was to wait for her to continue.

'I also know the media would be more than interested to discover she's hiding out in our cursed village, in the home of the local hermit. That would make for a great story, I imagine. Now, if the press get wind of it, she'll be out of here like a rocket. I've seen the way you look at her. I've known you for a long time and I don't believe you want her to go.'

'You're *blackmailing* me?'

'Blackmail is a very misunderstood word. Call it *gentle persuasion for the better good.*'

'Get out of my house—*now*,' he ordered, standing up so as to leave her under no illusions of his feelings. 'You're a cold-blooded woman, Daisy Reynolds.'

'I'm speaking the only language you're prepared to understand. Don't get me wrong, I like Adela. I even thought she might be good for you. I'm not asking you to serve up Norman for dinner. I just want you to help your village get back on its feet.'

'How dare you!'

Standing up and stepping closer to him, her eyes brimmed over with tears. 'Don't you understand, Gregory? Some of those people are slowly dying inside and they don't know what to do about it. If not you, then who? They've got nothing left to believe in, no money, too much time and too many crazy thoughts leading them in the opposite directions to where is good for them to be going. I love those people, Gregory. If I were cold-blooded, I would stand by and do nothing.'

His cheeks were flaming. 'Everyone has an angle, Daisy.'

'Why does that have to be a bad thing?'

'I'm nobody's saviour. You of all people know that.'

She brushed the palm of her hand against his cheek and whispered. 'Then expect to have those journalists pounding on your door.'

Gregory watched her shuffle out through the door and down the garden. The doorframe held his weight and he stayed there, looking out into the night long after she had disappeared from sight, battling the ache squeezing inside his chest; the invisible, cureless pain.

Chapter 25

DAY 7 - Sunday

Out of her bed at six that morning, Adela danced for an hour before taking a long, luxurious soak in Gregory's blissful Jacuzzi. Even without the fake fire burning in the background, the Jacuzzi room was enough to make her grin at its sheer luxury. It occurred to her as she was drying herself, the difference in her attitude towards this Jacuzzi today. She allowed herself to appreciate it, instead of dismissing it, like she had when she'd first arrived here. Slipping back into bed with her eReader, dressed in her leggings and long V-neck top, she read some more of her book.

Her notebook open beside her, she began taking notes alongside every page she finished. John had awakened another perspective in her and now she was seeing more in her grandmother's words than ever before. The peaceful background Gregory's home provided cocooned her, helping her to focus more on the writings and less on how they had affected her life.

By ten o'clock she was in the mood for a cup of tea and some hot, buttery toast. Gregory was sitting by the window in the kitchen, watching a small, brown, speckled bird peck at the seed cylinder hanging down from the bird table.

'Hey, you,' she said with a smile, flicking the switch on the kettle. 'Refill?'

'No thanks.'

'Your pool is amazing. What a lovely way to start the day. In fact, your whole house, Gregory, makes me feel like time has stopped, like all the hassles of the world are far away. I'm beginning to understand why you chose here to hide.'

'I'm not *hiding*. I told you before. You don't listen.'

Two minutes into the day and she'd already insulted him. *Fantastic.* 'In my own abominable way, I was trying to pay you a compliment.'

His stressed-out forehead relaxed. 'I know. Sit down. I want to talk to you.'

He wants me to leave. I'm not ready to go back out into that world again. Not yet.

'Let me butter this toast and I'll be with you.' In no hurry, Adela gently scraped the butter against the toasted side of the bread, ensuring each corner was covered. What would happen once she was gone from this odd sort of paradise? She wasn't ready to decide how to piece her life back together.

Had she only been here a week? Gregory was looking away from her again. Not a good sign. Please let her cheeks not redden like grilled tomatoes when he said it. She didn't want him to know he could have such an effect on her.

'We can sit here in silence if you'd prefer,' she said, lifting a half-slice of toast. 'We don't have to talk. Conversation, especially on sunny mornings, can ruin the ambiance.'

'Another insult?' His lips curved into a slight smile.

She snorted. 'What's one more, eh?'

'Indeed,' he said. 'I was thinking about the village. You were moaning at me to do something to help it, so my question to you is, "what"?'

'What can you do?'

'No, Adela, what can *we* do? You're still under my roof, that makes you part of this village.'

'Are you being serious?'

'I suppose so.'

Tapping her lips with her index finger, she mumbled. 'Hmmm, what could we do?'

'I may as well be honest; the part of my brain responsible for being nice, due to severe lack of use, has pretty much rusted away. I'm not the ideas man in this situation.'

'Well, from the age of three, I was party-planning for my entire doll collection, so between us I'm sure we can think of something,' she said, observing the pained expression on his face. 'Why are you doing this?'

'To give Daisy one less thing to complain about.'

'I've been here almost a week already. I'm only here for another couple of days, Gregory. I'm not sure how much we'll be able to achieve in that short space of time.'

'So you're not up for the challenge?'

'That's not exactly what I said.'

'You should take it as a compliment.' He nudged her gently. 'I wouldn't team up with just anyone.'

She tucked those loose straggles of her hair behind her ear. 'I wish I could say the same, but we'd both know that would be a lie.'

He laughed, his eyes turning soft.

'But seriously, I think I might have an idea. It's not much, but it might be fun.'

'What?'

'Let's just say, it will involve a lot of shopping, a torch, a weather forecast and a map of the village.'

Chapter 26

Adela was enjoying being outside of the mansion walls with the beardless Gregory. Women browsing around the shopping centre were lapping him up with their greedy eyes and filthy imaginations. Their expressions gave them away. Some deliberately trying to catch his attention, others simply admiring the view.

'Now that I have you in a public place, there's something I want to know...your mother informs me you fancy yourself as a bit of a mind reader.'

'My mother told you that?' he said, displaying his poker face. 'Nonsense.'

Adela's eyes narrowed. 'How would I know when you're lying?'

'You wouldn't.'

She rested her hands on her lap and huffed a little.

'See how you moved your body away from me there. Your whole body was twisting over to face me, then I said something you didn't like, and you literally turned yourself away from me, to reject me as you perceive I rejected you.'

'That's pretty obvious, even to us halfwits. Tell me something else.' The coffee tasted lukewarm and bitter. 'Read some of these people.'

'Okay, well see that woman over there, the one who's picking specks of dirt off her cardigan while her partner is chattering into her ear. I could pretty well guarantee you she doesn't like what he's saying to her. Instead of barking back at him, like she wants to, she is picking off the fluff. It's a displacement action.'

'What about that bloke over there by the railings?'

'See the way he has his thumbs tucked into the tops of his jean pockets. Notice what his thumbs are pointing towards. He wants you to notice how much of a man he really is.'

She made a face. 'Yuck. Creep.'

'And see how every man who walks past that hot-looking woman with the red handbag gives her a second glance? Do you know why?'

'Because she has legs up to her elbows, a gorgeous body and perfect lips?'

'Well, yes. But here's the reason why men think she's gorgeous. They find peachy bums like hers most attractive. A protruding backside gives a man the impression a woman is available for him.'

'That makes me feel dirty...'

'It's nature, pure and simple, although interestingly enough women's buttocks do have other purposes...'

'Such as?'

'Well, they store fat for feeding babies and also act as emergency food storage in case of leaner times.'

She laughed. 'I've never thought about my bum in quite as much detail before.'

'You can be pretty sure men have!'

'This shopping centre is having a weird effect on you.'

He raised his hands up in the air, palms facing her. 'You either want to know or you don't. It is what it is, Adela. If you don't want to hear it...'

Enthralled, she leaned forward. 'Are you kidding me? Go on!'

'Okay, well the reason men are attracted to her long legs is because of how fertile-looking they are.'

'How can legs look fertile? Are you lying to me? Damnit, I don't know how to tell!'

'No, I'm not lying! When a girl reaches puberty, her legs get longer, quickly. This is a sign she's maturing. It's all programming!'

'You men are weird.'

'Hey,' he said, nodding his head at her. 'It's not only us men that get taken in by the laws of nature. You women are just as consumed by your subconscious desires as we are.'

'Like how?'

'You like broad-shouldered men with muscular arms...all the better to protect you with. And small tight bums...all the better to make babies with. Oh, we are *all* part of nature's hilarious game of life. Doesn't it amuse you? It amuses the hell out of me.'

Nature's game of life didn't always seem so funny. She turned her empty coffee cup around in circles on the table using both hands.

He pointed to what she was doing. 'See how you're fondling your cup. Now, if I didn't know you better, I could interpret that as a gesture of things to come. It could be considered a courtship signal.'

'Ah, would you stop,' she said. 'For the record, I'm not trying to seduce you. Jeez, Gregory, I have enough problems.'

Adela removed her hands from her coffee cup and instead lifted out a mirror and a tube of lipstick from her handbag, all the time Gregory watching with interest. Applying a slow, deliberate layer of *rocket red* to her lips had never been more fun.

'Did you also know the use of lipstick is four thousand years old, invented by the Egyptians?'

She snapped the mirror shut. 'You're such a *woman*, Gregory...you know way too much about this stuff.'

His shark eyes bubbled with delight as he lifted his jacket from the back of the chair. 'Come on, we'd better

136

finish off this shopping. I promise I'll ignore any further seductive gestures you may direct my way.'

She gave him a steamy Hollywood actress look, pouting red lips and all. 'In your dreams, hermit!'

#

'Why are we stopping here?' Adela asked. 'Are you sure we've got time for this? We have a busy evening ahead of us.'

Gregory pulled up the handbrake and gave her a look that suggested he didn't know whether to kiss or shake her.

'I thought a walk on the beach might momentarily distract us from our future hell of shopping bags and gift baskets.'

'Hmmm, I like your way of thinking. This is the kind of stalling technique I can appreciate.' His hand felt warm to the touch as he escorted her out of the car. 'What a stunning sunset.'

'Yes, stunning,' he agreed, his eyes lingering a fraction too long upon her.

He helped her over the small stone wall. The air felt fresh on her skin. A mile of beach stretched before them and the ocean glistened invitingly. The sky was filled with swirls of yellows and oranges; the sun, relentless in its passion, pouring light upon them even in the final stages of its decent. Adela watched the waves lapping upon the sand, climbing closer to the shore with every sleepy and gentle attempt.

The beach was empty except for an elderly couple, owners of an over-excited Labrador who was splashing through the waves, chasing after his stick.

'I love the beach,' Adela said, burying a shell deeper into the sand with her shoe. 'When I was a teenager, my gang of friends and I would sneak away for a night every summer, pitch our tents in the sand dunes, share some bottles of cheap wine and generally be ridiculous.'

'You wouldn't want to know the history of the dunes,' he remarked. 'The stories they could tell.'

'This place is gorgeous.' Goosebumps prickled her arms. 'Do you come here often?'

'Is that the best line you've got?' Gregory picked up a small stone and skimmed it across the water.

She removed her shoes. 'Trust me, Hermit, if I was giving you a line, you'd know it.'

He grinned. 'What are you doing? The water will be freezing.'

'Ah, live a little.' She lifted the bottom of her dress and paddled her feet. 'Join me.'

'No way, it's cold and you're mad.'

She kicked some water at him. 'Chicken.'

'Hey,' he cried, jumping back. 'Stop it.'

Turning her back to the sunset, Adela stood, burying her feet into the sand, the water lapping around her ankles. 'What's the point of getting all the way to the edge of the water without going in? Where's the fun in that?'

Her words seemed to sting him.

'I have a heated pool at home. I don't need to endure sand in my shoes. Paddling isn't worth the hassle. Plus, the water has to be freezing. Where's the fun in *that*?'

'Take off your shoes, Hermit, and paddle with me.'

'Not on your life, crazy woman.'

'Do it,' she insisted. '*Or else.*'

'Or else, what?'

Adela wiggled both ends of her dress at him. 'Or else I'll go streaking down the beach and embarrass you in front of that couple and their dog.'

'Call that a threat?' He smirked. 'Go right ahead.'

'I'm not joking.'

'Neither am I.'

Damn him. She huffed a little and walked on. 'Fine. Be *old* all your life, see if I care.'

'Ahh, you're upset that I don't want to paddle with you.'

'I'm upset that you called my bluff.'

'Your threat was deeply misguided. I'm male, remember!'

'It was the best I could come up with under pressure. The cold must be getting to me.'

Gregory bent down and began removing his socks and shoes. 'Oh, you insufferable woman. It's all emotions and tricks with you. *Fine*, I'll paddle.'

Adela splashed around happily after that, successful in her mission to lure Gregory into the water. They made their way down the beach together, ankles splashing and conversation filled with teasing and joking, enjoying what was left of the setting March sun.

#

'I've never seen a person who can exhaust a credit card so spectacularly,' Gregory said, tying his fortieth red ribbon around yet another gift basket.

'Stop strangling that poor ribbon. Even your bows are mean.'

'Control freak.' He elbowed her. 'Are we crazy? It's the middle of the night, what are we doing? You have weird ideas.'

'Enough with your complaining, hermit,' she said, lifting up two baskets off the table. 'Come on, let's go.'

They filled Gregory's boot with the gift baskets and he drove them down into the village, the moon overhead following along for the craic. He parked along a side road.

'What time is it?' he whispered.

'Four o'clock.'

'Let's hope they're all sleeping like babies. Give Daisy and Elly a basket that *I* wrapped,' he said. 'The badly-tied ribbon will feed Daisy's need for complaining.'

Adela lifted another four baskets from the boot. 'She's not *that* bad!'

He grunted. 'Wanna bet? Come on, let's go.'

The two of them, like a pair of Santa's elves, crept about the village for the next two hours, delivering their gift baskets at the doors of randomly selected people. Gregory should have been tired, but Adela had infused him with enthusiasm for their project. He watched her giggle with delight as she placed another basket on the doorstep of yet another unsuspecting villager.

'This will create a bit of a buzz in the morning. They will *never* suspect you, Gregory.'

That wasn't altogether true. Daisy would more than suspect, she would *know*. Would this little stunt be enough to keep her off his back? What was he doing running around the village in the middle of the night? He didn't even like these people, yet he'd spent a small fortune and hours of his time packaging gifts for them. Why had he caved in to Daisy's ridiculous threats? Was he really so lonely after all? No, he was not. He'd simply come to the conclusion there was no harm in humouring Daisy and her need to save the world. Once Adela was gone, that would be the end of this façade, and his life would return to normal. Adela was the reason for all of this scampering about like a demented Santa. Women stopped having a hold on him a long time ago. He never believed any of them would again.

Chapter 27

DAY 8 - Monday

Adela signalled to John from the window to come into the kitchen for a bite of breakfast. Grilled bacon and poached eggs were crackling and boiling under Gregory's expert care.

'Did we really do all that yesterday?' Yawning was the only activity Adela's mouth particularly wished to engage in. Last night seemed like a ludicrous dream.

A powerful set of knuckles wrapped on the door. 'Hello?'

'Morning,' she said, yawning in poor John's face. 'Cuppa?'

John glanced at Gregory. 'I shouldn't really. I've just arrived...'

Gregory waved at him with the spatula. 'Oh, come on in, John.'

His shoulders relaxing, John dragged out a chair and sat himself down. 'It's been the strangest morning.'

'Oh?' Adela said, winking secretly at Gregory.

'I opened my front door to find a basket full of wine, chocolates, cake, fruit, flower seeds, lottery tickets, magazines and all sorts of things. All wrapped up with a big red bow.'

'Where did that come from?' Innocence oozed out of her.

John shrugged. 'Darned if I know. I called into Daisy on the way here and low and behold, she and Elly had one too. It seems a lot of the village folk were delivered a similar surprise.'

'Wow,' she said, feeling all warm inside.
'Amazing.'

Gregory placed a plate in front of John. 'You may as well have some breakfast while you're here.'

'Thanks, thanks.'

Adela stood up to get him a knife and fork. Gregory's body moved around hers, avoiding touching, yet close enough to each feel the presence of the other. A quick exchange.

He laid her plate on the table. 'What did Daisy have to say?'

'She wasn't her usual self at all. In fact, I did most of the talking. Daisy hadn't even opened up her basket. Margaret had already been on the phone, oohing and aahing about her presents. But just as I was leaving, Daisy's phone had already started to ring. The village had woken up to their surprise, everyone asking the same two questions…who and why?'

How could she be feeling so happy right now? What they'd done was a small thing. Nothing special. Yet Adela's insides felt aglow, as if a light inside her somehow got switched on. 'That's a crazy thing to do.'

John looked around. 'Didn't you get one, Gregory?'

'Not that I noticed.'

John's eyes moved around the room and then stopped, focusing on one spot. Adela followed his line of vision. One of Gregory's awful attempts at ribbon-making was sitting, abandoned, on the island. John looked at Adela, who was squirming at Gregory.

'I guess that means we're caught,' Gregory said, tucking into his breakfast.

Adela raised her index finger to her smiling lips.

John laughed, shook his head, and poured himself a hot cup of tea. 'Well, well. You pair of eejits! That's some influence your grandmother's book is having on you, young lady. Some influence, indeed.'

142

'We had so much fun, John, you wouldn't believe!'

John turned to Gregory. 'Even *you*?'

Gregory smiled. 'It wasn't the worst day I ever spent.'

'So what made you do it?'

Adela interrupted. 'I was moaning about how depressed the village was, focusing on all that curse nonsense. Gregory decided we should try to bring a bit of cheer to the place.'

'Hmmm.' John took a drink from his cup.

'Hmmm, what?' she asked. *John's brain...always churning.*

'How did it make you feel?'

How did it make her feel? Exhilarated, excited, happy... 'Alive.'

'And you?' he nodded at Gregory.

Gregory gave a slight laugh. 'You actually want to sit here discussing my *feelings*? Who are you, my *mother*?'

'Afraid you might have to admit you have any?' Infectious warmth spread across John's face.

'I'll tell you exactly how he felt, John...he was delighted with himself!'

'The reason I'm asking,' John said, rubbing his two hands together. 'Is because those feelings of yours, I thought you'd be interested in how they play a most important role in your life, even if you'd rather not discuss them over breakfast.'

Gregory frowned. 'In my experience, it's your feelings that tend to trip you up, get you into trouble.'

'No, Gregory, you have it all wrong. Have you ever used a map?'

'Sure,' he said with a shrug.

'Well, your feelings are the signposts leading the way along your roadmap to your best and easiest route ahead.'

Adela nudged Gregory. '*You* need a revised edition.'

'Hey,' he said. 'You can't talk, yours landed you *here*!'

'Tell us more, oh Great Master of Feelings,' she teased.

'Well, it's your intuition, your instinct. If deep inside it feels right and it feels good, then you're travelling in the right direction, but if it feels off, you may need to stop and redirect. We all know when we've taken a wrong turn. The wiser part of us knows. Our feelings guide us along, moment by moment, day by day, our whole lives long. That's why I asked how your secretive, night-time mission *felt*, I was wondering what it meant to you. I like to try to figure out which roads people are travelling. Maybe you felt superior to the rest of the village or you might have felt a kind of empathy for them. Two very different feelings…two very different directions.'

'You want to know how it felt to surprise the village?' Gregory said.

'I do,' John challenged him.

'My pockets felt light, my back felt sore and my eyes felt tired.' Gregory stood up. 'Speaking of directions, I'm getting the *feeling* that it's time I directed myself to my office to do some work.'

'Before you go, will I tell you how else it made me feel?' Adela said.

Gregory stopped. 'Sure.'

'Like I belonged, which is crazy; after all, I've only been here a week.'

Gregory opened his mouth but nothing came out.

'Hmmm, sounds like *your* signposts are pointed in a good direction.' John nodded. 'I suppose I should be greeting the morning myself. Thanks for the breakfast.'

144

'There's no rush, John. Sure stay for another while yet and keep her Highness company. Discuss your *feelings* a bit more.'

A throaty old man chuckle. 'Ah, if you insist.'

Adela poured John another cup of tea. Once she was assured Gregory was nowhere within earshot, she whispered across the table. 'Can you believe he did all that? The beard was holding him back.'

'From what Daisy tells me, young Josie McCarthy is mending buckets about you being here. Wait until she realises you got Gregory to step outside of Hermitsville. Did you shove him into some old phone box, twirl him around, and turn him into The Good Samaritan? From what I know of Gregory, and I try not to listen to idle gossip, but he is no fan of this village.'

'What idle gossip have you *never* listened to?' she asked, checking behind her to ensure the kitchen door was still closed.

'Why do you want to know?'

'You know why! Because I'm nosey.'

'And that's the only reason?'

She tried not to blush. 'For all your insight, John, you've a mind as dirty as the bottom of a school boy's pencil case. I'm living in the man's house; why shouldn't I want to know about him?'

He whistled instead of answering her question. 'One thing I do know is that Mr Sheridan is not acting like himself, nor does he even look like himself, and it's all because of *you.*'

'Please don't tell Daisy about Gregory being the one who organised the baskets. He didn't wait until four o'clock in the morning for no good reason. He'd hate for them to find out.'

'Afraid he'd lose his reputation as the coldest fish in town?' John drank down the rest of his tea before standing up. 'My, my, this is a day of surprises, let me tell

145

you. Funny that Gregory wouldn't admit his real motivation for last night.'

Adela's heart was thumping unusually hard in her chest. 'You think he was humouring me, don't you?'

John held up his hands defensively. 'Unusually generous for a hermit, I would say.'

'The whole thing was his idea.'

'Then I'm sure his motives were as pure as his filtered water.'

'You don't think I should trust him?'

'I was just wondering, that was all. Trying to figure him out. Anyway, I'd better be going out to do some work. Well done to the pair of you. Whatever the reasons, it was a mighty good gesture.'

But John's words had taken the shine off their little adventure, like a dirty scuff on a brand new pair of shoes. She was left wondering about the man with whom she had delivered all those baskets. In her desperation, had she begun to mould the hermit into the person she wanted him to be, not who he actually was? Cutting his hair, shaving his beard, forcing him out into the village, enticing him to do the biggest shop of his life, and even convincing him to tie all those terrible red bows. What on earth was she doing here? Playing pretend with a man prepared to play pretend, the two of them like actors stepping into each other's lives for a moment in time.

John had been telling her to listen to her feelings…well, her feelings were tainted with all kinds of darkness. She had drunkenly cheated on her own fiancé, of course she couldn't trust her own feelings. Even the clarity of John's words seemed to dissolve into nonsense. Maybe all of it was nonsense: her grandmother's book, John's advice, her developing friendship with Gregory. What could she really depend on to be true? Not John's misaligned ideas, not Gregory's smile and certainly not her own heart.

146

Chapter 28

Adela couldn't resist paying a visit to get a taste of Mad Margaret's reaction. How would the baskets fit into the woman's belief about the village being cursed?

Mad Margaret welcomed her with the warmth of an old friend, coming around from the other side of the counter and embracing her warmly. 'I'm so glad to see you again. You light the place right up, so you do! Did you hear about our gift baskets? They're the talk of the village. They put smiles on the faces of even the miserable feckers! Did Gregory get one?'

The sound of wind chimes jingled from the direction of the main doorway. 'No, he didn't. I mean, I heard about the baskets; John told us this morning, but nothing was left on Gregory's doorstep.'

'Well now, Adela, what would *he* need with a gift basket? Sure he could afford a swimming pool of gift baskets! I got lovely surprises in mine! Diamond hair clips, croissants, a silk scarf, lipstick... gorgeous. I'm itching to know who managed to keep it secret from me and Daisy.'

'I thought Daisy knew everything!'

'Not that she's saying. But even friends have secrets, I suppose!' Margaret's grin reminded Adela of a black cat stretching on the street, basking in the warmth of the sun. 'You can't beat a good secret to get the blood flowing through the veins.'

Adela laughed, picking out a fresh cake. Margaret refused to take any money for it.

'You'll never make money by giving away your stuff for free.'

Margaret grinned at her. 'You enjoy a nice slice of that with a hot cup of tea.'

Adela thought about the free cake. John would say it was the Universe at work, getting back what she'd given away. Could the world really have such magic going on behind the scenes?

Mad Margaret's smile stopped short of her face. 'What's wrong?'

'I hope nobody chokes on a mint or trips up over their fancy new basket and hits their head. You make sure you take care while you're here, sweetheart.' Margaret made some sort of a signal to the daft-looking fake blackbird, hanging over the door, alongside the wind chimes. 'Our village is cursed, don't you know!'

\#

Gregory didn't leave his office all day. Although tired, he was enjoying the pleasant feeling of calm he'd been experiencing since last night. After a busy twenty-four hours, he welcomed some time alone. Unused to the company of another person, much less a woman, Adela had crept under his skin.

A swim before dinner would refresh him. But Adela had the same plan, already relaxing in the Jacuzzi when he arrived. He waved to her before diving into the pool and swimming four lengths straight. *What was she thinking amongst those Jacuzzi bubbles? Would she have any idea what was going through his head?* He leaned up out of the pool. 'Did you get some sleep today?'

Hair piled up into a high bun, skin bare and shimmering, Adela could have been cut straight out of a magazine. 'Not really. I dozed a little. I was chatting to Mad Margaret earlier. She said to say hi.'

'She's a piranha, that one.'

'I think she's nice.'

A couple more lengths before he climbed out of the pool. 'Mind if I join you?'

148

Adela frowned, her lips tight. *What sort of body language was that?*

'What's the plan for tonight? Garden makeovers, window cleaning, house painting?'

She allowed him a half-smile. 'A bit of TV and an early night.'

'That's it?' The water was warm. He looked outside through the large glass panels. The sky was spring-like and bright; John had the shrubbery well-tended. 'All good things must come to an end, I suppose.'

'Indeed they must.' She closed her eyes, as if relaxing in the bubbles.

'What if I crack open a nice bottle of wine and make a fancy dinner to celebrate?'

'To celebrate what?'

'What happened to you since this morning?' he asked. *Her mind, it seemed, was hot and bubbling, like his Jacuzzi.*

'I'm in a bad mood.'

'But you were so pleased with yourself…what changed?'

'Pleased with myself? Because we did one supposedly nice thing for a few miserable people? You think that changes anything? Let me tell you, it changes nothing. We're still the same lousy people today as we were yesterday. Remember that before you go patting yourself too hard on the back.'

He moved closer to her. 'Why are you always trying to convince yourself that you don't deserve to be happy?'

'Why are you being so nice to me? You're a hermit, damnit. Start acting like one.'

'Excuse me?'

'Why did you do all that yesterday?'

'Because you guilt-tripped me into doing something nice for those eejits.'

'And why did you let me shave off your beard?'

'Why are you analysing the hell out of it? It was something to do. Why does the idea of my liking you cause you to react this way? Would you rather we spent the time hating each other?'

'No, I—'

What beautiful, conflicted eyes she had. 'Because despite my aversion to people, I *like* you, Adela. And I like that you guilted me into helping the village. It's good for a cynical, ageing man like me. You've been good for me.'

Smiling humbly, she reached out and touched his face. 'You do look so much better without all that extra hair. And you're not old.'

He laughed, thinking of John's conversation about feelings being the roadmap of your life. How did that work? In what way did Adela fit into John's theory? How would he feel when she walked out his door? What direction would he be travelling on his roadmap then?

Chapter 29

'Ground nutmeg.' Adela fingered through each ingredient Gregory had placed on the counter top. 'I've bought at least four jars of ground nutmeg in my life and never knew what to do with it.'

Gregory laughed, removing ginger, a lime and a red pepper from the fridge.

A bottle of rum? 'I wouldn't have thought you'd be trying to get me drunk again so soon.'

'You got that right.' He passed her a knife. 'Here's a tip; you should always keep good knives in your kitchen. It will make all the difference to how you feel about your cooking. The preparation takes time so it's important to enjoy it.'

'Note to self: must have fun in the kitchen!'

'Of course, the process of having fun while cooking begins with one very important thing.'

'What would that be?'

'Music!' He gave his hands a quick wash and then opened the cabinet in the corner of the room. 'Shuffle okay with you?'

'You can tell a lot about a man by his "shuffle".'

Yet another female pop song blasted into the room.

The laughing began, Adela couldn't help it.
'Another interesting song choice. Know all the words, do you?'

He sang along, waving the wooden spoon in the air like a microphone.

'And the hermit can sing…well, of course! Enough showing off, weirdo! Now, what will I do first?'

151

After setting his wooden spoon aside, Gregory handed her the mushrooms, pepper and the ginger. 'Chop those up, please. Slice the ginger small, like you would garlic.'

'So what's this meal we're cooking?'

The chopping board was pulled out, on which he placed the first raw chicken breast. 'Foreign Holiday Chicken.'

'Foreign Holiday chicken, eh? Can we have tiny paper umbrellas in our drinks too, like Elly's googleberry juice? Wow, that's one hell of a sharp knife, Mr Sheridan.'

'Good, isn't it,' he said, pointing to the pepper she was chopping. 'Did you know that one red pepper has more vitamin C than an equivalent-sized orange? They're excellent for the immune system.'

'No, I can't say I've ever studied up on the properties of a red pepper.'

'Did your mother really not want you in her kitchen?'

'No. It was her domain only.' Adela watched him slice through the second chicken breast. How it could have been, standing alongside her mother, learning tips to pass down to her own daughter, ideas that might have made Adela's cooking life a little more interesting or inspired. 'My mother's a good woman; she just has her own ways.'

'Doesn't every woman?' he said, lightening the mood a little.

'She's never been a very capable person.' Adela scooped up the chopped peppers and placed them into the designated bowl. 'Small things get her flustered. She thinks I'm off my head climbing mountains and wanting to surf. She doesn't stray too far from her house. Her neighbourhood is her world. I think that's why she

152

doesn't really understand mine. It's too big, too uncomfortable for her.'

'She's afraid?'

'Yeah, I suppose she is. It's always, "don't do that or don't do this". Yes, when you say it, she's pretty much afraid of everything. I guess I found it hard to understand because I was always so excited about life. She would fret and I would pat her on the shoulder and tell her not to be worrying. But when I needed her to pat me on the back and tell me not to be worrying, it never even occurred to her. Somehow my worries made her worries worse. It's always been about her, even when it's about me.'

'So who helps *you*?'

'My sister and my friends. I like to deal with things on my own, when I can. I like to be independent, this week being the obvious exception.'

He handed her across a medium-sized glass bowl. 'We're going to mix some of these ingredients in here. I printed out the recipe for you to follow.'

Continuing to watch, he helped her now and again as she made up the marinade. 'Didn't you ever cook with David?'

A tablespoon of brown sugar in her hand, she shrugged. 'He was worse than me. We were minimalistic in the kitchen. Lots of pizzas, the odd spaghetti bolognaise from a jar if we got really adventurous!'

'You must miss him.'

'Of course. It seems I'm a great mountain climber but a terrible fiancée.'

'Don't you worry, it'll all be okay. David will come around. With domestic goddess-like qualities such as yours, he'd be crazy not to!'

#

Adela watched the flicker of the solid cream candle, sitting in an ornate beige candle holder. The dining room was warm and inviting, with its thick carpet and

153

luxurious flowered beige and cream wallpaper. Double doors opened out onto the outside patio area, which was surrounded by raised flowerbeds and baby trees. The dining table was long and low, made of marble. This room was connected to the sitting room by a huge wooden wall that could be slid open or closed, as it was tonight. 'This is delicious.'

'Thank yourself…you made it!'

What was David doing right now? No contact from him since their last wretched phone call. The insults he had pelted at her. Then again, she supposed, hurt could do that to a person.

'How have your parents dealt with recent events?' Gregory said, pouring her more wine.

'The same way they deal with everything.' Although grimacing was not good for the complexion, Adela couldn't stop herself; the mere mention of her parents put all her face muscles on high alert. 'My hypocrite of a father ignored me, on the understanding that my mother would say all that needed to be said on the matter. My mother took to her bed for the first three days and has been using it as a reason to cry every time I speak with her. If she's not upset, she gets angry. She is the ultimate victim, especially because of her large neighbourhood of friends. She's always been a victim in some shape or form. I've just given her a particularly valid reason to be one this time.'

'My father does that too. He drinks and smokes his way through his day. He accepts that for himself, as if there is nothing else. He has set such limits on his life, it drives me mad.'

'So your father's lack of drive gave you your ambition to have all this?'

'I suppose so. Interesting, how it can work like that.' He laid down his knife and fork. 'What's your relationship like with your dad?'

'Difficult.' She shrugged. 'He worked a lot; although it turns out he's an excellent multi-tasker…when it comes to work and women.'

'Does your mother know?'

Adela nodded, thinking back to the drunken night with the waiter, the parts she could at least remember. She remembered her acute embarrassment at learning of her father's inappropriate actions, followed by the strong desire to drown in a large bottle of forgetfulness. 'She knows about some of it; she resents my father, makes him suffer because of it, but part of me thinks she's grown comfortable in her discomfort. She gets to play the victim while feeling superior to him, and he has to constantly make it up to her. It's a deeply unbalanced relationship…always has been. My sister and I presumed when we got old enough, they'd separate, but they seem to prefer to live miserably together than apart.'

'People are weird.'

'They sure are.'

'And you wonder why I'm a hermit!'

'I'm beginning to see what your way of life has to offer.'

Gregory lifted his glass. 'Cheers to crazy childhoods.'

He looked extraordinarily handsome in the candlelight. 'Cheers to us, Gregory. To surprisingly good times.'

The heat of the alcohol poured through them.

'Your list of rules really went to hell.'

'It did, didn't it?'

'Thanks for letting me stay.'

'You've been reading your grandmother's book with some dedication. Isn't she all about the gratitude?'

Adela's eyeballs did somersaults. 'Yes, all about the gratitude.'

'How did you fake the book tours and talks? How did you manage to answer people's questions?'

'I got really good at repeating back to them what they asked, giving me enough time to regurgitate words and phrases from the book. I got away with it, but I was stressed out all the time, wondering when I'd get caught out. Do you want to know something terrible?'

'Of course!'

'I grew to hate the words in that book. I had to pretend they were so full of wisdom but to me they were empty. I resented everything about that part of my life. I even blamed my grandmother for leaving me those damned diaries.'

'Lying is stressful. If you weren't so beautiful, you never would have got away with it.'

'That makes me feel worse,' she said, patting the sides of her mouth with her napkin. 'But being here, meeting John, listening to his version of the writings in the book, without the worry, the fear and the stress of all the lies; it has changed something. It's like I'm hearing this stuff for the very first time, even though I know I'm not. Does that make any sense?'

Gregory laid his own napkin on the table beside his plate. 'My mother says life's messages are hidden everywhere; that life is like a treasure hunt, and we find the clues to each new piece of treasure when we're ready for them. The invisible then becomes visible, as life's magic is slowly uncovered. The messages are everywhere, in poems, in songs, in books, in paintings, in conversation, in coincidences even.'

'It's a lovely idea. Do you believe it?'

'As you say, it's a lovely idea.'

'While I was travelling around the world, I kept meeting people who would want to talk to me about all that stuff. Do you know what I felt as I listened to them, as I watched light shine from their eyes?'

'What?' he asked.

'Envy. I was jealous of their belief in some kind of magic, the kind *I* was meant to be selling to *them*.'

'My mother believes in it.' Gregory lifted his glass to take a drink. 'I do think it helped her get through separating from my father. She didn't have it easy, starting over.'

'Nancy looks strong; I can see her strength, even in the way she wears her clothes.'

'You'd never imagine she's gone through what she has in her life. She attributes her courage to an inner connection to something bigger. I don't know...'

'John believes in it too.' That next sip of wine tasted so delicious, fruity and velvety sweet. 'It's like he's on the other side of a glass door with no handle and I love listening to him, but I still can't find the handle that will open the door the whole way.'

Sitting here, talking to him felt nice...safe. She watched as he stood up and disappeared. Time didn't seem to have a place here. No schedules, no panic, no lies.

Music started from nowhere, filling the room with slow, seductive sound. Gregory re-appeared, pausing in the doorway, watching her.

'Dance with me.' He reached out his hand.

'I'm not dancing with you, Gregory.'

'Dance with me.'

'Whoever heard of a dancing hermit?' *This was crazy. She only ever danced alone.*

'You know you want to,' he whispered.

Putting her hand in his was easy. His grasp was confident and strong. They moved closer together. One arm wrapped around her waist, he pulled her towards him, their bodies swaying to the rhythm of the song.

She hummed the words, her lips close to his chest. The melody cast her memory back to those times as a teenager, lying on her bed, listening to that same song on repeat, feeling its essence deep within her in a way she hadn't yet even understood, and creating in her younger imagination a perfect moment such as this.

Gregory traced his hand along her back, with every touch pressing her clothes against a part of her skin as if it had never before been touched. His fingers rested against the nave of her neck, the palm of his hand on the top of her back, its warmth tempting her, caressing her.

Adela breathed in the woody smell of his aftershave. The shape of his body was so new and inviting against hers. This music, those words, they wrapped life up in a perfect moment of life itself. Eyes closed, they danced, holding onto one another, getting lost in each other, leaving everything else behind.

Chapter 30

DAY 9 - Tuesday

The rain pounded against the large kitchen windows. Gregory's hair was still wet from the shower he'd taken after his strenuous work out. He'd needed it. What an evening they'd had. Dinner, wine and dancing. But so much more had happened between them; something had remained beyond the last drops of wine in the bottom of the glass and the smudges of chocolate desert on the table. Holding her in his arms, he'd known Adela could have asked anything of him and he'd have said yes.

Anything.

This was not what he wanted.

She was from her world and he was from his. This week was not real, their lives merely temporarily suspended. Yet last night, when they'd talked about themselves, they hadn't been so far away from one another. This hiatus meant he had begun to question his choices. He thought back to when he was young. His childhood was filled with dress up, grand imaginings and playing pretend. While he watched from the stairs, his father stealing coins from his piggy bank, Gregory had dreamed of living in a house similar to the one he now owned. He knew even then that he would never scrounge for loose change at the bottom of a jar.

But his rich imagination was catching up with him, like a set trap. He had shunned the world in place of tranquil solitude, away from the mess of human emotion. In spite of that, JB had delivered Adela to him, with all her beautiful possibilities, like a Trojan horse.

'You got up then,' Adela greeted him, running her fingers through her messy hair and tidying some of it back behind her ears. 'About time.'

He liked her sense of humour. 'I've never been able to sleep in. Half-six is the latest I make it to.'

'Ugh,' she said, pouring herself a glass of filtered water. 'We're like chalk and cheese, you and I, Gregory. I hate mornings.'

Like chalk and cheese, she'd said. 'How's the head?'

'Not too bad. I didn't drink too much, considering.' She gulped down half the contents of her glass.

Yet she'd danced with him for longer than had been good for both of them. He should have stuck to his own rules. "No friendship, no prying, no stealing inside." Why hadn't he continued to believe she was some kind of raving alcoholic? Had he forced her to leave that very first day, he would have felt relief to watch her walk out his front door. With hateful understanding he realised he was already missing her, even as she sat in front of him, chatting casually over breakfast.

'JB's coming over,' he said. 'Harry was crying in the background and the poor sod sounded exhausted.'

'Did he mention his gift basket? I'm surprised we didn't see him yesterday.'

'No, but he was probably too tired to notice it on his way out the door. He's more likely coming over to enjoy a quick afternoon siesta.'

She laughed. 'Is that a regular occurrence?'

'Only since Harry introduced himself. Sometimes JB brings his swimming trunks too, has a sleep, a swim, relaxes in the Jacuzzi for a while, gets me to make him pancakes and then leaves half dizzy with panic at the thought of yet another night ahead of a screaming baby and no proper sleep.'

160

'And you said you weren't a hotel. How wrong you were, Gregory!'

Her voice sounded cheeky when she said his name. 'That's okay; I've a very limited guest list.'

'Thanks for a lovely night, by the way,' she said. 'It was fun.'

Is that what it was? He watched her entwine her legs, a gesture used by women to draw attention to their long-limbed assets. She needed no such gestures…he'd already noticed.

Silence.

Adela lifted herself carefully off the chair in order to open the bag of croissants sitting on the counter.

'Today's plan is to get dressed and head into the village for yet another walk. Exciting, eh?'

'Knock, knock.' JB's head appeared. 'Who's going to make me a cup of coffee? You wouldn't believe the kind of night I've had.'

I could say the same myself, Gregory thought, watching JB trying to use Adela as a pillow.

'Poor you,' soothed Adela, between giggles.

'Pancakes?' Gregory asked him as JB huffed and puffed some more.

'Yes, please,' JB said, taking a seat. 'Why are babies so mean? And Julia has turned into her *mother*. My life is hell.'

'Shhh,' Adela whispered. 'Of course it's not, JB. You know what you both need?'

'What?'

'Enough distance from Harry for a few hours to remember why you love him.' Adela patted his hand. 'In fact, why don't you suggest to Julia that Gregory and I will babysit for the night and you two can go home and sleep or swing from the chandeliers, whichever you prefer?'

161

'What?' Gregory could see Norman lift his head. 'Babysitting?'

'Yes, Gregory, *babysitting*. Have a little compassion. Even hermits were babies once. Daisy told me all about you, remember?'

Gregory chose to ignore her taunting. 'Are you sure Julia won't mind handing Harry over to the pair of us? Julia and I don't exactly…gel.'

'Mind?' Using the table as a makeshift pillow, JB rested his head on it. 'Julia would let *Norman* babysit if it meant her getting some proper sleep.'

Gregory shook his head in irritation as he beat two eggs together. Adela mimicked him. JB began to snore.

#

'Well, Daisy, how are the knees today?' Adela asked, sitting up on one of the bar stools.

'Creaking, same as plenty other bits of me.' Daisy raised a pint glass up against the light to check for smudges and continued polishing it with a tea-towel. 'You'll have heard about the mysterious deliveries?'

'What a silly notion,' Adela said, slapping her hand on the counter. 'That was definitely someone with too much time on their hands.'

'Ah, get away with you, young one. What are you like?'

'You don't even want to know, Daisy. You don't even want to know.' Adela checked her phone quickly. No messages. 'Did it create a bit of a buzz about the place then?'

'Oh, they were buzzing like big, fat bees all right; are you kidding? Presents *and* a mystery to solve. They're not the brightest bunch though. They think it was Paddy McGuinness's wife Gloria from two miles south. Ever since she got new windows in, they're convinced she won the lotto!'

162

'I'm prepared to give this Gloria the credit, if she's prepared to take it!'

'And how's our Gregory doing? Stiff and tired, I suppose.'

'He's very well rested, Daisy. He'll be grateful you've taken such a keen interest in his well-being.'

'Argh,' Daisy sniffed. 'You tell him from me there are flowerbeds alongside his barn need attention before summer. The barn might be prepared to sit like a big, empty lump in the middle of the village, but the ground would appreciate a few flowers. Get John on the case and he'll have it looking good in no time.'

'How did you know it was us?'

Her frown lines burrowed deep. 'I'm ugly and old, not stupid.'

'Stubborn, I might agree with, but ugly and old definitely not.' Adela interlaced her fingers. 'I was chatting with your BFF, Mad Margaret.'

'You were hardly out the door and she'd rung me. She thinks you're simply gorgeous.'

'Is she really as wild as she seems?'

'And the rest!'

Adela smiled, thinking of Margaret's hand with three perfectly manicured fingernails and a thumbnail with tiny stars glued on for extra sparkle. 'Can I ask you a personal question?'

Lips pulled together like a string purse, Daisy looked out at Adela from under her bushy eyebrows. 'You can ask; I may or may not answer.'

'Are you happy, Daisy?'

'Happy?'

Adela nodded. 'Yeah.'

'Now what sort of a question is that?'

'I'm interested.'

Her tea-towel thrown aside, Daisy's elbows rested on the counter. 'Am I happy? Hmmm, I haven't been asked that question before.'

'First time for everything, eh Daisy!' Trying to sound cheery, she was unsure of the woman's reaction.

'Do you think I wouldn't be happy because of Elly?'

Adela gasped. 'Oh, no. Of course not.'

'I'm sure you look at her rolling her imaginary snowman head and think I must have the life from hell...'

An uncomfortable cough tickled in Adela's throat.

'But do you want to know something weird?'

'What?'

'Sometimes, it's *her* gets *me* through the day. She's always been quirky and lovable. She just needs a bit more attention than before but I have great friends in the village who help me. So, while I'm not, jump for joy kind of happy, I do okay.'

What response wouldn't sound fake or patronising? 'Good, I'm glad.'

Daisy stood up and shuffled towards the pub door. 'Elly's having her afternoon nap. I'm going to lock up this place for a few minutes. Come with me, I want to show you something.'

Adela followed her through a narrow door and passageway and up three small steps where she unbolted a heavy wooden door. Inside was Daisy's sitting room, the most cosy and delightful room Adela had ever seen. On its walls hung exotic, colourful treasures and glorious photographs, from mountains at sunset to tropical ocean fish.

'Daisy, where did you get all this stuff? It's amazing.'

'Sit yourself down and I'll make us a nice cup of tea.'

164

Adela observed the pottery and ornaments as Daisy boiled up the kettle in the small kitchen next door. She arrived in carrying a tray with a hot teapot and two dainty china teacups and saucers.

'You look at me and you see an old woman doing old woman things. You're trying not to feel sorry for me, yet it's written all over your face. But we live a thousand lives within a lifetime. I travelled around the world, Adela. I spent a year in Peru, two in Indonesia, six months in Guatemala. I worked in bars and restaurants. I got paid for my photographs sometimes too. I slept on beaches, hadn't a care in the world and I got to see things that would make your toes curl.'

'What a life you've had.' Even Daisy's teacups were printed with an interesting pattern of green and gold.

'This room is my other life. When our village gets too small, I escape to Africa or India. Some evenings, I'm climbing the route to Manu Paccu or I'm sitting by the river with my friends, Lucio and Grecia. The world is a beautiful place, Adela. So when you ask whether I'm happy, the answer is mostly yes.' A cloud passed across Daisy's face. 'Then other times I'm frustrated because my life is disappearing as fast as I'm pulling pints in this bloody awful village pub.'

'Will you ever leave, do you think?' But even as Adela asked the question, she knew the answer.

'Some mornings I want to pack my bag, ship Elly off to my brother in Scotland and lock up this place, without a clue as to where I'd even go. But then I realise I'm not twenty-five any more. I'm sixty-five, with a mother who needs me, so I close my wardrobe door again and ring one of my friends for a chat instead or go for a walk along the river.'

'Why did you come back here, Daisy?'

'Why, indeed? Perhaps my instinct told me Elly wasn't getting any younger. I had many homes, some for one night, others for years, and I may again someday. This is not as romantic as living my life on the wings of the birds, but there you have it—it is what it is. Some people never get to do all I've done. And you know what? This village may have its problems, but its people have helped me when I've needed it and helped my mother when I wasn't here.'

Adela felt a sudden urge to squeeze Daisy's hand. Daisy was not the woman she portrayed herself to be. Her home was an Aladdin's cave, her life a tapestry of rich colour. Adela had so quickly dismissed this village as a place hardly entitled a spot on the map, yet every day brought her another surprise, another unexpected delight. 'I'm beginning to understand what you see in this place.'

The cloud had passed, Daisy's eyes were now clearer. 'Then while we're talking, can I ask *you* a question?'

'Sure.'

Back straight, shoulders back, eyes on the target. 'The gift baskets were a great start…but tell me, Adela, whatever's next?'

Chapter 31

Adela milked the cup of tea. 'I swear to you, John, I've never drank as much tea in my life as I have in the last few days.'

'There's worse you could be drinking.' He lifted his own mug and sat back into his chair. 'You shouldn't be here. I don't want to go giving you this sore throat.'

'When I didn't see Gregory's shed door open, I had to investigate. I told you I was nosey.'

'And you are.'

'Do you need a doctor or anything?'

'Ha, I do not. I'm drinking some nettle tea, and some honey and lemon. That'll do the job nicely.'

'Can I make you anything to eat?'

'You're okay. I'm defrosting soup for later.'

'Capable as always.'

'Would you rather I fussed like a needy child?'

'No.' Fussing always felt appropriate whenever she was sick. A tradition, long since upheld with every croak and groan. 'I've come from visiting Daisy.'

'How's the auld divil?' he asked, coughing up some phlegm into a tissue.

'Better than you.' Adela cleared off his breakfast dishes from that morning. 'Did you tell Daisy it was us who delivered the baskets?'

'I did not. I told you I *wasn't* nosey. I can't believe you'd try to insult a sick, old man.'

'Well, sick old man, any pearls of wisdom for me today? *I* can't believe you even have philosopher quotes on your toilet seat!'

'Specially made,' he said. 'And on my toilet roll. The toilet is a good place to set goals.'

She giggled at the image of John daydreaming about the Universe next to a roll of two-ply toilet paper. 'You're so weird, John.'

'I know! Now what would you like us to talk about?'

She thought about Daisy. 'How to be happy.'

'Here's my view of happiness, for what it's worth! You want to be happy? Then *choose* to be happy, right here, right now. Sometimes people try to *do* all these things to make themselves happy, but it's never enough. There are not enough shoes, handbags, video games, bars of chocolate to fulfil you.' Even through bloodshot eyes, John had a way of looking at her. 'But here's the thing— you don't need any more handbags to make you happy. All you need is to choose how you want to feel. Choose happiness. We're back to that idea of perspective again. That's how to be happy, Adela. It's a frighteningly simple concept.'

'You're totally weird, John.'

He shrugged. 'I'm okay with that! Well, now we're on the topic, what does happiness mean to you?'

'I used to be happy when I was writing. These days I guess I'm happy when I'm dancing.'

'Ah, yes, that's good too. A practical example of happiness. Dancing is creative. Defining your passions and then living them is a good way to enjoy happiness. If dancing is your passion, then dance. If writing is your passion, then write. If fishing is your passion, then fish.'

'But shouldn't someone aspire to more than catching a few fish in their life? How will that make them happy?'

'Once again, you're missing the point of why any of us do anything,' John said, waving his finger in the air, as if conducting an imaginary orchestra. 'The purpose of our lives isn't to be the most famous or the richest, the purpose is for us to have the *experience*, to feel the beauty of whatever we decide to connect with, to grow and evolve, to be whatever we choose to be. We rate each other on scales of wealth and success, but we can't possibly understand what success is to another person. Success is the most personal choice of your life, as is happiness.'

'So success to someone who has a desire to catch fish is to simply catch a really big fish?'

'It's the process of trying to catch the fish that is the most worthwhile part. Once the fish is caught, the desire grows to catch another, even bigger fish, and that's fine, but if you aren't happy holding the fishing rod, get off the boat.'

'Get off the boat?'

'Yes, get off the boat.'

But Adela wanted more than a fishing analogy. 'What then?'

'Discover your passions, examine them, feel them, follow them and enjoy them. What greater purpose could there possibly be? Life is to be felt and enjoyed. We often miss that point, because we get so bogged down in drama and responsibilities. Think back to our conversation about energy and the law of attraction. Passion and desire without focus can be deadly; they can attract all sorts of trouble into your life.'

Didn't she know it!

John continued. 'Be clear about what you are asking from the Universe. The Universe has no sense of humour; its swirling soup of cosmic energy is waiting to give you what you want, but most people haven't understood this well enough or defined their passions clearly enough to ask. When you are clear in your focus, your road map will guide you well, you will feel good, you will feel happy and you will get what you truly want.

But you mustn't get bogged down in the details, trying to control every single move. Focus on the end result and let the Universe figure out how to get you there.'

'You have a lot to say about happiness,' she said. 'Is that it?'

'Not quite.' He searched for a tissue in his pocket. 'To be happy, it may help you to understand your life is not about *you*, as much as it is about the lives of the people you touch.'

'I'm sorry, John, you've lost me. How is *my* life not about *me*?'

'Relationships are a tool we use to define who we choose to be. You can't *express* love until you have someone to love. Do you want to show generosity, hate, selfishness or even happiness? You can only show these things through your relationships with others and with life itself. How you decide to *be* in relation to the life surrounding you is what defines you.'

'I'm totally screwed then,' she said, wishing it didn't feel true.

'Giving service in your life to others is a way many people feed their souls, show their love from the inside out, and find a way to be happy. The reason all of this works is back to what I told you before…it's because we are all connected…we are all part of the one thing. If I am kind to you, I get this kindness returned…my heart understands this.'

'How do you know all this to be true, John? When did you learn how to be so happy?'

He cleared his throat. 'I had a wife who knew way too much about everything, one of those clever-clogs you couldn't stand except that she was so great. In-between her dirty-minded jokes, she nurtured me with gentle wisdom. I was a pretty dark character in my earlier days. Time is so often treated with disrespect. People can't seem to see beyond the dents in one's skin or the grey of

170

one's hair. Youth certainly has its moments, but freedom can often be the ultimate gift of ageing.'

'You really believe that?' she said.

He shrugged. 'Society is so focused on all we lose as we get older, it doesn't put any value on what we gain. But this leads us back to the whole perspective thing again. If you believe time will decimate you, then that's what you experience. I choose to believe something different. See how our conversations bring us around in circles...the circle of life, Adela. It goes round and round and never ends.'

She looked at John with a love that overwhelmed her heart. 'You're fabulous, do you know that?'

'Ah, thanks.'

'Daisy wants you to plant flowers along the sides of the barn. She told me to mention it to you.'

'I'd have to discuss that with Gregory.'

'Why has he abandoned such a beautiful building?'

John scratched his forehead. 'Self-preservation.'

'What does that mean?'

'That place hurts him, Adela. That's all I'm prepared to say on the matter. If you persist on maintaining a large nose, then ask him yourself.'

'You must have driven your wife crazy, refusing to be a gossip. Jeez, John, throw me a bone here.'

His eyes closed halfway. 'What's your interest in the barn?'

'Well!' She leaned forward a little. 'I've decided I want to organise a village party in it.'

'A village party...in *Gregory's* barn?'

'Yes.'

'Are you crazy?'

No doubt about it! 'Probably.'

'You're stark raving bonkers, is what you are.'

'A great big party.'

'And what's better is you'll probably do it too. You'll get him to agree to it. Gregory, throwing a party for the village in his barn! My...my...that'll be the day.' John opened one eye for two seconds, stared at her, then closed it again and rested his head, grinning from ear to ear. 'Can I tell you something, Adela?'

'What?'

'My wife would have loved you!'

Chapter 32

'We meet again,' Adela said, watching the girl like a hawk.

Toni stopped rummaging through her backpack and glared up at Adela through heavily coated lashes. 'I'm busy.'

Adela thought of John. 'So I hear.'

'What's that supposed to mean?'

Observing the young skin, painted nails and dyed hair, Adela decided to sit down on the rock next to her. 'You're unhappy, I get it. But stealing from an old man? *That* I don't understand.'

'What are you talking about, woman? I didn't rob no one.'

'Yeah, because you were *caught*.'

Toni stood up and grabbed for her backpack. 'Screw you, Elvira.'

Elvira! The cheeky minx! 'Screw you, Elvira? *That's* your response?'

Those young cheeks burned like hot coals. 'I'm a thieving little bitch, is that what you want to hear? I could also drink you under the table, so what? You think I care?'

'Hurt yourself all you like, Toni. But leave everyone else alone.'

'Don't think you can look down your nose at me. I may be a screw up but I don't plan on being one forever.'

'You don't?'

'No way. I'll show them all. Just not yet. I've another few years of screwing up ahead of me first.'

Adela grinned. 'Hold on a minute here…you're telling me you're *choosing* to be a screw up?'

'No, I'm telling you I *am* a screw up, but I have no intention of *remaining* a screw-up. You may not think it possible, but I intend on re-inventing myself at some point.'

Adela helped herself to a quick chuckle. Toni's face softened, revealing a prettier side to her features.

'This image the village has of you…you *like* it, don't you?'

Toni's downbeat shoulders shrugged. 'It gets their attention.'

'You need their attention?'

'Why are you so interested anyway?' she said, swinging her backpack back and forth.

'I'm a concerned and nosey citizen.'

'Is that why you were going on about robbing John? It was John you were talking about? I saw you two together…'

'He's my friend.'

'How sweet.'

Adela frowned. 'Don't do that.'

'Well, don't talk to me as if you expect me to be nice to you. Haven't you realised by now—I'm not one of the nice ones!'

'Whoever told you such a thing?'

Toni hugged her backpack to her chest and laughed. 'Gotta go. See you around, Elvira.'

#

'We're babysitting at six,' Gregory announced as Adela shut the kitchen door. 'Julia must be desperate.'

'I hope you're good at this baby business because *I* don't have a clue!'

'Why did *you* offer our services as an established business if you never got the proper training?'

The softness of the couch felt good on her tired body. 'You saw the state of our friend. That's why. Where are they going?'

Gregory sat on the chair next to her. 'Here!'

'What?'

'They plan to avail of the services of the other half of my house while you and I tend to Harry in this half. They're getting a takeaway delivered to the dining room, then relaxing in the Jacuzzi with a bottle of bubbly, then taking themselves off to one of my guest suites for the night.'

'That actually sounds quite lovely. Six o'clock, eh?'

'Yep. I have a stew in the oven. It'll be ready in half an hour. Interested?'

From the delicious aroma drifting across the kitchen, there was only one answer to that question. 'Hmmm, yes please.'

'What was the craic in the village?' he said. 'Did you call into John? How is he?'

'Oh, he'll live. He's the healthiest sick person I ever came across.'

'Oh?'

'No, he is sick, but sick without self-pity. That's a new one for me.'

'He's some man, all right.'

Adela glanced out the window. 'Why has John left that field empty when he's done so much with all the rest?'

She noted how instantly Gregory folded his arms.

'It was meant to be an orchard—'

'Like the ones in your paintings?'

'Yes, like those.' His shark eyes returned, more grey than blue. Cloudy amid the mist of his silence.

'So why is it still a field?'

'I'm not sure if I want an orchard.'

'Sounds lovely to me.' She pulled off her shoes and curled her feet in around her. 'I have a question for you…'

'What now?'

'Considering I'm doing nothing else, I'd like to open up your barn to the village for a day. I was thinking we could throw a party in it.'

'No, Adela.' Those grey clouds swirled in his eyes as he stood up. 'You're always pushing.'

She uncurled herself and followed him to the oven. 'It would be brilliant. I have this plan—'

'You and your plans! I don't want to hear any more plans.'

'What's the big deal? The barn's just sitting there, empty. It's only a party. I could practically organise it in my sleep. You wouldn't even have to do all that much.'

Picking up the oven glove off the counter, he began speaking to it. 'She wants the *hermit* to host a party for the village. Could this woman be any more incredible?'

'*I'll* host the party. I just need the barn to do it.'

He turned to her. 'No.'

'But—'

He raised the oven glove to the level of her face. 'Absolutely not. The barn stays as it is.'

'Why?' Adela shouted. 'What's the big deal? It's a stupid building. Why make a fuss?'

'Stop, Adela. I won't change my mind.'

A scowl rippled from the back of her throat. 'I honestly don't know how Norman puts up with you.'

'He overeats to compensate.'

'Please, Gregory?'

He concentrated on his stew. 'I know you tend to get your way a lot, Adela, but not this time. Sorry.'

#

She sulked through every spoon of her dinner, with each sigh thinking he would relent, but Gregory didn't budge.

In fact, to her dismay, he reverted back into his hermit-like behaviour, more than content to eat in silence.

No longer able to bear it, she had to speak. 'Seriously, Gregory! I could understand you not wanting a party in your house, but it's a frigging barn!'

'Well, it's *my* frigging barn and I said no.'

Where would he keep the key of that barn? Gregory's full set of keys was lying on the counter top. Adela had to get inside. What was the big deal anyway? Hermits made up the rules as they went along. 'Then at least tell me why you're being so selfish about it.'

He slammed the spoon down into his bowl. 'Because that's who I choose to be.'

'Then make a better goddamn choice.'

'Now listen here; I—'

'Knock, knock,' JB shouted, opening the kitchen door wide. 'I'm sure that was the soft, silky tones of a couple delighted more than life itself to be minding our precious bundle of joy.'

Gregory almost growled.

Adela threw a dirty look in his direction, before turning her attention to JB. 'Where's the gorgeous, little man?'

JB placed the car seat down on Gregory's marble table. 'Would you believe he fell asleep on the way over here?'

Harry's cheek was cold to the touch, the only part of him peeking out from under the thick, blue blanket. 'He's a dote. I can't wait to see him awake.'

'Be careful what you wish for.'

'Julia! Nice to see you again.' Adela embraced her warmly. 'Congratulations on landing two of the most gorgeous men in town.'

JB's eyes went a little wide and he laughed nervously. 'You're a hoot, Adela.'

Julia's voice was more high-pitched than Adela remembered. 'I hear you're back on the market.'

'I suppose that's one way of looking at it,' Adela said warily, moving her attention back to Harry. *A hello would have been nice!*

Julia threw a look at JB that could have drawn blood. 'I've always hated that JB's college friend was so hot and successful. You're extremely attractive, damn you.'

The woman was blunt. 'As are you, Julia.'

'And you two seriously never…you know?'

'Julia!' JB face flushed all the way up to his scalp. 'No, never.'

Suspicion injected into ever pore, Julia's glare was frightening. 'Why not? Are you not interested in ridiculously attractive women, JB?'

'Jesus, Julia, would you give it a rest!' he cried. 'We *really* need to have sex. You always get like this when it's been too long. Leave poor Adela alone.'

Julia turned her attention to Adela. 'Well, I would prefer if his college friends were short and ugly. I'm sorry, I'm just being honest. It's also obvious you've never squeezed any nine pound human out of *that* body. Enjoy it while it lasts.'

JB snorted. 'Sometimes, Julia, darling, you don't have to say every single thing that pops into your neurotic mind.'

'Nothing neurotic about it. Even *I* can't stop staring at her. Nobody should look that good without airbrushing. I *hate* you being single again. Yes, well anyway, thank you for offering to babysit.' Julia tucked the blanket a little tighter around Harry. She pointed to the blue bag at her feet. 'Nappies, babywipes and cream are in the front. His cartons of milk are in the side pocket. All you have to do is pour them into those bottles. It's easy peasy. I've left a list. Browse the internet for anything you can't figure out. Any questions?'

'What time do we feed him?'

Even the look Julia gave to her watch would have threatened time. 'At nine o'clock. Roughly every four hours after that, although he doesn't always make it. It's all on the list.'

Julia's appearance and behaviour was manic, her hair was hardly brushed and milk stains spotted her jeans. How did that sleeping bundle of beauty manage to turn a grown woman so wild?

'In which room will I set up the travel cot?' JB asked.

'Adela's,' Gregory said quickly.

The babysitting had been her idea; she conceded. 'Mine, thanks, JB.'

'Hurry up, honey,' Julia squawked. 'Let's get out from under their feet while he's still sleeping. Thanks for the use of the other half of your house, Gregory. Forget we're here. Like—seriously.'

This time Gregory let out a nervous laugh.

'Bye,' whispered JB, tiptoeing back into the kitchen. 'Thanks again and good luck.'

Before they knew it, Adela and Gregory were left alone; them and this tiny person who had reduced his parents to a pair of escaped convicts. They stood watching Harry sleep, his plump, pink lips and his soft, clear skin.

'I don't know what all the fuss is about,' Adela whispered. 'He's really rather charming.'

Gregory's hair definitely had a few more grey flecks running through it, whether it was the Julia effect or ultimately the Harry effect, she wasn't sure. Time would tell.

'I'm not sure I *trust* him.'

179

Adela snorted, still agitated with him for the barn incident. 'Only *you* could mistrust a baby.'

'He's like a deadly bomb…waiting to go off.'

They kept staring at him until Harry let out a little yelp.

'Ah, so cute,' Adela cooed, bending down to touch his cheek once more. His eyes shot open. 'Hello, there.'

Harry's lips started to quiver.

'Oh, no, schhh, don't cry, little one. Go back to sleep. Schhh….'

'Waaa..'

She looked at Gregory. This was going to be a long night.

'Listen, kid, go to sleep and we'll all get on fine.'

'His name is Harry,' she said, nudging him.

'Waaa…'

'Take him out, then.' Gregory nudged her back.

'Sorry, Gregory, you'll have to do it. I don't actually *do* babies.'

'*Now* you tell me.' He unclicked the straps and gently lifted the screaming Harry up onto his shoulder.

Harry let out a loud burp and puked a mouthful of pasty regurgitated formula all over Gregory's shoulder.

'This babysitting idea was your suggestion, remember?'

Somehow managing to find a cloth after a quick rummage in the baby bag, Adela wiped the sick off his shoulder. 'You have your roles, I have mine.'

He glared at her as Harry's cupid lips attempted to suck on his collar. 'You and your bright ideas.'

All she could do was to return his glare and pray Gregory would quickly send the crying, puking infant back to the land of Nod.

Chapter 33

DAY 10 – Wednesday

Adela lay diagonally across the bed, her head at the wrong end. Her body felt paralyzed. She couldn't think straight. What was wrong with babies? How could they treat adults this way, night after night? It was no wonder Julia was a basket case. Harry was breathing gently in his sleep. *Oh, yeah, now you'll sleep! Nice one, Harry.*

Adela sat up, gently lifted up her dressing gown and socks, crept out of the bedroom and tiptoed to the kitchen. 'Ugh,' she said out loud, to vocalise her complaint.

After a bit of fumbling, she switched on the baby monitor and looked out the conservatory window. What a beautiful spring morning. Pity she was too tired and grumpy to appreciate it. Poor Julia and JB. Her attention was drawn to the table, set for two. Somebody had been busy making breakfast. Her nose sniffed greedily at the smell of sausages and bacon emanating from the oven. Coffee was already percolating. Exactly what she needed.

Please don't wake up, Harry! She poured herself a delicious cup of strong, black coffee. *Let me get my act together and then you can torture me some more.*

Gregory appeared at the door. 'You look like you need the whole pot.'

'*You* slept through the other two screaming sessions. That child needs a teat inserted directly into the cow. And nobody should have to smell such a nappy at four in the morning. Babies have absolutely no manners.'

181

He laughed, opening the oven. 'You are a grumpy one this morning. I made you some breakfast; might cheer you up. Sit down and I'll bring it over.'

A further gulp of coffee tasted warm and smooth. 'Are the other two still hiding out? I wouldn't blame them.'

He laid the warm plate in front of her. 'I brought them up breakfast in bed. They were giggling like two school kids.'

She ate her breakfast quietly, amazed at how irritable she was feeling. What a lightweight she was. She tried to think of John's advice about a person getting to choose their thoughts. She knew her thoughts were small and selfish. *Poor Adela, mean baby.* So what would John advise—that she instead focus on how good JB and Julia were feeling this morning, instead of how sore *she* was from lack of sleep? Okay, she had to admit, focusing on this made her feel slightly better. They had done a nice thing for two other people. Think about that, Adela, and not your selfish and fuzzy brain.

'You were really good with Harry,' she said, undecided whether or not to demolish the final piece of toast.

'He's a cute little fellow, despite his inability to hold his own manners.'

She laughed. 'I guess we shouldn't hold that against him, not for another while anyway.'

'No, I suppose not.'

The warmth of more coffee pouring down the inside of her throat helped with the kick-start. Yes, the lights were beginning to switch on in her brain at last. 'How did you get so good with kids?'

He pretended to breathe on his fingernails before rubbing them on his shirt. 'I have certain hidden talents, Adela. Stay another week and you never know what else you'll discover.'

Another week? He wanted her to stay another week? The thought was like balm to her soul.

She raised her good eyebrow. 'Think you could handle it?'

He looked at her, unsmiling. 'I may be prepared to take the risk.'

Another week away from her hellish life. Why not? 'On one condition.'

'What?'

Knowing he could read her, she kept her facial features firm. 'You show me around the barn.'

'Adela, no!'

'Look, Gregory, if you don't show me around, I'll have to find a way to sneak in there myself, and neither of us want that, so do it, okay?'

'You're incorrigible.'

'Yet no longer grumpy.' John was right. A different perspective lent itself to change of the greatest kind. The essence of her grandmother's wisdom was definitely sinking in.

'You're full of sorcery and magic, woman.' He frowned at her. 'Don't think I'm a push over for you.'

You will let me into that barn, Gregory. Oh, yes, you will.

The monitor switched mode and she could hear tiny cries coming from the speaker. 'Harry's awake. I'll go get him.'

'For a woman who doesn't do babies, you managed well enough,' he remarked, still huffing.

'I guess they're an acquired taste,' she retorted, stretching her arms high up into the air. 'Like hermits!'

\#

Gregory turned the key in the barn and pushed open the door. *How had she convinced him to do this?*

Adela walked in behind him. 'You never mentioned it was so beautiful.'

He hadn't mentioned a lot of things. Funny, how it hadn't changed. It was exactly how he remembered it. Yet, why would it have changed? Perhaps he believed time itself was enough to change it. He didn't want to be here. He should have sold the damn barn.

'Wow,' she cooed. 'This place is amazing.'

That had been his intention.

Adela opened the door into the huge kitchen. She walked along the large open plan section, touching the wooden tables and the couches. She pressed down on the counter and glided her fingers along the dusty cash register, observing a number of rooms off this main one.

'Picture it: music playing, food being cooked in the kitchen, some white lights twinkling from the ceilings, hot chocolate for the children, served with fluffy pink marshmallows, dancing over there, maybe a swap shop in that room, where people could bring what they no longer use, and swap it for something else, a chill out room for the introverts who still want to be part of it all…something for everyone.'

It was the brightness in her eyes that killed him, knee-deep in her vision, every detail, every corner filled with something more.

He'd seen such a look before.

'Can you imagine?' she said. 'Daisy taking photographs, John sharing gardening advice, kids dancing, JB and Julia relaxing as the neighbours play with Harry. Toni trying to steal the cutlery. Mad Margaret terrified everyone was going to have fun! It would be great.'

'Okay, let's go,' he said, moving towards the door. He was finding it hard to breathe.

'Go? But we've only arrived. Can't you see what I see?'

'No,' he said flatly.

She stopped. 'What is this place, Gregory?'

'This place is *nothing*, Adela,' he said, his frustrations getting the better of him. 'See for yourself, it's empty…hollow.'

She came towards him. 'What happened?'

'Nothing happened, that's the whole point,' he said, glaring at her. 'Stop with your questions.'

'You won't scare me into retreat, Gregory. What happened to you? What is this place all about? You've abandoned it, yet you carry it with you. Why?'

'It's never enough for you, is it? You asked me to show you the barn, so I showed it to you. But you keep pushing.'

'Someone has to.'

'What's that supposed to mean?'

She leaned against one of the tables. 'You cut everyone off, living up there in your great, big house, convincing yourself that you don't want anyone, then you roar like a monster from some outdated fairy tale if anyone tries to get close.'

'I've told you before, I don't need saving.'

'You're like a bear with a wounded paw.'

'I don't need saving, you stupid woman. Why won't you listen?'

'Of course you do,' she shouted back at him. '*We all do.*'

'You want to save me, Adela? You wouldn't know where to start.'

'You think *I* want to save *you*? You think that's what this is all about?' She laughed, shaking her head. 'I don't want to save you, Gregory. You don't get it, do you?'

'Get what?'

She moved closer to him. 'I want you to save yourself.'

Save himself? She knew nothing about it. She was a woman bloated with random words that kept tumbling out of her overused mouth.

'Stop it.' He turned to her. 'Use the damn barn then, if you're so insistent.'

'That's it?'

'You got what you wanted. Still not enough for you? Why am I not surprised?'

Her hands searched the air in frustration. 'You're *that* determined not to talk about it?'

'There's nothing to talk about.' *Leave it, woman. You can't fix this. Go away.*

'But you'll help me with the party?'

'No.'

'If you're not prepared to talk to me about it, then at least stop sulking. It doesn't suit you.'

He'd had enough of her today. He'd simply had enough. 'The key is on the counter. Do what you want with the barn. Burn it to the ground for all I care.' He stormed out, away from Adela and away from the wretched barn.

Chapter 34

Adela stamped her foot in frustration. Why did Gregory have to ruin it? And why was she trying so hard to organise a party for people she hardly knew? Yet something inside kept urging her to continue. Was that the internal road map John kept talking about? What was the mystery surrounding this building? Gregory acted as if the barn was a place of torture. Yet it was the kind of place that could bring a village together, help create something from the nothingness surrounding it. It did not have the dinginess of Daisy's pub. There was something special about this barn and Adela got hot just thinking about what it could become for their Village Extravaganza. She needed to speak to Daisy so she locked up the barn, made her way across the road and opened the door of the pub.

'Well, look at herself. If it isn't Ireland's Most Talented Babysitter!'

Adela bowed; a couple of old men chuckled.

'JB has a bigger mouth than yours, Daisy! Is there anything you don't know?'

'Whatever I don't know about today, I'll no doubt learn about tomorrow,' she said, cleaning a poor glass to within an inch of its life.

'Can I have a bit of a chat with you?'

'Of course.' Daisy came out from behind the bar and limped across the floor to one of the empty tables in the corner. 'What has you looking so excitable?'

Adela leaned across the table and whispered. 'I've decided what the next thing will be; I want to throw a great, big party for the village.'

Excitement added a few extra wrinkles to Daisy's face. 'Ooh, now there's an enchanting idea.'

'Gregory's going to let me use his barn.'

'He's *what*?'

'What do you think about that?'

'I think he must be in love with you.'

It was Adela's turn to choke. 'Excuse me?'

'That's what I think,' she said, matter-of-factly, sitting up straight.

'Don't talk nonsense, Daisy. Get your mind out of the gossip clouds and focus on the matter at hand, which is a party. But I can't do it without you. You have all the connections. Will you help me?'

Daisy's face was the perfect picture of delight. 'You betcha I will. What kind of party?'

Adela explained her vision of the swap shop, the food, the hot chocolate, even Daisy taking photographs. 'It'll be great.'

'How's the old barn looking?'

'A bit dusty,' Adela admitted. 'But fabulous once you can see past its abandonment issues.'

'It's the perfect venue.'

Adela knew she shouldn't ask but Gregory had given her nothing and she had to figure out what that barn meant to him. 'Daisy…'

'I see a twinkle in your eye, Adela.'

'What's the history of the barn?'

Daisy rested her hand upon Adela's. 'As you've gathered by now, I'm a nosey person, like yourself.'

Adela nodded. 'Sure.'

'But the odd time I understand when a story doesn't belong to me. This is one of those times. Be patient. Let him tell you when he's ready. It's his story to tell.'

Suitably humbled, she murmured her agreement.

'I'm not trying to be harsh with you, but some things are not fit for over-the-counter, lunchtime gossip.'

'Okay.'

'Suffice to say, him letting you use the barn is proof enough of how deeply he must care about you. I never thought those doors would open again. I guess even Gregory is still capable of surprises.'

'He's a good man, Daisy.'

'I know, sweetheart. It just takes a bit of digging to get to his gold.' Daisy gave her a warm pat on the hand.

'He's kinder than you might think.'

'It's okay, you don't need to convince me. Now, how are we going to organise this barn party?'

Adela removed a small notepad and pen from her handbag. 'The only way I know how—we'll start by making a list!'

#

Adela decided to take a walk down through the forest before heading back to the house. Her mind was buzzing with ideas for the party, but her thoughts were soon interrupted by Toni sitting precariously on the bridge, her legs facing the river below.

What was the girl doing? Trying to get herself killed? Adela approached her. 'Elvira here. Fancy another walk?'

Her words knocked the young girl out of her daze. Toni turned, one eye open and one closed. 'Naw.'

But Adela couldn't just leave. Instead she sat on the thick lip of the bridge, next to her. 'Can I buy you an ice-cream then?'

'In March?'

Adela shrugged. 'Why not?'

'You want to buy me an ice-cream?'

'Yes,' Adela said, watching the water rush by below them.

Toni shook her head. 'I'm not six, Elvira. We're not building sandcastles at the seaside.'

'Fine.' Adela jumped down off the bridge wall and walked towards the shop, without looking back. She wondered if the news of the barn party had yet spread. Would Margaret be sprinkling the barn in holy water or banging up more signs, her head filled with dread and wonder? As for Toni, the girl was hard work, sitting on that wall, almost daring the village not to notice. Adela went into the shop and two minutes later returned with two mint chocolate cones.

She came up behind Toni and nudged her. 'I bought you one anyway.'

Toni rolled her eyes but smiled, reluctantly taking the cone from her. 'I suppose you still want to go walking?'

'I do,' Adela said, starting to move.

Twisting her body around, Toni leapt off the bridge wall. 'You're deceptively bossy, Elvira.'

The paper came off easily from the bottom of her cone. 'I've been called worse.'

'What are you doing here anyways? You staying with the mad dog?' Toni glanced in the direction of Gregory's house.

'The mad dog?'

'Yeah, that bloke they all talk about.'

'Gregory…yes, I am.'

'What's his game? You his bitch?'

'No, I'm not his *bitch*. You've quite the appetite for the gossip yourself.'

Even Toni's grin seemed dulled. 'Why are you being so nice to me?'

'You call this *nice*?'

She got that faraway look again. 'The village will be talking about you and all, if you keep buying me ice-creams.'

Adela was amused at the irony. If only Toni knew! Idle village gossip was the least of Adela's worries. Yet, at Toni's age, life didn't really exist beyond the village.

'Do you like school?'

Toni licked a stray stream of runny ice-cream from the side of her cone. 'Some of it. The rest doesn't make much sense to me.'

'How do you mean?'

'Like why because I'm sixteen, I'm told I have to sit all day in a classroom learning about history. The past was great and all, but get over it...it's done. Too much dwelling.'

'Then what would you propose?'

Warmth returned to the girl's eyes, like she'd opened a big heavy door and let herself back inside. 'That kids get to do what they're naturally good at, and stop trying to force everyone through the same door. Praise their talents, don't always be telling them they're rubbish at the stuff they're rubbish at. Not everybody likes the same stuff, you know? This system treats us like we're clones...all trodding along in one direction. We don't all fit that mould, not when we're thirty or forty, and certainly not when we're sixteen. I don't get why the world is so convinced we should.'

This girl had more between her ears than how to pick locks.

'You're not so dumb, Toni.'

She shrugged miserably. 'Tell that to my history teacher!'

#

'Adela!' JB waved to her.

Adela noticed how relaxed JB looked as Harry cooed from the comforts of his buggy.

'Well, how's my little angel now?' she said, touching Harry's fingers. 'Your son could drink and poop

191

for Ireland! I dread to think what he'll be like when he's a teenager. You'll be broke.'

JB laughed. 'Thanks again for your babysitting services. You've no idea how happy we were to get a night off.'

'Oh, even after one night with dear old Harry, I can somehow imagine.'

'Well, what's the story with you and my hermit friend? There's no mistaking the glint in his eye. You've made mincemeat out of him in a week!'

She gave JB's arm a pretend shove. 'Would you stop! You're as bad as Daisy. We're friends, that's all.'

'And when are you leaving?'

Why did she feel embarrassed all of a sudden? 'I'm sticking around for another few days.'

JB grinned. 'Oh, are you indeed?'

'It's not what you think. We're organising a village party in the barn for this weekend.'

'I must be going deaf, I thought you said the barn?'

She knelt down to smile at Harry and avoid looking at JB. 'I did.'

'Gregory agreed to it?'

What was this mystery nobody wanted to share? 'Yes, he did. Care to tell me why you sound so surprised?'

JB shrugged. 'He didn't want anything to do with the place.'

She was no longer in the mood for Gregory and his dramatics or the irritating way the people around here caressed his secrets for him. 'Well, he's fine with it. So keep the weekend free as you've a party to attend.'

'Any word from David?'

Adela's humour was plummeting fast. 'Afraid not. Listen, JB, I'm going to go. Hi to Julia and I'll chat to you soon.'

She walked away, knowing JB was watching her. People had so many questions, yet when she asked any, nobody would give her the answers. Gregory and the mystery of his barn, well, she didn't care to know if he didn't care to tell her. She would concentrate on the party and leave the dramatics to the past. She would go home and face Gregory as if there had been no argument, no storming away, and no issue with the barn.

Same old, same old…she would pretend.

#

Adela's intentions were quickly thwarted when she opened the kitchen door to find Gregory's mother, Nancy, sipping tea at the table.

'Adela, lovely to see you.'

Before she knew it, Nancy had wrapped her thin arms around her for a hug.

'Nice to see you too,' Adela said, looking around. 'Where's Gregory?'

'In his office…he got an email…it couldn't wait.' Nancy gave a dismissive wave of her arm.

Adela removed her coat, placed it on the back of a chair, and sat down.

'What have you done to him? He's in a ferocious mood.'

'He didn't tell you?'

'No, but *you* will.'

Adela smiled. Nancy's eyes drew her in. The warmth of her face, mixed with her elegant movements and older woman's beauty, Adela immediately felt at ease with her. 'We had a fight.'

'About?'

'I want to throw a party for the village, you know, to get a bit of community spirit flowing. Gregory didn't—'

'Still talking about the damn party, are we?' Gregory's jaw was rigid, his hand holding onto the door as if he wasn't ready to commit to being in the same room as them.

Ignoring her son's obvious discomfort, Nancy rubbed her hands together. 'A party sounds wonderful. I still own a house in the village, so I presume I'll be able to come too?'

'That would be great,' Adela said, trying to sound calm.

'Let me guess, Gregory doesn't want to go to the party and you were trying to convince him? Don't be wasting your time arguing about a—'

'It had nothing to do with that, Mother.' The door closed with a bang. He leaned against the inner doorframe and turned towards them, arms folded.

'Then why were you fighting?' Nancy said.

'Because I want to have the party in Gregory's barn.' *Nancy was a social animal. She would knock some sense into her son.*

'*Gregory's* barn?' Nancy said, her tone sounding shocked.

Adela couldn't avoid the expression on the older woman's face. 'What have I said? What's wrong?'

No longer smiling, Nancy repeated, 'Gregory's barn.'

'It was never *my* barn…not really.'

Tears formed in Nancy's soft eyes. 'I think a party is a very good idea.'

'What?' Gregory frowned. 'You can't be serious?'

Nancy removed a tissue from up her sleeve. 'Then what's your solution? Ignore it? Give it away? Leave it there to rot? It deserves to be used, son.'

'I don't want it to be used,' Gregory said firmly, grabbing Norman's lead from the chair. 'Sorry, mother, but I need some air.'

Twice in one day. Adela closed her eyes as he let the door bang on his way out. What had she got herself into, jumping from one complicated situation to the next?

'Nancy, I'm sorry if I've upset you all, but nobody will tell me why the barn is such a difficult subject.'

Tissue tucked between the cup and the palm of her hand, Nancy held the warm cup against her cheek. 'You saw inside it?'

'It's lovely.'

'Yes. Gregory put his heart and soul into the place. It was meant to fix everything.'

A shiver ran through her. *Meant to fix what?*

Nancy looked at her straight in the face. 'Gregory wasn't always this way. He was happier before.'

'Before what?'

Her expression reminded Adela of young Toni, gripped by shades of despair.

'Before the death of his twin sister.'

'Oh, Nancy…I'm so sorry.'

Nancy patted her on the hand. 'That's okay dear, it is what it is.'

'When did she…?'

'Almost four years ago.' She paused. 'Seems like yesterday in some ways, yet so long ago in others.'

'I'm sorry. I didn't know…'

'Of course you didn't. How would you? People don't like to talk about death.'

'What happened…'

'My little girl's name was Susan…even as a child, she was never strong like Gregory. Growing up, although he was the younger, Gregory propped her up, kept her going. He transformed the barn for her, to give her something to love, something she had control over. Susan, you see, never really felt she had much control of her life. The children's father was a hazard to the health of any young and innocent spirit. His drinking, his humours, at first the children didn't understand them. Then they learned to tolerate them. Gregory had a special way about him. You want to know what saved *him* from the damaging effects of his father?'

Adela swallowed the lump in her throat. 'What?'

'The depths of his imagination.' Nancy smiled, travelling back in time. 'His father used to constantly beat into them words of poverty, neglect and despair. Gregory chose to ignore the sentiments of an ignorant man. Even at his young age, he knew life was about more than what was being dished up to him. His telescope revealed treasures of grandeur and hope…

…Susan's had no such glamour about it. All she saw was a sad little girl coming last in every race. Gregory and I would play pretend, dress ourselves up, visit the finest kings and queens, travel all around the world. We would live in a castle one day, on a yacht the next, we would sail down the Amazon, build a house made of gold or a pyramid of sand and diamonds.'

Adela couldn't imagine Gregory with a twin.

Nancy continued. 'Susan was deeply affected by her father's bitching and whinging. She allowed him to get inside her head and he was determined to prove to the world that she had the same vision of it as he. We used to distract Susan, and for a time she came along for the ride, playing pretend with me and Gregory. She was a master baker; she would sprinkle ingredients together, producing spectacular cakes, as we imagined we were preparing a feast for our banquet. It was she who taught Gregory to cook. But to Susan it was always pretend.'

'That's so sad.' Adela was at last beginning to understand why Gregory had turned his back on the world.

Nancy continued. 'Susan grew more and more frustrated, angry at the holes in her socks, the emotional mine fields, the arguments over every lost penny. She

196

wanted her dad to change and was unable to separate his grievances from her own. I should have taken her away from him sooner but I was young and naive. It took me time to navigate a better direction for us all. But it was too late for Susan. By then she was living inside a fog of depression. I thought she was being a teenager. Gregory knew better. For years, he acted like a sergeant major, cajoling her out of bed, insisting she eat, not tolerating her empty behaviour. At times, I felt like she was already beyond repair, but Gregory would not give up on her. He had abandoned hope for his father, but he couldn't bring himself to do the same with his sister.'

'How truly awful.' Adela glanced out the window, wondering where Gregory had gone. He'd told her none of this, nobody had.

'Gregory had been helping her overcome her demons. She trained to be a chef. After a few false starts, she was working, had a small flat, things were looking up. Then she lost her job and everything began to unravel. Gregory was so desperate to save her from the black hole inside her mind that he bought her the barn and put a fortune into renovating it. It was going to be Susan's nirvana. But on the day it was due to open, Susan went missing. Whether it was the stress or what, we'll never know, but my little girl took herself down to the river. It was a sunny morning, I always remember that. There was a giant rock in the middle of the river, Riverman's Boat, they used to call it. Kids used to picnic there in the summers. Susan's picnic was a bottle of pills. She wasn't discovered for three hours. Gregory found her. By then it was too late.'

All Adela could think to do was to reach out and touch this kind woman's shoulder. 'Nancy, I'm so sorry.'

A dab of her eyes. 'Me too, dear. Every day, I'm sorry. What could I have done to help her, to save her, to change the script of her young life? The guilt and the

197

emptiness are so paralysing. I hope you never know that feeling. It's the most relentless thought in your head, and nothing you can do or think or feel can change even a moment of what happened. It's over. She's gone. Life will never be the same.'

'I'll cancel the party in the barn, of course. I didn't know...'

Nancy scrunched up her face, revealing the truth of her age. 'You, my dear, will do no such thing. Gregory has been cancelling the party for the last four years. You need to push this with him, Adela. Maybe that's why you came into his life, to help him move forward. He's stuck, you see. He can't allow himself move forward without her. He needs someone to push him.'

Adela thought of that same conversation she'd had with him earlier. She wanted to run out into the night, to find him and tell him she understood. 'Are you sure it's the right thing to do?'

Nancy nodded firmly. 'I insist on it.'

Chapter 35

Gregory removed the marinated pork chops from the fridge. Cooking would distract him from his irritation. Walking certainly hadn't.

'Can I come in?' Adela appeared at the door.

'Grab a knife,' he said, pointing towards the potatoes.

They settled into the food preparation in silence.

'Did my mother stay long?'

'Long enough.'

He didn't want this tension. 'I know I overreacted.'

'No…you didn't,' she said, continuing to peel.

'My mother told you, didn't she?'

'Yes.'

Okay, Adela knew about Susan. He waited for the questions, for the fuss. All he got was the continued sound of chopping and peeling.

Norman nudged his way into the room, took a loud slurp of water with his thick tongue and sat beside Adela. She bent down to his level and blew him an air kiss. 'Hello there.'

What now between them? Talking about Susan was not what he wanted. Going back inside the barn was not what he'd ever intended. He removed a chopping board from the press and began slicing into the spinach, feeling her next to him, even though she was standing a foot away. Adela rinsed two hacked potatoes under the water, the spray hitting all sides of the sink.

'You treat your spuds with such contempt.'

She picked one up. 'What's wrong with it?'

'It's half the spud it used to be.'

'Hey.' She nudged him, smiling.

'I'll help you with the party.'

A momentary pause from potato hacking. 'You will?'

'You'd only aggravate me until I said yes anyway, so I may as well make it easier on myself.'

Her open-mouthed laugh showed off a perfect set of teeth. 'It's only been a week and you have me figured out already.'

'I should have added "no cheap flattery" to my list of rules. Not that you cared a damn about my rules.'

'Not a toss,' she agreed, washing the last potato and throwing it into the pot.

#

Adela could hear the noise of the crowd before she even opened the pub door. Although used to large gatherings under much more stressful circumstances from her book tour, she found herself feeling irrationally shy and made a quick beeline for Daisy.

'You're rushed off your feet tonight,' she said, squeezing between groups of people. 'Maybe I'll come back tomorrow.'

Daisy chuckled. 'That would be a terrible idea. These people are here for *you*! I put word around about the barn and everyone was intrigued. You've already met John, Margaret and Nigel, but I thought it was important for you to get a feel for the rest of the village. Now don't kill me, but—'

'Good evening, Adela!'

She looked across the bar. 'John! I wasn't expecting to see you here.'

John lifted a tea towel and swung it over his shoulder. 'Didn't Daisy tell you? I'm barman for the night…well, for an hour or two anyway!'

She turned to Daisy. 'What's going on in your conniving little mind? I think I need to watch my step with you!'

Daisy patted John's shoulder as she walked past him and joined Adela on the other side of the bar. 'Follow me.'

They arrived to the same table by the window as she had sat with Gregory. 'I'm having a raffle tonight with a prize of a hundred euro and the only way people can acquire a ticket for this raffle is if they come and introduce themselves to you and sit with us for a quick chat.'

What an idea! 'Do people ever refer to you as Crazy Daisy? Because if they don't, they should.'

'A bit of crazy makes the world go around,' Daisy said, wiggling her thick fingers.

Making herself comfortable, Adela watched as Daisy informed the villagers that the application for raffle tickets was about to commence. She gave a quick wave to Elly, who was painting a face onto a balloon with some pink lipstick. What was she doing in this place, trying to solve its problems instead of solving her own? This was a ludicrous situation within a ludicrous idea. The whole plan was, well, ludicrous!

Daisy flopped back down on her seat. 'Okay, who's first?'

A man in his mid-fifties, almost the shape of a pint glass, with broad shoulders and thinner hips, lowered himself down, pausing before his backside was finally planted on the chair. 'Daisy certainly doesn't need this introduction, but I'm Brian.'

'Nice to meet you, Brian. I'm Adela.'

Daisy tapped on the table. 'Okay, Adela, shoot Brian a question.'

What on earth? Words stumbled around Adela's unprepared mind. 'I...em...well...what's the last film you watched?'

Brian bent his head slightly. 'I can't rightly remember. I don't actually own a TV, you see.'

A big cheer from the bold Daisy. 'The girl struck gold.'

'You don't own a TV? How do you live?'

The man's grey hair sat like a puffball on his head. No thinning there. 'I listen to the radio mostly, while I'm painting.'

'You're a painter?'

'I sure am.' He nodded proudly. 'Nothing like painting at dawn, birds chirping, the cold nipping at your fingers, out in the middle of nowhere, painting up a storm. The mightiest feeling in the world. Way better than TV. Although I do sneak down to Larry's the odd evening for a watch of that car show. Very entertaining, that show.'

'Do you make a living out of the painting?'

'No, no, no, no,no,' he said, shaking his head. 'I used to work in the chicken factory down past Newmills, but it's been closed almost three years now. I'm not that kind of painter. Could you imagine it?' No, I like to clog up my own house with paintings, I'd never expect anyone else to do the same.'

Daisy winked at Adela before handing Brian a ticket. 'Thanks and good luck in the raffle, Brian.'

'Ah, Jesus, is that it? Sure that was grand. Thanks very much,' he said, folding the ticket up and tucking it into his wallet.

It had never occurred to Adela that someone would choose not to own a TV.

'Next.' Daisy's voice boomed. 'Mary, how are ya? I'm surprised aul Brian got in there before you.'

A tidy looking woman with pointed features, Mary's brown hair was scraped back in a bun, not a stray hair in sight. 'I know, the rascal! I'm dying to know, what's this all about?'

'We're the ones supposed to be asking you the questions, Mary,' Daisy said, nudging Adela.

'I know, but I've never liked surprises, Daisy. I like to be in the loop.' Mary made a circle with her finger.

Could Adela actually be beginning to enjoy herself? 'Mary, what annoys you most about your life?'

Mary lifted her drink and took a sip. 'You want to know my answer?'

'I do.'

Her fingers rubbed unnecessarily against the sides of her already neat hair. 'I've no job, my house is as clean as any house ever needs to be and I'm bored out of my frigging head.'

'Your face just turned a kind of purple.' *There was plenty of emotion bubbling beneath that bun.*

Mary patted her cheeks, her eyes wide in her head. 'Jesus, it's hot in here.'

'Well, now, Mary, that definitely deserves a ticket.' Daisy ripped one off the ticket book and handed it to her. 'Thanks for your honesty.'

'It felt good to be asked the question. Another couple of drinks and goodness knows what I'd be telling you!'

Daisy leaned across to Adela once Mary was out of earshot. 'We call her Mary, Mary, Quite Contrary. She carries a pair of rubber gloves in her handbag, swear to God! Well, what do you think so far?'

Adela giggled, high on the feeling this weird raffle ticket venture was giving her. 'I'm loving it.'

Daisy caught John's eye and whistled at him.

Adela gently bumped against her. 'Okay, what bizarre question can *you* think of to ask the next person?'

Awaiting Daisy's answer, Adela found herself glancing towards the door of the pub. What was Gregory doing tonight while she was trading tickets for secrets? Was he thinking of his twin, the woman who had broken his life while retreating from her own? Was it fair to take over a dead woman's barn? His own mother believed it not only fair, but necessary. Adela wasn't sure. She hadn't expected when she came to Gregory's home, carrying her jumbled life with her, she would also mess around with his.

Chapter 36

Gregory was finishing up in his office when Adela returned home.

'Well, did you and Daisy spend all evening plotting how to take over the world?' he asked, closing the office door and heading into the kitchen.

Adela's eyes were sparkling. 'Even better; Daisy managed to convince the villagers to share some of their secrets with us.'

'Why did she do that?'

'She decided I couldn't invite a load of people to my party whom I know nothing about. Well, let me tell you, I know a whole lot more now than I did a few hours ago. People are pretty fascinating.'

'They're a particular fascination I've been quite well able to live without.'

'Cuppa?' she asked, lifting out the filter jug to fill the kettle.

'Why not?'

Her face was animated. That glossy hair, those Everest legs, and a pair of sea-green eyes able to bring a man to his knees.

'You know the funny thing? Those people seemed to enjoy it too. They liked being asked about themselves, having someone take an interest in their thoughts, their dreams, even in the things they detest.'

'You're surprised?'

She lifted two cups off the mug tree. 'I suppose I thought they might think us cheeky. We *were* cheeky, so I wouldn't have blamed them. Daisy's hilarious.'

'Do you know why I think they were so happy to talk to you? My view, for what it's worth…'

'Oh, I can't wait to hear what *you* have to say on this matter, considering your general hatred of people!'

Gregory took the hot cup of tea from her. 'They want to be *heard*. Fat people, short people, nice people, angry people, they all want the same thing…for someone to listen to them…to really hear them.'

'If you know that, then why are you so *hard* on them?' Adela lifted herself up onto a stool at the island.

'Just because I get the basic concept doesn't mean they don't annoy me. Nobody goes out of their way for anyone else. People are inherently selfish.'

'I disagree.'

'I tried to make my sister feel like the world cared about her, but now I think she just knew more than I did; that nobody was really listening to her, nobody cared except for her mother—and a brother who only cared because he was genetically encoded to do so.'

Adela's mouth opened but nothing came out.

'I was so angry at you, trying to get involved, to care about the barn. But then Susan kept popping into my head. She would have liked what you want to do.'

'It must have been the worst time,' she said awkwardly.

'It was. Susan used to get so sad. No matter what I did, I couldn't find a way to piece her back together. The barn was meant to be her new start…she, unfortunately, had other plans.' His own heart grew angry, a recurrent problem of his.

'How come *you* escaped when she couldn't?'

He let himself think back. 'When I was eight years old, my mother came to me, tears still in her eyes, after my father had kicked a hole in the door in a drunken rage. She got out my paints and painted the word FREEDOM onto my wall. She was crying the whole time. She held me in her arms and said, "I want you to see that word every day, Gregory. Don't ever let anyone say you can't be free. You can be as free as you choose to be…it all starts in here." I never forgot the look in her eyes or those tears washing through the makeup on her face. I detached myself emotionally from my father after that. I chose to be free of him, even when I wasn't. Life tore Susan down, day by day, until she retreated so far inside, the rope wasn't long enough to pull her back out.'

'Then don't make that same mistake,' she said.

'I'm as free as I can be.'

'You really think so?'

'I don't blame myself, believing I could have done more to help her; I leave those empty feelings to my mother to waste her time over. I did all I could for Susan.'

'I'm glad.'

'It's something different to guilt. I can't really explain it. It's like a feeling for which nobody has yet invented a word. Anyway, the original point was about people and their foolish need to gather an audience around them, to have others make them feel justified. But, I'm glad you enjoyed yourself tonight. I suppose they're not the worst people in the world.'

'They're nice,' she insisted.

'Then why don't they look after their houses and shops and gardens? Why is JB always complaining to me about the poor state of the village? Why is Margaret obsessed with curses? Not that I care, I rarely see it…but still.'

'Is being perfect the same as your definition of being nice? It's no wonder you don't like anyone.'

'I'm just saying it's a clean-up you should be organising, instead of throwing them a party. Don't you think half of them probably drink or lounge about eating cake too often as it is? Now, you know I've agreed to offer up the barn for your big party, but those people need more than being occupied for a couple of hours to distract them from their miseries.'

Adela tapped her fingers on the sides of her cup thoughtfully. 'But a party will make them happy.'

'Feeling useful would make them happy. A party will entertain them adequately enough for them to forget how unhappy they are.'

She jumped down off her seat.

Oh, he'd annoyed her now. It was her turn to storm off. What were the pair of them like? 'Come back,' he called.

She turned to him, a smile forming on her lips. 'I'm getting a notebook out of my handbag, Gregory. Relax!'

'Oh,' he said, feeling a little silly. 'What are you doing now?'

She shook the pen rigorously. 'Oh, no, Gregory, it's not what *I'm* doing, you don't get off the hook that easily.'

'What do you mean?'

'Well, my dear landlord of sorts, because of that grand idea of yours, you've landed yourself a place on the Organising Committee!'

'You've got to be kidding me. Nice try but no way. I said I'd give a bit of help, but that's where it ends.'

'Oh, yes,' she said equally firmly. 'It's time more than your credit card did a bit of charity work, don't you think?'

'You're the bossiest woman I have ever met. You think you can have anything you want, don't you?'

Hand on her hip, she stared at him. 'Are you telling me, Gregory Sheridan, you're not up to the challenge?'

'Psychology 101,' he said. 'The answer is still *no*.'

She flipped open her notebook. 'I'm only here for another few days. Can't you grin and bear it? *Please*?'

'Oh, enough with the begging, it's painful,' he said, raising his hands in mock defeat. 'Look, I'll have a couple of brainstorming sessions with you about what you can do, but that's where I draw the line. No being part of your Committee, none of that rubbish. But I'm available for cups of tea and related conversation. Agreed?'

Could her wink have been any cheekier?
'Your wish is my command.'

Chapter 37

DAY 11 – Thursday

Adela walked past Gregory's office, noticing the door ajar. She stopped and back-tracked a couple of steps before pushing the door open a little more and stepping inside. What a spectacular office, with its solid desk and chair, rows of books, a beautiful seat by the window, and even a fireplace. But her eye was drawn to the large painting on the wall above the mantelpiece. The word, so relevant to her now, would have meant nothing to her a day ago.

FREEDOM.

Gregory's greatest desire.

A coldness passed through her. Was she again making up *her* version of his life? Perhaps he felt perfectly free and choosing to be a hermit had nothing to do with the death of his sister. But why would anyone choose to tear themselves out of society as if human connection meant nothing? He was so strong and capable. She felt protected around him. What difference did it make to her how he really felt about anything? She would be leaving soon, once their party weekend was over.

Time to leave his office. She carefully pulled the door back the same way. Gregory intrigued her more and more but she had to be careful not to let the fantasy of these two weeks cause her more pain than pleasure. Maybe she should have anonymously booked herself into a hotel, let the world drift by without affecting any part of it, instead of trouncing around, making all kinds of mess. Still, she would not leave, not yet anyway.

Was David thinking of her? Had he thrown himself into the arms of someone else as easy retaliation? Adela fought the desire to go onto the internet and look him up. Instead, she needed to concentrate on her party weekend. The more she thought about Gregory's idea, the more its brilliance appealed to her. They had chatted late into the night, her scribbling down note after note. They spoke about the different raffle ticket owners, Gregory filling her in on some further details about them. A firm image had formed in her head about what she wanted to do.

Gregory was finishing a lap when she pushed open the doors to the pool.

'I'm off to John's for lunch,' she called. 'You'll be happy to know I'm bringing my notebook with me.'

'John's welcome to you, slave driver,' he said. 'See you later.'

The next few days may actually be fun, she thought, as long as the village welcomed their ideas.

#

'Elvira, you busy?' Toni asked, pushing out her right cheek with her tongue.

'I have a few spare minutes, if you're interested.'

'I wanted to show you something.' Toni looked away, hopping from one foot to the next.

'What's going on, Toni? You need to use the loo?'

'Naa,' she said. 'Come on.'

Adela followed her. Toni was clearly nervous. *Where were they going?*

'My mother doesn't like to cook, so I get control of the kitchen most days.' Toni chattered all the way there. 'I do a mean roast chicken.'

'You cook roast chicken?'

The young girl nodded. 'Sure do. Come on…this way.'

They hopped over a half-tumbled stone wall.

'Where are we going, Toni?'

'Not too far away now.'

Adela stared down at the girl's worn runners. 'I'm a terrible cook.'

'Why?'

'I don't know how to do it well. I get timings wrong and I get stressed.'

'A lame excuse.'

'Lame?'

'Download a recipe. Start with one. Learn how to do it well. That's not difficult. You shouldn't be lazy about your food.'

'Being chastised by a sixteen-year-old delinquent!'

Toni opened a wooden gate. 'We've arrived!'

Adela looked around, her eyes taking in all that lay before her. 'What is this place?'

'I guess you could call it my secret garden.'

'This is yours? You did all this?'

She nodded proudly.

Adela couldn't believe the beauty of what she was looking at. Rose bushes, azaleas, shrubs and even a vegetable patch and herb garden.

'This is…beautiful. Where did you learn to do this?' She turned to look at Toni, whose expression had changed. Her face was illuminated with pride and happiness.

'The internet is my paradise.'

'Well, don't just stand there,' Adela said in a pretend stern voice. 'Show me around.'

They spent the next half hour chatting about Toni's fruits and vegetables, about her young plants and trees, and all the flowers beginning to blossom around them.

'Where did you get the money for all this?' Adela thought of Toni's attempted break-in to John's house.

'I know what you're thinking, but I'm not a thief. I don't drink or smoke half as much as I pretend I do and any pocket money my Ma gives me goes towards this place. When Nigel caught me hopping John's wall, I was attempting to steal from him, but not like you all thought. I could never afford to buy proper plants, like they have in them garden centres. You've seen John's garden, it's amazing. All I wanted was a few cuttings from some of his plants. I've grown most of this garden from cheap packets of seeds and cuttings and stuff. That was all I wanted off John. I'm not a thief, Adela. Not really.'

'So why didn't you ask him?'

Toni looked taken aback, as if the thought hadn't really occurred to her. 'Ask him?'

'Yes! John would have given you all the cuttings you wanted. Did you tell Nigel what you were doing?'

'I tried. He has no tolerance for me since he caught me throwing my mother's ironing board out the bedroom window.'

'I won't ask.'

Toni frowned. 'Best not to.'

Adela sat on a seat Toni had made out of a tree stump. 'But look at this place. You have real talent. Why would you waste your time getting into trouble?'

'Trouble finds me. People don't treat me the way they treat you.'

'And you're perfectly innocent in all of this?

Her expression held pain as raw as an open wound. 'I haven't been innocent for a very long time.'

Chapter 38

'So what do you think?' Adela asked John as he laid down two toasted cheese sandwiches on the table.

'I don't know why anyone hasn't done it before now. It sounds so simple when you say it.'

'We're pulling this together really fast, so I need your help. Gregory said you're not to turn up at his house until next week; your services are required for a much more worthy cause. He'll still pay you, of course.'

John grinned. 'He's a saint underneath it all, I'm sure.'

'I hope it doesn't go wrong and fail miserably.'

'Go wrong? You're a powerful creator, Adela. It's time for you to create! Failure is an illusion, don't you see? Creation is the purpose of your life, it is the reason you're here. It's the same for all those people. They can create a different village; they simply have not believed it was possible until now. They've allowed the threat of a curse to shake their beliefs. Show them they have a right to create for themselves. Allow them to demonstrate their own creative skills. Focus them, get them to push their boundaries, and push your own at the same time; that's what this thing called life is all about. Exciting, isn't it?'

Something clicked in her. A new understanding. Her fear of failure vanished. What was there to really be afraid of? She had to keep her vision strong enough that they could see it too, or at least their version of it.

'John, I want you to make a list of ten people who have nice gardens in this village or who would be good solid helpers to clear out the overgrown areas and turn them into something attractive.'

'No problem at all.'

'Will you contact as many of them as you can and I'll be back across to you in an hour to see how it's going?'

'Of course.'

'By the way, Nancy told me about Susan.'

John raised his caterpillar eyebrows. 'Oh, did she now?'

'What was Susan like? Did you know her?'

'I've known Nancy for years. Susan's death hit Nancy and Gregory hard. Susan adored Gregory when she wasn't in one of her moods. Nancy's had her share of heartache over the years. It doesn't show on her.'

'True. She's so charming and warm.' Adela smiled. 'Is that why Gregory stopped engaging with the world?'

'To lose your twin like that; how would any of us react?'

It was hard not to wonder about the man Gregory would have become had he not spent so much of his life trying to save that of his sister.

'On another topic, I have something to tell you.'

'Oh?'

'Young Toni is actually more green-fingered than light-fingered. She wasn't breaking into your house that day; she was trying to get a few cuttings from some of your fancier shrubs and plants.'

'What a relief...and a surprise!'

'Here's another surprise...' Adela scrunched up her nose. 'Will you add her to your list of helpers?'

John smiled...no doubts, no questions, and no judgement. 'It would be my pleasure.'

After another round of thanking John, she left him to his list. This town would be littered with lists by the weekend!

Next stop, Daisy's, where Adela explained the revised plan.

'Now, *that's* what I was trying to make happen,' Daisy exclaimed. 'And a party at the end to celebrate everyone's hard work. Brilliant, Adela.'

'We're not there yet,' she said. 'I need your brain for another half an hour.'

'Of course! Elly will be grand snoozing over there in the corner.'

Adela ran through her lists of requirements, Daisy's contact book was produced and lists of people to help with a variety of tasks were made by the two excited women.

An hour of solid business later. 'Daisy, what's wrong? You look like you're about to cry.'

Daisy patted her chest and blinked. 'Talking about these people and all they can do, there is so much talent among them. Yet that is never what we speak about when I meet them on the street. We talk about the weather or about what has happened to whom. A town full of creators, who knew?'

Adela gave Daisy a big hug. 'Come on, Missus, no time to sit here and get emotional about it. We've got serious work to do.'

'How are we going to pay for all the paint and flowers and stuff? I used my spare cash on the raffle.'

'I know how.' Adela gave a salute to the sky. 'My grandmother!'

Chapter 39

DAY 12 - Friday

Adela spent the next twenty-four hours either talking on the phone, knocking on doors, shopping for supplies or updating her lists. The people of the village got swept up in the excitement, cancelling plans, bringing forth their ideas, offering their equipment, time and services. A firm plan of action was set in motion. The village was due the makeover of a lifetime.

Adela bumped into raffle ticket Mary on her way to the barn. 'Well, Mary, are you all prepared for tomorrow?'

Mary's bun was sitting off centre at the back her head. 'I'm not sure what good I'm going to be. I haven't worked in years, Adela. A bit of cleaning is all you'll get from me, so don't be expecting miracles.'

'Are you kidding me, Mary? Miracles are exactly what I'm expecting! By the end of this weekend, you'll be one of the most satisfied women in Ireland!'

'You're promising an awful lot!' Mary mustered a grin through her pale cheeks.

'Miracles, Mary…miracles,' Adela repeated, walking away. 'See you tomorrow at nine.'

Whistling all the way to the barn, Adela was shattered but delighted. Tomorrow couldn't come soon enough. Practically everything was now organised. Earlier that day, she had collected the plants, compost, tools and paint from the nearby garden centre. Gregory had driven her to pick up all the stuff. He really got stuck in with her, even though it would have killed him to admit it. Putting aside his issues with the barn, he'd acted professionally and with total commitment. She could see how he'd done so well in his business life.

The door of the barn creaked open. Adela could hear Gregory sliding something across the floor. Most of the arranging of Sunday evening's party had been done by him. All work was to finish at five o'clock on Sunday, everyone was going home for an hour to get cleaned up, and then the celebrations were starting at six.

'My, my, you have been a busy boy!' The barn was no longer covered in its layer of dust, it now smelled like lemons, its windows sparkling and its floors shining.

'The cleaning crew I hired did most of it, but I'll be happy to take all the credit.' He appeared from one of the small rooms, covered in grime and dust but with a big, happy grin. 'You better not even think about taking out that notebook of yours. I'm done for the day.'

Unable to resist, she walked over to him and wiped her index finger across his forehead. 'You missed a bit.'

'Oh, you'll pay for that,' he said, threatening her with his grimy cloth.

'No,' she squealed, running away from him. 'Don't you dare!

But he made chase as she scurried into one of the side rooms. 'I'm trapped.'

'Yes, you are,' he said. 'And after Sunday, your notebook is *getting it.*'

'Very threatening behaviour, Mr Sheridan.' She leaned her shoulders up against the wall, her hips tilted outwards towards him.

He moved closer to her, cloth still in hand. 'You deserve it, slave driver.'

Another step closer. Despite the cool temperature of the barn, Adela could feel the heat of his body.

'You don't scare me,' she said, her eyes not leaving his.

'Well, you scare the hell out of me.' He dropped the cloth, moving closer again so that he was almost touching her.

'What's my body language saying now? You being the expert, and all.'

His eyes crackled with the colour of the sky on a bright spring day. 'See how you flicked your hair away from your face? You *want* me.'

She repeated the action, with the other side of her hair. 'Oh, yeah, you think so?'

'I do.' His hand touched her cheek.

'You must be mistaken,' she said. The rush was intense, like every cell in her body had thrown itself into a wild, primitive dance.

'I don't think so. The way you're tilting those dangerous hips of yours towards me…you *really* want me.'

'I have to point them somewhere.'

'And as for those eyes…they could burn a man to his very bones.'

'That doesn't sound healthy.'

'You're telling me.'

They stared at one another, his hand gently brushing her waist. David, her book, the problems in her life, all faded away. She could see the hunger in his eyes…as he could in hers.

The sound of crashing came from the hall. Gregory pulled away from her, the spell broken. Adela took a couple of deep breaths, trying to restore some kind of order, before walking out behind him.

A smiling John greeted them. 'Afternoon, folks. I thought I'd stop by with some newly-potted plants.'

But it was not John who Gregory was staring at. It was the man standing beside him.

'Oh, and this fellow. It seems he wishes to talk with you, Gregory.'

Adela fussed around her dear friend, almost as much to hide the blush of her cheeks and the heat struggling against her clothing, the ache of that last moment still quivering within her.

'My, my, this place is lovely,' John continued. 'I've been chatting to some of the younger ones, and even they are coming out to help tomorrow. According to my weather App, although it'll be a bit on the chilly side, it's going to be dry and bright all weekend.'

Stepping forward, Adela put out her hand. 'Sorry, I don't believe we've met. I'm Adela.'

The man cleared his throat, and shook her hand. She could feel the sweat from his palms on her skin. How tall he was, and thin, like a wafer. This was the man from the pub to whom Gregory had acted so cold.

'Nice to meet you too. I'm Barry.'

What was wrong with Gregory, standing next to her, fidgeting? Adela placed one of the plants John had carried in with him into the corner, next to the window. 'These are beautiful, John. You've been working hard.'

'We all have.' He winked at Gregory. 'Even you, eh.'

'Even me, John.'

Barry placed his full attention on Gregory. 'Can I have a quick word with you—in private?'

'Come with me, Mr Philips. You'll be amazed at what Gregory has been getting up to in these little rooms.' She led John into the same room she'd run from moments ago.

'Who's the man and why have you brought him here?' she said, once she had closed the door behind her. 'Did you see the scowl on Gregory's face?'

'Barry heard Gregory was opening up this place for the weekend. He asked me if I'd soften the entrance. What could I do?'

She scratched her neck. 'Yes, yes, but who is he and what does he want with my hermit?'

'*Your* hermit?'

'You know what I mean. Stop stalling!'

John sat down on the couch that ran along the window. 'Barry was Susan's boyfriend.'

'Oh,' Adela said, sitting next to him. How to set the cat amongst the pigeons. Gregory would be a bag of fun after *that* conversation.

'From what I believe, they had a falling out after Susan died and haven't spoken since.'

'Tricky.'

'Yes, tricky,' John agreed.

What would have happened had Susan changed her mind before swallowing that first pill or had someone gone in search of her sooner? Would Susan now be making pots of tea and serving delicious slices of her homemade cakes in this lively, bustling barn? Who would Gregory have become, had he not chosen to detach himself from the pain of the world around him? He was putting on a good show, but this was hard on him, his twin sister's ghost all the time dancing on his shoulder.

After ten minutes, Gregory opened the door. 'You can come out now.'

'Thanks,' John said cheerfully, as if he was unaware of any change in the atmosphere. 'I must leave you now. Things to do. See you all tomorrow. Don't have too much fun without me.'

They waved John goodbye and returned to the barn to gather up their stuff. She wanted to ask him, but found no avenue to begin the conversation.

'Stop looking at me like that,' Gregory said, nudging her as he walked past to collect the array of dirty cloths scattered about.

'Like what?'

'Like you feel sorry for me.'

221

'It's not *you* I'm feeling sorry for,' she said, deciding to give him the space he needed. 'It's your *shower*. Even Norman won't recognise you, you filthy beggar. Come on, let's finish up here and get home.'

#

The sun was dipping into the sky as they walked together down the lane, in the direction of the house. Adela was chattering away. He liked listening to the lilt of her voice. She affected him; he could put it no other way. He couldn't imagine life from the other side of this stir she'd created in the village. But he had to be realistic and not run away with himself. Adela was hiding out here, recovering from a broken heart. This wasn't some holiday romance, this was real life. It wasn't like him to become ridiculous about anything, much less a woman. Even Norman had fallen under her spell.

'What's going on inside your head?' She linked her arm through his. 'I'm almost afraid to ask.'

'He was Susan's boyfriend...'

'Okay.'

'John told you?'

She nodded.

'He came to make amends. He heard about the barn being used.'

'I'm sure what happened to Susan was hard on him too.'

Gregory could feel himself stiffen. 'The morning she died...he'd had a fight with her. He was jealous, you see. He didn't like that she'd been handed the keys to the barn. He never really loved her. He should have been glad for her but instead of minding her, he made her feel guilty, unworthy. He laid the guilt on thick and strong...he admitted it to us in those first couple of days after she'd died. He denied it afterwards. Bastard.'

'People fight, Gregory. Do you think it's right to blame *him* for a choice your sister made?'

222

'He should have protected her,' he said, pulling his arm away. 'The barn would have helped Susan get through. The responsibility would have been good for her.'

'So you've continued to hate him all this time?'

'Yes.'

'What did he say to you today?'

Words were nothing but a weak, after-the-fact way of relieving guilt, of filling a void. 'That he was sorry. Back then he'd been suffering from depression too. He'd been selfish but he really did love her.'

'And you don't believe him?'

'You know how his life went? A year and a half later, he met someone else, got married and they have a young baby. Barry gets to live happily ever after.'

'You resent him for being happy?'

'I resent him being happy when Susan's dead!'

'What would it take you to feel better, Gregory? Barry's head on a platter? Misery and pain for the rest of his life?'

'You don't understand.'

'Maybe not, but hating him comes back on you, that's one thing I do understand. You will never find peace in your soul if you keep wishing pain for him. He's human too, like the rest of us. Yet you blame him for his flaws and you blame Susan for hers. You're angry at everyone for everything unfair in your world.'

'Maybe I am. So what?'

'Here's the news, Gregory, it's time for you to grow up and take responsibility for all the blame you so easily dish out to others. You have everything, yet you have nothing. Susan is gone. You're afraid. Accepting her death would require you to have to live again and you're way too comfortable being the victim of your crappy family. Stop being a bloody victim, and give people a break.'

'You're too harsh, Adela, do you know that? You're too damn harsh.'

'Someone needs to be and everyone else who loves you is too afraid to say it like it is. I refuse to see you as a victim, so get over yourself.'

'My sister's dead.'

'But *you're* not.'

They walked in silence along the road all the way to the trees at the edge of his land. Gregory let her words sink in. Of course he blamed Barry. And yes, he blamed Susan…and his father. It felt justified but also left him stuck. He didn't want to be stuck anymore. But without his anger or even his detachment, what would there be? Love? Vulnerability? Those words were difficult for him.

Before they reached the gates of his driveway, he stopped.

'Although it pains me to say this…thank you.'

'You're welcome.' She linked him again, a smile curving onto her lips.

'I know I have to try to accept what she did.'

'What other sane option do you have?' She leaned her head against the side of his shoulder. 'Susan didn't do it to hurt you. Can you imagine what that level of desperation must feel like?'

'She's gone. That's it, isn't it? Susan's gone. The rest is irrelevant.'

'Yes, Greg. She's gone, but it doesn't mean her life meant nothing.'

They stood in silence together, leaning against one another, watching the sunset.

'That's one hell of a sky, don't you think?' she said.

One hell of a sky. He was able to notice its beauty because he was standing next to her. Adela was all the perfect elements of life rolled into one beautiful, strong woman. Gregory's mind felt a glimmer of hope, her harsh words blowing away the turmoil, allowing him to notice life, as if seeing it from another set of eyes. A subtle calmness greeted him, like a long-lost friend returning home.

Together they watched the blending of the oranges, yellows and pinks.

She looked up at him. 'Thanks for this last couple of weeks. My real life has seemed very far away. I never thought I'd be saying this but I've enjoyed the break.'

'It's been an *experience*.'

'Hey.' She punched him lightly. 'Is that the best you can do?'

He could say so much more to her. Put his arms around her, press his lips against hers—finish what had started earlier in the barn. What had this woman done to him?

'Are you kidding me? The whole place is talking about you. Nobody can understand why you're organising the village to within an inch of itself. You've charmed Daisy and John, Mad Margaret and even Mary, Mary quite Contrary. Hell, you even managed to force *me* out of hibernation. You know how to hide out in style, Adela, that's for sure. There's just one thing…and it does slightly ruin the illusion…'

'What…'

'You snore like a son of a bitch, Ms Winters. An overweight, beer-bellied, middle-aged man would have nothing on you. You're like a steam train once you get started.'

'And to think I was prepared to share my sunset with you!'

He refused to let her walk away from him, blocking her at the fence. 'Typical woman. You give and then you take away.'

Her face turned pale and her smile disappeared.

'What? What did I say? It was a joke—'

But she was looking past him. He turned around, the back of his house now in view. An unfamiliar car was parked diagonally across the path.

'Who's that, I wonder?' he said, trying to see more clearly.

'David,' she said quietly.

As the sun lowered itself down, Adela and Gregory walked together in silence up the pathway, both pairs of eyes glued to the door of the black jaguar as it opened.

Chapter 40

Even from a distance Adela could see the furrows of his brow and the angry squint of David's close-set eyes. Her stomach churned as she wondered how in the hell she was going to explain all of this away. She hadn't told him she was staying in some rich guy's mansion for a couple of weeks. Had she left last week, nobody would have found her. Oh, no, clever clogs herself had decided to save the world, instead of making any attempt to retrieve the ashes of her badly burned relationship. But who was she kidding? She had stayed because it suited her. Cursing her own selfishness, Adela wished she could retreat to Gregory's pool, sink down into the cleansing water and not come back up for air until her life was back in balance.

Of course she wanted David to forgive her, but this way she had to face the drama of having further lied to him. Once again, she would be the bad guy. There would be grovelling involved. She hated that she owed it to him.

'Well, well, well,' David muttered as she came closer. 'You even changed your hair colour, I see!'

'Hi.' What should she do, try to hug him and act like this was the best moment of her life? Would this aggravate him or would standing before him like a limp ragdoll, not showing him any recognition of affection, be the choice to drive him into a fit of anger? She couldn't tell what he wanted her to do. This moment could not be about her, this moment was all David's.

She opted to walk up close to him and try to take his hands; an awkward balance of intimacy, somewhere between the two. But David kept his hands firmly by his side. Now she became the limp ragdoll.

'What exactly is going on here?'

The truth spread too eagerly on her cheeks, but what she felt for Gregory was only part of this dream, it wasn't real life. David was. She had to try to fix what she had broken.

'Nothing,' she said, aware of how filthy Gregory looked from all his cleaning. 'This is Gregory. Gregory meet David. Gregory is a friend of JB's. He gave me a place to stay so I could get my head together and figure things out.'

David glared at her hermit. 'Could you give us a bit of privacy, if that's not too much trouble?'

Gregory nodded, glancing at Adela before opening the back door of the kitchen and closing it behind him.

'You expect me to believe this is innocent?'

'I expect nothing, David.'

'You were *here* the last time we spoke?'

Bitterness chilled the insides of her heart. 'You hated me enough already. What was telling you going to achieve?'

'Honesty.'

'Why exactly are you here, David?'

He looked around him, almost as if he was in a daze. 'Good question. I wish I knew the answer.'

'You know I'm sorry for what I did. I never meant to hurt you.'

'Come on, let's walk. I'd rather not stand on some dirty stranger's doorstep discussing my relationship.'

So he still thought they had a relationship? That was something, she supposed. 'Sure.'

They walked back the way she had come with Gregory, mere moments ago, past the place where they'd shared a sunset together. Now the goose bumps were high on her skin and the pretty reflections of Gregory's garden had dissolved into the darkness of the night. Everything about this new moment was colder and darker.

Being away from the house softened David's approach. 'I came here because I missed you.'

Nagging conflict battled within her. Guilt? Shame? She had become close friends with both, going to sleep night after night, wishing David would come back to her. Now here he was and she wasn't sure what she was supposed to feel. Were the nerves in her stomach causing such a fuss they left no room for anything else?

Adela took a deep breath. 'I need to explain something to you. You asked me why I let myself be seduced. I've been asking the same question. I can't keep blaming my father's lousy behaviour for enticing me to drink myself into oblivion. I'm too old for those kinds of excuses. So I was using this time away to try to figure out a better answer.'

'Okay…' he said hesitantly.

'Remember when the publishers convinced me to treat my grandmother's book as my own?'

'Yes.'

'I should have listened to my own instinct, David. Instead I listened to everybody else.'

'So you're blaming *me*?' His eyes widened and he started to walk faster.

Adela had to run a little to keep up with him. 'Slow down. Wait. Please, listen to me, would you?'

'Well, frankly so far I don't like what I'm hearing.'

'I'm blaming *me,* David. My decisions, my choices. I didn't go with my gut feeling back then. I was swayed by the lure of publication and excitement. But I hated the lies. They've shadowed me the whole time.'

'It didn't seem to stop you from continuing to lie. Your truth must be stored away deep, Adela.'

How could she convey her image of life to him? His view was so different to hers. If only she had John's way with words to make David see she wasn't a terrible person, she was simply struggling to find her way? She had discovered a world of knowing inside of her which she couldn't find a way to express.

'You can't pretend you hadn't noticed how I'd lost my spark, David. Didn't you want to talk about the bags under my eyes, the night-time trips to the kitchen, wide awake when I should be asleep and sleepy when I should be awake? I was sinking into a great big hole so without light I almost couldn't see. The waiter forced me to stop and look at everything. Every part of me needed to stop and take a breath.' She could never tell David she was beginning to feel grateful for that silver-tongued devil. David would never in a million years understand.

Never.

'And now that you're having this *life-changing* look around, what exactly do you see?'

She paused, wishing he could glimpse inside her heart, hoping he could understand who she was, beyond her mistakes. 'I see the importance of being aware of how things make me feel.'

'What the hell are you talking about?'

John and his spade popped into her mind. 'I'm climbing out of the quicksand. I'm starting to grab colour where I can. You should too, David. I'm pulling apart those clouds before they come down any lower. I couldn't keep pretending. It was pulling me away from myself. My granny had life sussed, but I don't and I can no longer pretend I do. I'm actually okay with that. I want to figure out the best way to live my life and maybe someday I'll write my own book, who knows? But they will be *my* words, *my* wisdom, not stolen from the diaries of someone else.'

'You felt this way the whole time? Why didn't you tell me?'

'I tried to but I could hardly admit it to myself.'

'I didn't suspect a thing. You're an astounding liar.'

His words stung her. 'Try having people treat you like you're something you know you're not. They expected me to be perfect. My hair, my skin, my clothes, my answers. Life got unstable and I reacted. The waiter meant nothing. I was trying to escape.'

'From me? Do you still want to escape?'

'No,' she cried. 'Of course not. I made a mistake, David. That's not who I am.'

His features softened. He moved closer to her and reached out to take her hand in his. 'Part of me wants to hurt you as much as you've hurt me.'

'I know.'

'The other part doesn't want to lose you.'

She waited for him to continue, feeling worn out, like there was nothing else to say. 'So what now?'

He gave her hand a squeeze. 'Do you love me?'

Her hesitation lasted but a moment. 'Of course I do.'

'Well, how about you try to convince me over a drink and maybe something to eat?'

Gregory would be waiting for her. 'Give me a sec, okay?' She took out her mobile; he answered on the second ring.

'Hi, it's me,' she said, afraid of the panic rising in her chest when she thought of him.

'Are you okay?' His tone was soft.

David was listening intently to every word.

'Of course. I won't be back for dinner. David and I are going to get something to eat.'

'Oh…sure. My mother is on her way. She's staying over tonight, so she can be fresh for the morning. You're still okay for the weekend, Adela?'

Tears welled up at the back of her eyes. The weekend felt spoiled now. 'Try stopping me.'

'Okay,' Gregory replied, his voice tight.

231

'See you later, then. Bye.' Blinking away the tears, she forced a smile upon her face. 'Let's go see what we can find to eat.'

'I came across a restaurant about ten miles from here. Looked okay.' David once again took a firm grasp of her hand. 'Have you been looking yourself up on the internet?'

She tried to make a joke of things. 'That's a very personal question, David!'

He frowned. 'I'm being serious.'

'No, I don't want to read any of it. The public hate me, they feel sorry for you and they think I'm a liar and a cheat.'

'Yeah, pretty much. I've been hounded by press looking for my side of the story.'

What was Gregory doing? Peeling spuds? Tossing the salad? Getting David back was what she wanted, of course it was. But she was uncomfortable with David residing in Gregory's world. When she was with John, he rationalised life into a clear path ahead. When she was with Gregory, she was able to forget the before and the after and simply enjoy the present. But David *was* her before and her after. The two simply did not fit.

Chapter 41

'Gregory, will you stop taking it out on the pots and pans? What's wrong with you? You're not still annoyed with Adela about the barn, are you?'

'No, Mother, I'm fine. Coffee?'

'Yes, please. I'm looking forward to the weekend. I called into Daisy on my way. The pub is buzzing and Daisy's the queen bee.'

David would want her back. Of course he would. A man would be a fool not to want her. Gregory slammed the lid onto the kettle. 'Coffee?'

'For the second time, yes.' Nancy leaned against the island. 'Where's Adela?'

'Out.'

'Out with the owner of the fancy car I saw speeding out of your driveway?'

'Yes, Mother, out with her boyfriend, if you must know.'

'David's here?'

'How do you know David?'

She waved dismissively. 'They're a pretty famous couple in certain circles. He has a voice like melted chocolate. It's his job. He does voice overs. So he came for her. Romantic, is it not?'

Romantic? He slammed the coffee jar onto the counter. 'Oh, very.'

'Actually, he's a real jerk, if you ask me. David squeezed the situation for every ounce of publicity he could. Maybe it's beginning to dry up so he has to reignite the machine, so to speak.'

'You think so?'

233

Nancy shrugged. 'Maybe.'

'Either you do or you don't.'

She poured some milk into the black coffee he'd passed to her. 'Maybe that's what I *want* to think.'

'Why?' Gregory's brain wanted to explode, not sit having coffee with his mother. He wanted to run out and grab Adela away from David and his flashy car, to lock all the doors and make the rest of the world go away.

'No mother wants her son to get only a glimpse of loving someone.'

'She's not mine to love.'

Nancy sighed in defeat and they brought their cups of coffee over to sit on the couches. 'Do you think she'll go back to him? What was she doing with the waiter in the first place if she loves David so much?'

His head was pounding. This felt like reopening old wounds. Life had chased him with these feelings for years with Susan. Her depression had kept him swimming forever in unpredictable waters, never knowing when an unexpected current could try to swirl them both under. When she died, the fear died with her, yet in its place was something much more torturous. The realm of the absolute. No hope, no change, no more possibilities.

Memories, when they were all he had left, were the most unsatisfying of all, for pain clung to them like bitter cold. Gregory had chosen to bury that life, memories and all. Adela had shovelled her way in, beginning to allow him to picture a life held together by more than money. But the reality of Adela's situation had now landed on his doorstep. She would leave with David, and he would become one of her memories, something that would no longer really exist.

#

Adela glanced at David from above her menu. She wasn't hungry, yet she knew she should eat. She had explained

234

her plans for the weekend to him on the journey to the restaurant.

'What do you owe those people? You should pack your bag and come home with me tonight.' David closed his own menu and lifted a toothpick from the plastic container in the middle of the table.

'No, David. I have to see it through. I was the one who started it, I can't walk away.'

He stabbed the table cloth with the sharp end of the toothpick. 'Because that wouldn't be like you...'

His bitterness travelled deep into her stomach, as if she'd swallowed it. 'This isn't going to work if every time I speak you're going to make me suffer. I hurt you, I get it. But that doesn't mean you become entitled to keep hurting me back in lots of tiny ways in an effort to get even.'

His eyes were on fire, his jaw rigid. 'Jesus, Adela, give me a bit of time, would you? I'm trying here. Forgiveness has never been my strong point.'

You're telling me, she thought, squirming with despair. 'This sucks, David. This really sucks.'

'Don't you think I know that?'

A waiter appeared, tall and a bit gangly, but with an impish smile and large hazel eyes. 'You guys ready to order?'

David looked at her. 'What would you like from this handsome young man?'

Her stomach felt queasy; she ignored his taunts. 'I'll have the soup, please.'

'Are you sure soup is all you want from him?'

'Yes, thank you,' she said, smiling weakly at the waiter.

David ordered a steak and the waiter left quickly, obviously sensing the tension.

'You don't trust me, I get it.'

'And what about this Gregory fella? What the hell is the story with him? Don't you have any sense of right and wrong, Adela? Staying in his fancy house, how did you think it would make me feel? It's like you *want* to antagonise me.'

At that very moment, she wished she could spoon-feed David her soup…up his nose. But of course, she kept on having to remind herself his anger was justified. She had broken his trust; of course there would be consequences. For now she was tired and wanted to climb into bed and sleep. Tomorrow she had to be bright and bubbly. Like a superhero, she had to don her mask and be more than which she believed she was currently capable.

This evening had sucked all the energy out of her, leaving nothing but regret and resentment. She thought of John and his cosy kitchen, his kind words and generous time, tears threatening to add extra salt to her soup.

'I wasn't thinking very rationally two weeks ago, David. I was offered a place to stay by a friend and I took it. No strings attached, no hidden agendas, just a kind gesture to which I agreed. Please try not to make more out of it than it is. Gregory is a nice man who was kind to me when I needed it. I'm going to do a bit of cleaning and painting and tidying in his village as a way of saying thanks, and then I'll come home to you. It's clear you still need a bit of space from me. You need to decide if you can live with what I did to you, because I'm not sure you can.'

He grabbed her hand. 'Of course I can. Why do you think I tracked you down and came here? Come home with me, please, Adela? How can we make things better between us if you're sleeping under another man's roof?'

'I need to finish what I started.'

'Even now, I don't come first with you.'

Not a spoonful of her soup could she swallow.

'You'll never stop blaming me. This isn't going to work.'

'Well, whose fault is that?'

'Yes, yes, it's my fault. I was only asking for a couple of days.'

'You know what I think, Adela? I think you're terrified of returning to your life and you're trying to avoid the consequences. Once the media get you back in their sights, you'll be hounded and questioned and you can't stand the thought of it.'

'You're wrong, David. I will face the media and their questions, but I'm trying to figure out my own answers, I'm trying to do the right thing. You may as well know that I intend to give my granny the recognition she deserved.'

'Like hell you will.' He slammed his knife and fork down onto the table. 'Don't you dare change the rules now because you're suffering from an attack of conscience! You'll be an even bigger laughing stock...we both will. We'd never recover.'

She laid down her spoon. 'I'm tired and I don't want to be here. We're not going to sort this out in one night. I have an early start and you have a long drive ahead of you. Let's just go.'

'Fine.'

A fifty euro note from her purse would be more than enough. She could feel the eyes of the gangly waiter on her back as she left the money on the table. She couldn't escape quickly enough, away from people, away from David and his demands. It was all too much to take in. Was this really the way couples behaved? Was this the man she had chosen to grow old with? But tonight was not the night to ask such questions. Too much had happened. The answer would be tainted.

They drove back in silence. They were about to pull into Gregory's driveway when David stopped the car.

'This wasn't how I meant it to be.'

She gave a half-nod. 'Me either.'

'I know I need to forgive you. It's hard.'

'I understand.'

His fingers interlaced with hers. 'So I'll see you on Monday then?'

Exhaustion was taking aim at her. 'Thank you.'

'I don't reckon I've got much choice. You're a firm woman when you set your mind to it.'

Returning a weak smile, the knot in her stomach loosened slightly. 'Think of this weekend as my community service!'

'Okay,' he said, squeezing her hand.

The rest of the short journey was made in silence, neither speaking until they reached Gregory's front door. 'It feels weird me leaving you here like this.'

'I'll be back before you know it.'

He paused, as if to decide what to do next. Taking her in his arms, he held her before planting a kiss on her lips. 'I'd almost forgotten what you felt like.'

Another false smile as she wondered if Gregory could see them from the conservatory window. 'See you Monday.'

David drove away. She checked the time on her watch, relieved to have a bit of distance from his demands and blame. Two days left before she would return home. She opened the back door and went inside.

Chapter 42

'Hi,' Gregory said from the chair in the corner of the kitchen.

Adela jumped. 'Jesus, Gregory. Why are you sitting in the dark?'

'I wasn't sure you'd be coming back.'

She switched on the lamp in the corner and sunk into the couch across from him. 'Weird day, huh?'

'Yeah.'

She could see his bottle of beer was almost finished. 'Want another?'

'Sure.'

This was a different kind of silence as she went to his fridge, removed two bottles and pulled off the tops with his bottle opener. She handed him one, but as he went to take the bottle from her, she kept hold of it. Their eyes met.

'You okay?' she said, still holding the top of his bottle.

'I'm okay.'

She released her hold on it and sat down.

'How does this work? Do I ask you how it went?' he said, laying his empty bottle on the table.

She took a hard slug of her drink. 'I cheated on him. It wasn't wine and roses.'

'But he wants you back...'

'I think so. He's awfully angry though.' Her legs curled up under her feet.

'How long are you staying?'

'Until Monday...if that's still okay?'

239

'Of course.' He rubbed his hand against one half of his face.

'Are you tired?'

'No,' he said, a little too loudly. 'No, I'm not tired.'

'How's your mum?'

'Intrigued by your guest. She loves a happy ending, does my mother.'

If only she could take Gregory by the hand and bring him to her. Why couldn't they forget everything else and go back to how it was earlier? But she had to remain where she was. Throughout her evening with David, she'd wanted him to go home without her. Gregory complicated everything. Before his entrance into her life, her prime focus would have been to make things right with David. Now, when she looked at David, all she could think about was Gregory, and when she looked at Gregory, she was overcome with guilt. This hideaway was meant to simplify her life—it hadn't.

None of John's wise words seemed to make any sense to her now. When she was cocooned in the small, safe world of John's kitchen, she had the world figured out, but once a challenge came along, her notions crumbled to nothing.

'I'm sorry for coming here,' she said quietly.

'Why are you sorry?'

'You know why.'

Gregory stood up. 'You flatter yourself.'

'Where are you going?'

'To bed.' His tone almost sounded like a challenge.

'Don't go like this.'

He moved closer to her. 'I'm fine...we're fine, Adela. I'm glad you're getting your happily ever after. I'm glad he's giving you a second chance. You're a wonderful person, you deserve it.'

'Gregory, I—'

Placing his finger against her lips, he silenced her. 'You don't need to say anything.'

Her eyes filled with tears.

'It is what it is. You understand that as well as I do.'

She nodded.

'Goodnight, Adela.'

She allowed herself to cry properly for the first time all day once he closed the kitchen door behind him.

Chapter 43

DAY 13 – Saturday

Gregory took a swim at six o'clock the next morning, his way of trying to shake off his lack of sleep. Breakfast was easier to eat alone, before either of his guests awoke. Back to his old routine. The silence should have satisfied him. Had she killed the hermit in him for good? He would never let JB do this to him again. Bringing a woman like Adela into his home and expecting him to be unaffected.

He went into his office, turned on his laptop, went online and searched for stories about David. His mother wasn't wrong about this man stuffing his face in front of every camera imaginable. Adela's dalliance was indeed big news. Gregory closed down the lid. He observed the word painted on his wall. He'd been looking at that damn word for so long, trying to map his route to it. He had an idea in his head of what it meant. Money equalled freedom. True enough. His wealth allowed him to act as free a leaf on a windy day. But money, it seemed, was a mere piece of the puzzle.

Susan hadn't felt free a day in her whole, miserable life. He should be grateful to have made it this far, so much further than she ever got. But that wasn't how this whole game seemed to work. The rules of his game were not the same as Susan's. Her happiness was not his happiness. Freedom was as far from inside the walls of his home as ever it was, and no amount of painting those seven letters on every available space was going to change that.

'Good morning,' he said, facing the two women who were chattering in an excitable way, suggesting the events of yesterday had vanished from their minds. But the flicker of a glimpse from Adela as he was opening the cupboard told him otherwise.

'Have you seen Adela's agenda for today, Gregory? She presumes we all have the strength of ten men.'

'No doubt you'll prove her right,' he remarked lightly, grateful for the hard work ahead of him. It would do his mind good.

'We're all meeting at nine?' Nancy checked her watch.

'Yep,' Adela said. 'You still have time to apply your makeup.'

'Makeup is hardly necessary for what we're about to do,' Gregory said.

Nancy tutted at her son. 'So clever, yet so much to learn.'

Adela grinned. 'I'm going to head over to John's for twenty minutes before we all meet up in the square. I'll see you there at nine.'

#

'Are you ready to get to work, John?'

'I've been ready for the last two hours. I'm an early bird. I brought everything over to the square already, so come on in and have a cup of tea with me before it all kicks off.'

Adela was grateful for the offer. She proceeded to spill her guts to him about what had happened the previous day. 'David doesn't want me to come clean about the book.'

'I suppose he doesn't want you to get hurt.'

'Whatever I do, I can't keep going the way I was. The publishers have probably already dropped me, I've just avoided hearing about it. You know what, John?'

'What?'

'I'm okay with that.'

'You're an honest girl who got stuck in a web of lies and now you're trying to cut yourself free. I respect you for it, Adela. You're listening to life and beginning to understand its language. You're making progress, even if it's difficult.'

'You always know how to make it sound okay. It's a real gift you have.'

'As you know, I've been in a worse place than you ever were. Growth can be sore on the bones. When I went to England, what got me through was the good grace of the couple who let me become their lodger. They saw more in me than I saw in myself. Aidan S. Bryant was the man's name--my philosopher friend. He let me help him out in his garden in exchange for cheaper lodgings…

…He taught me so much about caring for plants and vegetables. He helped me move my focus to something more worthwhile. I fell in love with gardening whilst living in that small house with those generous people. Without them, I sometimes wonder whether I would have made it. It healed me. Then I met their niece.' His eyes glimmered.

'Your wife?'

Her photograph on the wall met his attention. 'She was so many things to me when she wasn't driving me crazy bossing me about the place. Back then, I needed the structure she demanded from me. She was a whirlwind of a woman.'

'When did you know you were in love with her?'

'Would you believe I can still remember exactly when? We were sitting having a drink with her friend, Sarah, I think her name was. Sarah was going on and on about her husband, moaning this and groaning that. Well, when Sarah left, she took my hand, looked at me with such love, and made a statement I carry with me to this very day…'

244

'What did she say?'

'She said, "I won't ever be your victim, John, and may you never be mine. I'll never look on our relationship as something I intend to squeeze dry or wear to the bone. You and I both separate and together are a mighty force. We don't *need* each other so let's not be afraid of it, of losing it, ruining it, and instead let's enjoy the heck out of it." With those words and that sparkle in her eye, I was a goner.'

Adela squeezed his hand. 'She sounds like an extraordinary woman.'

'I've impeccable taste, don't you know!'

'I'm going home to David on Monday.'

'Jeez, you could try sounding happier about it.'

'I get the feeling David would like me to eat humble pie for the rest of my life. He stuffed so much of it down my throat last night that I'm still gagging from the taste.'

'Don't you regret what you did?'

'You'll think I'm weird if I tell you the truth.'

John rubbed his hands together. 'Oh, goodie. I love weird.'

'Part of me does. Then there's this other part of me that needed something to shake me from my tree. I regret hurting David, of course. But I couldn't imagine not coming here, not meeting you, Daisy or Gregory.'

'What a fine thing to say.'

'The downside is my relationship with David doesn't seem so straightforward all of a sudden. He was sitting across from me last night and I found myself wanting to be home with Gregory instead.'

'Now we're getting down to it. I don't even need to ask how Gregory feels about you. The change in him is extraordinary.'

'Help me, John! What do I do?' *If anybody could help her, it was him.*

'How do you feel? It's time to examine your road map.'

'But what if my road map is wrong? It's calling me to go in more than one direction. That's no system at all.'

'Do you know what I would do if I were you, Adela?'

'What?'

'I would stop ranting about how confused you are. Have you ever heard the idea that prayer is you talking to God/the Universe whatever you wish to call the Intelligence which exists around and within us, and meditation is you listening to the reply?'

'Praying doesn't sit too well with me, I'm afraid.'

'Ah, praying is just an expression for posting your request to the Universe. But your answer doesn't always come in the way you may think it would. You may hear the words of a song, or receive a phone call or meet a stranger. It may also help if you quieten your mind and listen, be still, tune in like a radio, to feel your easiest way forward…

…Meditation sounds like a grand yet unattainable idea, but all it means is to focus your mind to allow the bigger wisdom of life through. You meditate when you dance or write; painters do it when they pick up their paintbrush and think of nothing other than their job at hand. Gardening is my meditation. I fully immerse myself in the act, and when my thoughts rush in, I smile at them, I mentally pet them like an eager puppy, but I do not let them jump all over me. You should use the next couple of days to try this. Hard work is the perfect meditation.'

'You're so clever, John, but why can't you give me straight advice? Should I go back to David? Should I come clean to the public about my granny? What would *you* do?'

246

He giggled, nodding his head. 'I don't live in your heart, Adela. My advice would be based on *my* life, not yours.'

'Yeah, okay, *fine*.' She raised her eyes to heaven.

He stood up and placed his cup in the sink. 'Every day of your life, you make choices. You get to decide what you want to make of life. Every thought, every action will build something. What is it you wish to create, Adela? That is the question I would be asking myself. This choice of David or Gregory, Granny's book or the lie, it boils down to that one question. Your life isn't all about David. Your happiness is not based on having David or even Gregory. You do not need either man to complete you, contrary to popular belief...

...You need to understand you are already complete, and from this position of strength, choose where you wish to go next. You cannot make grand life decisions from a position of fear, because this fear is an illusion that will likely steer you wrong. Be well inside yourself first, and then you will never again wonder if your map is upside down.'

'Easy to say, John, but not so easy to put into practice.'

'It boils down into one simple sentence. Want to know what that sentence is?'

'What?'

'The most important love affair of your life should be with yourself.'

She scratched an itch on her nose. 'Why does that feel a bit depressing?'

'Because you don't get the significance of what I've said.'

'Seems I'm making a habit of it.'

'Be true to yourself, love yourself, take the time to listen to your own inner voice, be kind to your needs, and everything else will fall into place. Don't expect David's

247

forgiveness to complete you, or Gregory's love. You may get those things or not, but ultimately your life is about whatever you choose it to be. Love yourself or hate yourself. Be kind or condemn who you are, but who you are is who you have chosen to be. If you don't like it, choose to be something else. It begins and ends with *you*. Not David. Not Gregory.'

Adela felt the sudden urge to hug her friend. 'Thanks, my little fountain of knowledge.'

John grinned relentlessly. 'You're more than welcome.'

The time on her watch said they needed to go.

Chapter 44

Gregory couldn't believe his eyes as he walked towards the town square. At least ninety people in tracksuits and clothes of all colours and textures were gathered together. Adela, Daisy and John were handing out the lists they had compiled, including the names in each group and what each group would be working on.

Some would be tackling the green areas, planting all the shrubs John had purchased. Others would spend the day cleaning. Anyone with a bit of extra talent was designated a specific task; mending, fixing, building, painting. Daisy had contacted the owners of some of the now-empty buildings on the main street and sought permission to paint the window sills and clean up the windows, as these places made the street feel jaded and old.

Gregory watched Adela organising people who she'd never met two weeks ago. Her friendly yet confident approach made them want to please her. She was extraordinarily good at it. He could see how she had got away with her charade for so long on her book tour. Adela was a natural born leader. His heart made itself known to him as he approached her. He wanted to run from this pain she was causing him, this desire to be close to her.

But trying to run away was no longer an option. Should he tell her how he felt? Would it be fair? Was to love another person really what he wanted? He'd lived for so long by himself, needing no one. Would this rush of desire wear off once she returned to David? Were these feelings even real or was she a convenient doorstep fantasy?

Adela greeted him with a smile and a pair of disposable gloves. 'Hi stranger. You're on John's team. He's been bending my mind already this morning, so beware!'

Gregory winked at her. 'Thanks for the advice.'

John waved over at him and Gregory made his way towards his group of co-workers, Josie being one of them. Cheers, guys, he thought, making a mental note to kick someone's ass for doing that to him.

John handed him a trowel and explained his plans to create flowerbeds at the entrance to the village. One of the men had been working on a wooden sign to hammer down into the ground next to the beds. They had plenty of digging and weeding ahead of them. Once the entire team of ten was gathered together, John led them along the pathway.

Josie nudged her way up beside Gregory. 'Full of team spirit all of a sudden, are we?'

Gregory glanced at her. 'Sure, why not, eh, Josie?'

Her fury was evident by how hard she was stomping on the ground.

'I've been seeing Mark McDaid. Do you know him?'

'I can't say that I do.'

'Sure you do. The McDaid's from behind the bridge.'

'Oh, yeah, I think I went to school with him. Nice fella.'

Josie pushed up her sleeves as she walked. 'How long is your *friend* staying?'

'As long as she likes.'

She stopped on the path, almost tripping up Nigel, who had to swerve to avoid bumping into her. 'You even cut your hair and shaved that lousy beard for her? I mean, what the heck?'

'Don't make a scene,' Gregory said, nudging her forward. 'Come on.'

Tears sprung from her eyes. 'I had to accept your terms and conditions, no exceptions.'

John was looking back at them. Gregory turned to her. 'Don't make me the bad guy here. Don't make me have to spell it out for you, Josie.'

'Why should I make it easy for you to walk away? You got me when it suited you and then you—'

'I never promised you anything. You wanted to believe my feelings for you were more than they were.'

'You're a cold-hearted bastard,' she hissed.

'Well, while we're being so honest, you were convenient.'

'At least I'm not a cheating, lying slut, like *her*.'

He stopped. 'What?'

Josie blew her nose. 'You think I don't know who she is? How backward do you believe us to be, Gregory? Some of us even have *broadband*.'

'Don't take this out on her.'

'The village sweetheart. Ha, what a joke! I see it now. She's doing to you what you did to me. You shaved your beard, pretended to give a damn about this hole of a place, and all with the intent of seducing a woman who will stamp on your wizened heart and not even remember your name when she's done with you.' Josie laughed, her eyes turning to slits. 'You know what you were for her, don't you?'

He gave no response.

'Convenient.' Josie's face was contorted with hatred. 'The last laugh's on you, sucker.'

#

Adela tapped her index finger against John's back.

'Where's Toni?'

251

He stood up, groaning as he did so. 'She never turned up.'

'You're kidding me? Right, where does that imp live?' Adela pulled off her gardening gloves, rolled them up into a ball and shoved them into the pocket of her rain jacket. 'If I have to drag her out kicking and screaming, she'll be here.'

'You're scary when you're mad,' John said. 'I'm almost afraid to give you directions.'

Adela marched down the street, around the corner and up the hill a little, before turning into the small cul de sac of squished-together houses. Number 22 was drab and miserable, much like the rest of them.

The doorbell was hanging out of its socket so Adela banged on the door. No reply. She rapped on the badly-conditioned wood. Again nothing.

Opening the letterbox, she tried to look in. All she could see were coats and bags lying about the hallway. 'Toni.'

A ruffling noise. Someone was coming. Adela moved back from the letterbox and waited.

The door opened. A woman with the worst roots Adela had ever seen popped her head around the door. 'What do you want? Who do you think you are, knocking at my door like a beggar?'

M-O-M was freaky.

'I'm looking for Toni.'

'What's the little bitch done now?'

Adela stepped back even further, the energy of this woman disturbing her senses. 'Nothing.'

The woman put her head back inside the house and Adela could hear her blow her nose. 'You're fucking right, nothing. She ain't here, but if you see her then tell her to get her skinny ass home.'

The door was shut in Adela's face. She walked away wondering what had happened in that woman's life.

252

What a world Mommy dearest lived in. Although the sun was warm on her face, Adela caught a shiver. She wanted to find Toni more than ever. Her first stop was the forest but Toni was nowhere to be seen. Why hadn't she appeared this morning, as promised? What must life be like for the girl, sharing it with such a woman as had answered the door? Where did John's theories about the universe fit into Toni's life? Try as she might, Adela could not see the perfection in the design of Toni's situation.

Next stop…Toni's secret garden.

When Adela found her, she was lying right in the centre of her garden, out cold, covered in an old blanket. She had obviously slept there all night.

'Wake up,' she said, nudging the young girl.

Toni yawned before pulling the duvet over her head. 'Go away, Elvira. You shouldn't have come here.'

The grass next to her was dry enough to sit on. 'I called to your house.'

'You met my *mother*?'

'I did.'

'Invite you in for the tea, did she? Now go away. I want to be alone.'

'Like hell, I'm going anywhere. Nobody wants to be alone, Toni. I'm sitting here until you get yourself together and come with me. We have work to do, girl. I intend for you to impress the pants off our friend, John.'

'I'm not part of your little project, so stop trying to save me; you make me want to puke. You don't know me, you sure as hell don't care about me, so off you go and do your thing, I'll do mine, and we'll get along fine.'

Adela pulled a blade of grass. 'How long has your mother been sick?'

'My entire life.'

'Has she ever tried to get help?'

253

Rising from under the duvet, Toni's eyes were red and puffy. 'She gets help, she feels a bit better, she empties the pills into the bin, she sinks back in and the cycle begins all over again.'

'Well, you can't stay here all morning, useless, like your mother's pills, lying at the bottom of the bin, stuck between the stinking carrot peels. I'm not asking you to come with me because I'm trying to save you, I'm asking because I *need* you.'

'Don't patronise me, Elvira. You don't need me.'

Adela put her hand gently on the girls arm. 'You're part of it, whether you think you want to be or not. I'm leaving here on Monday, so this is all the time you've got left to call me names.'

'You're leaving already? Don't you like it here?'

The truth of the question burned inside of her. 'Of course I do, but I've got to go home.'

Toni looked into her face, her eyes wild and dark. 'Okay, I'll come.'

Chapter 45

Adela scrubbed and cleaned to within an inch of her life all morning. At one o'clock, they all stopped for a lunch break. Mary Mary quite Contrary and Mad Margaret together produced an impressive array of sandwiches and buns for everyone to eat. Gregory had given them a key to the barn the previous day in preparation. The villagers oohed and aahed at the beauty of the building from the inside. The sun shone through the windows, and despite an abundance of dust particles in the air, the people relaxed and enjoyed themselves.

'A cup of tea and an egg and onion sambo never tasted so good,' said Nigel, who, true to form, was dressed in a blue and red Superman t-shirt and a pair of faded denim jeans.

Gregory approached Adela with a large coffee pot in his hand. 'You'd think they were at a wedding, chattering away, proud as anything, the lot of them.'

'Nice, isn't it?' she said, putting out her cup for a refill. 'You make an excellent waiter.'

'Was that a come-on?' he teased, batting his eyelashes at her.

'Do you think you're funny?'

'Oh lighten up. I was joking.'

For her, it didn't feel so funny. 'Some of us have feelings, Gregory. Take it easy on mine.'

'You think I'm heartless?' He laid down the pot onto the nearest counter.

'You think I'm a slut?'

'Of course not. Would I make the joke if I actually believed that?'

Damn, he had her there. 'No, I don't suppose you would. I'm not a slut, for the record.'

'You've been so prickly since David's arrival. What did he say to you?'

'He's not a bad man. It would be easier if he were.'

'I don't need a rundown of David's merits, thank you very much.'

Maybe I do. 'How's gardening with John?'

'Between you and me, I think he's enjoying bossing me about.'

'Even *he* must have his flaws!'

'Hey, just to warn you, be careful to avoid Josie,' he said. 'She's gunning for a fight and you're almost as unpopular with her as I am.'

'Why do I *always* get the blame? What did *I* do?'

'You came to live in my house. That alone was enough. You got further as a stranger than she did as my dedicated sex machine.'

Adela flinched. She didn't want to hear about him and Josie. 'Oh, Jesus, look at her giving me filthy looks from across the room. She'd better not try to stir up trouble with me…'

'Hey, calm down, crazy lady. Let her be. She's venting, that's all. It's the effect I have on women; it's not her fault. If anyone's to blame, it's me.'

Adela shook her head. 'You are a nasty piece of work, do you know that? Making jokes off the heartache of the girl. If John is right, it'll come back to bite you in the ass. Karma, remember? You read about it in my most brilliant book!'

'The book that came with the free gift of an extra-large can of worms!'

'Don't remind me!'

'John's in his element, directing the show.' Gregory waved across at Toni, who was devouring a slice of chocolate cake. 'You were right about her; John thinks

256

there's nothing like her. She has already told him all about some garden she grows. Although personally, I wouldn't trust her with my bag of carrots.'

'Gregory!' Adela nudged him. 'Give her a chance. Look at what people thought about you!'

'So polite of you to use the past tense!'

'Have you met Toni's mother? It's a miracle Toni's here at all, judging by *that* piece of work.'

'No, but speaking of mothers, have you seen mine?' Gregory asked, pointing across the room. 'Look at the way she's chatting with John. She doesn't smile like that at everyone!'

'And the lipstick's still in tact,' Adela remarked, checking the time. 'It's nearly two o'clock.'

'Will I round up the troops?'

She touched his shoulder. 'Great, thanks.'

He glanced at her hand, resting against him. 'You're welcome.'

#

'Daisy, what a bad example you're setting! Less eating sandwiches and more rubber gloves and sweated brows, that's what we need,' Gregory whispered in her ear.

'Hey, you, cheeky hermit. Enough of your chat.' Daisy threatened him with the crusts of her sandwich.

'The truth hurts, eh, Daisy! You women do love your food.'

'Pity Adela didn't remove the stubble from your *mouth* while she was at it,' she said, nose up in the air. 'Your mother must have taken the wrong baby home. She should try sending you back, not that you're even worthy of a credit note, I'd say.'

'Still a bit of life in the old girl yet, eh Daisy! Time hasn't made any less of *your* mouth, it seems.'

'Ah, but thanks for letting us use the barn, Gregory. That's one less smack you deserve on that bony, little ass of yours.'

'I'm a kind soul beneath my bony ass.'

'And modest too.'

'How are you managing with Elly?'

Daisy swallowed her bite of sandwich. 'She keeps me young.'

'Are you able to cope?'

'I manage, Gregory. Now enough of that talk, it sounds strange coming from you.'

'I'm sorry I haven't been around for you.' He touched her elbow.

'I'm sorry for blackmailing you into organising this.' She shrugged. 'You had it tough with Susan. Despite my jokes and recriminations, I understand why you wanted to hide away from it all. Sometimes I too wish I had that luxury.'

'I suppose it has been selfish of me. I couldn't stand that she was…'

This time Daisy took his hand. 'I loved her too. She was a great girl, full of passion.'

'Why did she do it, Daisy? I still don't understand why she thought it was her best option. I'm afraid of never being able to forgive her for doing what she did. I would have helped her, but she chose to…'

'Depression eats up the soul, Gregory. You have to let all the blame go. Nobody in their rational mind would end the opportunity to experience a perfectly good life. But you can't imagine what her feelings were. You will drive yourself crazy trying to control what cannot be controlled.'

'Thanks.' He squeezed her hand. 'And thanks for all you've done for Adela while she's been here. I really appreciate it.'

Daisy frowned. 'She's a good girl. The man who gets her will be smiling a grand happy grin the rest of his days.'

'You've never been a subtle woman.'

'Who has time for subtle?' Her wink was intended to be natural, yet it looked more like the beginnings of an eye infection. 'And while we're having a moment of ridiculous sentimentality, it's good to see you getting out. I'm glad Adela was able to shake you off your perch. It's been a long time coming.'

'Poor me, eh!'

'I'm being serious. You think Susan would want you to ignore life? Ain't nothing to be gained from refusing to participate.'

'You were always good at the old lectures, Daisy,' he said with a smirk.

'I'm just saying, that woman is good for you.' Daisy curled the last bits of bread into her mouth. 'She's good for all of us.'

'Enjoy it while it lasts. She's leaving on Monday.'

'*Monday?* Why?'

'Her life doesn't begin and end on my doorstep, you know.'

'But it's so soon. We'll hardly even be rolling into bed after the party by then.'

He watched Adela move from person to person, her face glowing. *Why did she have to be so damn gorgeous?*

'Alas, her fiancé awaits,' he said sharply, squeezing Daisy's shoulder before walking away.

#

The working day was over. Adela laid herself into the huge en suite Jacuzzi bath. Her body felt like someone had tried to pull it apart. She closed her eyes and relaxed. She needed to start packing. Soon there would be no more Gregory sitting in the dark, waiting for her to return home, no more cups of tea by John's roaring fire, no more mad plans with Daisy. Instead she must begin the gruelling task of shovelling up the mess she'd made.

She needed to see what the world was saying about her, to get her bearings before the onslaught. Gregory was

259

making a meal for her tonight. Tomorrow would be filled with the final day of work and then the party, which meant there would be less time for dining together. Tonight, without either of them saying as much, was the beginning of their goodbye.

Her thoughts were interrupted by a loud knock on her bedroom door. 'I'm in the bath,' she called.

The bedroom door opened regardless.

'Adela?' It was JB.

'I'm in the bath,' she repeated.

'You're going back to him? Seriously?' he said from the other side of the door. 'Gregory just told me. Why?'

'Because he's prepared to forgive me, why do you think?' She stood up and grabbed the large towel, wrapping it well around her.

'But you slept with someone else!'

She opened the door. 'Thanks for your vote of confidence.'

JB was pacing the floor. 'But I was sure...'

'You were sure *what*?'

'What about Greg? You're going to *leave* him?'

'Do you expect him to keep me, like some sort of indoor plant?'

He blinked rapidly. 'It's just...you changed him.'

'Yes, I cut his hair and shaved off his beard.'

'Stop dismissing what I'm saying. Nobody gets to that place with him. Nobody, not even *me*. Don't you dare dismiss the importance of that.'

'Hey,' she cried. 'You weren't trying to help *me* by bringing me here—you were trying to help *him*.'

'It was both, you silly fool. I never forgot the way you two were together, all those years ago. The spark was instant, so instant even *I* couldn't miss it.'

'That's not true, JB. Sure...I liked him, but he walked out on me and never looked back.'

'He got a call from the hospital.' JB sat on the edge of the bed. 'Susan tried to kill herself that night. I was sworn to secrecy so I couldn't tell you.'

'Oh.'

'What's so special about David anyway? His voice is overrated.'

Adela laughed. 'I wouldn't be with him if I didn't love him. The way I feel about Gregory, it's all wrapped up in this two-week plan to escape from my problems. You want me to love him because *you* love him, because you want him to be happy. But I don't intend on making any more stupid mistakes, I've made enough of those already.'

'Oh, who cares? Stay anyway.'

'Stay? This is not my life, JB.' His hand felt warm as she held it. 'Gregory is a hermit. He took a holiday for a couple of weeks, that's all. We can't keep our real selves on hold for much longer.'

He sighed dramatically. 'I believe he's making you dinner.'

'Yes, I believe he is. But before we eat, I've got to get dressed and then do some packing.'

'Julia will be devastated you're leaving. She keeps asking me to organise another babysitting session!'

'Poor Julia. You need to get your shit sorted, JB, and find someone proper to mind Harry.'

'I know, I know.'

'Gregory doesn't need me as much as you think he does. You all feel desperately sorry for the oddball hermit, but I wouldn't if I were you. He's in better shape than the rest of us!'

'Here's your real phone,' JB said, removing it from his pocket and handing it to her. 'I'll see you for the clean-up tomorrow. I hope David won't be expecting any rigorous make-up sessions with you on Monday morning, because, let me tell you, your head will be feeling like it's going to explode. The entire village will be bending over back ways to get those drinks into you. By the way, beware of Dirty Micky, if he's about later. He's a desperate man altogether after a couple of whiskeys.'

She thanked him for his concern and hugged him goodbye. Once she was sure he was out of earshot, Adela turned up the volume on her MP3 player, lay down on her bed and imagined how she would say goodbye to her hermit.

Chapter 46

Gregory poured her a glass of wine.

'Thanks,' she said, lifting her knife and fork. 'I wish I hadn't looked myself up on the internet.

'What's the verdict?'

'They make it sound like nobody ever made a mistake before.'

'Ah, but well-paid gurus should be beyond reproach.'

'You read that too?' she said miserably.

'Yeah.' He wished he could cut her off from the judgement of those people. They didn't know any part of her.

'I was never a guru. I was never unaffected by life. You know how the publishers covered themselves?'

'How?'

'I have the same name as my grandmother. In the acknowledgements, they worded it so I was giving the wise words of my granny credit, which technically meant it wasn't false advertising, even though it was.'

'Hmmm. What are you going to do?'

'Contact my agent and tell her I'm coming clean. She can speak to the publishers and let them all continue to bitch and curse about me.'

He cut into his steak. 'And David?'

'He'll bitch and whinge about it for a while too. I'm sure I'll be attributed to potentially ruining his career, but he'll get over it. He'll have no choice because I'm doing it. People won't take me seriously now they know about the waiter. I can forget about a writing career, it's time to move on.'

'I've read your stuff; you're obviously a talented writer, with or without your granny.'

'Writing was always a passion of mine. I've been writing stories since I was kid. That was why I got hooked into granny's diaries in the first place. But—'

'But what? You have an audience, Adela. People recognise your face. That's why I believe they want so desperately to know where you are, and why you did what you did. You intrigue them. Your looks are so striking; they won't want to give up on you. But you need to play this right.'

'Play it how, Gregory? I don't know how to play it. While I might have been inspired by my granny's writings, I didn't create them or really understand them.'

'They will say—so all that inspiration led you to land on the lap of a waiter?'

'In the beginning, I thought I understood it all, but life has since showed me otherwise. My thoughts weren't in line with my actions. There is a better way to live than the way I was living. It took me to come here to really understand my granny's messages. Life is what you make it—those words repeat in my brain, but they only made sense to me when John started talking about life being an opportunity to create. Life really is what we create it to be. In fact, how mine has turned out only proves to me how true my granny's words are.'

'So how do you turn it around?'

She took a sip of wine. 'I need to accept all that has happened, not to judge myself too harshly. I need to decide what I want my life to be, who I want to be. Then I have to use my road map to ensure every choice I make is in line with this. You're right, if I want to be a writer, a true one, not a fake one, then that's what I need to put my focus on. Not hiding from the world, but embracing it, whatever the consequences.'

'I think I need to accept all that has happened too. Decide who I want to be. Embrace the world, instead of hiding from it. Our circumstances are different, yet our solutions the same.'

'How did it feel watching the village eat and drink inside the barn?'

'Strange. Sad. I just have to get used to making the jigsaw with one vital piece missing.'

'It's hard for you.'

'I made it harder.'

'Don't we all?'

He smiled. 'You understand me. I like that.'

Adela speared tiny pieces of each food item onto her fork. 'You can choose to be free of the guilt and pain, just as you once chose not to.'

He watched her stabbing her food. 'It can't really be that simple.'

'I'm beginning to realise it can, for both of us.'

'Habits are funny things, don't you think? Guilt has been my humble servant. If I wasn't feeling guilty about my anger towards my father, I was feeling guilty about my ability to cope with life while Susan struggled. Susan died and I was soaked in my contempt for humanity. When I think of my life in that way, I wonder how I ever expected to be free.'

They ate quietly, against the light of the flickering candles.

He wanted to tell her not to leave, but he also understood she had to go. Their lives had connected for a fraction of a lifetime, a very precious set of moments, but time was destined to play itself out in a way that would hurt them as well as help them.

But how he wanted her to stay with him.

'The village already looks so much better. Cleaner and fresher. The sign Nigel made is beautiful. I never knew he was so talented.'

265

'Did you see Brian's paint job? Really professional workmanship. It's a pity he can't get a job.'

'And as for Mary and Margaret's baking— *delicious.*'

'They'd almost compete with you,' Adela said. 'This village is bursting with hidden talent.'

'Pity so much of it is hidden.'

'You could do something about that, you know. When I'm gone.'

'Oh, no you don't! Not another plan.'

She laughed. 'Maybe. Have another glass of wine.'

'Trying to get me drunk so I'll say yes to anything?'

'Anything?'

He gave her a stern look. 'Don't do that.'

She blushed. 'I was joking. Sorry.'

'This isn't easy for me, Adela. I'm trying to do the right thing, but you push me with your teasing. It's okay for you; you're going back to *him.*'

'It doesn't feel very okay,' she said quietly. 'Nothing about leaving here feels okay.'

'So, what's this plan of yours?' he asked, not knowing what else to say to her.

'Well,' she said, 'the village has a high rate of unemployment, which means lots of people with too much time and not enough money. But what if you organised for someone to open the barn, just like Susan intended? Even if it was only to sell tea, coffee and cakes.'

'You're kidding, right?'

'When do I ever joke about such matters? It's a beautiful building and it would be a boost to the village. Daisy's pub caters for the drinkers, but there's nothing except the coffee machine in the shop for the teenagers, the elderly, the women pushing around babies all day or

266

even couples who wish to stare into each other's eyes over a coffee slice and a hot chocolate.'

'Mary did open a nice enough coffee shop a couple of years ago, but it was closed six months later, after the fire.'

'Yes, but I'm not talking about a big money making venture, Gregory. You don't need the few extra quid earned through selling the odd bun or two. What if you treated it like a community project? The barn was lying there empty as it was, but this way people would have an affordable place to socialise and connect with one another.'

'You're seriously asking me to open up the barn full-time?'

'Yes, and there's more,' Adela continued, her eyes beginning to shine. 'The barn could be the place where people come to share information and barter their stuff. You could have a big noticeboard where people post up in what way they are prepared to help someone else. The villagers could begin sharing information, saving money, helping each other and feeling useful in the process. Daisy could show them how they could help others, as well as what help they themselves might need. Someone could be a fantastic plumber but be useless at ironing. Another could be a fantastic cook but god-awful at painting or hanging pictures. Another could be a brilliant organiser, but a terrible gardener.'

'You're the one with the ideas, *you* do it. Take the keys. In fact, take the whole barn.'

'Stop joking, Gregory. People could really help change each other's lives if they began to understand the benefits of seeing themselves as part of something bigger. Helping each other, no money involved; just time, a bit of effort and a desire to feel useful. You could even run classes, and each week someone could teach something new.'

267

'I'm a hermit, remember?'

She tutted. 'I thought you wanted to be free? Money alone hasn't given you your freedom. Maybe helping them might help you. It might be what you need to recover from Susan's death. John told me happiness can come from giving service to others, from focusing your life on what you put out rather than take. I believe that's how you can feel free. You've wanted to know how to feel it for a long time…now you know.'

'Who are you, my counsellor?'

'You did ask!'

'What if I need *you* instead?'

She laughed. 'You and I, Gregory, we are a strange pair. You don't need me. I know how strong you are. You've the strength of a hundred men. That's what I so love about you. You don't need me and I don't need you. John taught me that. And you know what? That's okay. In fact, it's more than okay. Who wants to be needy? Not me and certainly not you.'

'So you want me to help the needy folk of the village instead?'

'No! I want you to help them to stop focusing on this curse of theirs and to begin to see their own strengths. Every big change has to start somewhere. You could organise different weekly events. Storytelling on a Saturday morning for parents with kids hanging from every leg.'

'Storytelling?'

'Yes and swap shops in one of those rooms every Sunday. Why shouldn't we share our stuff? The world needs less waste and changing that must start somewhere. Why not *here*, beginning with a change of attitude? "Survival of the fittest" thinking hasn't worked for us. The world is more unhappy, more dangerous and more greedy because of it. People need to come together. Why shouldn't they come together *here*?'

'Life isn't all gingerbread houses and hugs, Adela. You're expecting a lot with that plan of yours.'

'You believe we shouldn't expect a lot? *You* always expected to have a lot of money? Was that wrong?'

'No.'

'My vision is for those people to feel less alone and part of something bigger, like they did today. They will all get the opportunity to show off what they're good at and some of them might even discover talents they weren't aware of, potential that may have lain dormant while they wasted time flicking through their hundred channels in the desperate search for a valid distraction from the boredom inside of themselves. Take John as an example, a man full of wisdom, not to mention his gardening skills. He is wasted having cups of tea alone.'

Gregory thought of all those times he watched John work from his kitchen window, never inviting him inside, keeping himself so completely separate.

They heard a bang at the window. Gregory jumped up. 'What the…?'

He opened the back door, but before he could go outside Josie came barging past him and with her the smell of too much drink.

'Well, well, isn't this cosy?' Josie shouted, her face dulled by excessive alcohol. 'Candles and everything! How nice.'

'What are you doing here?' Gregory asked impatiently.

'I came to see the little whore in action for myself.'

'What did you call me?'

'Oh, I know all about you, Adela Winters. Gregory told me earlier when we were gardening together. About David and the waiter, and some, what did you call it again, Gregory? Oh, yeah some rubbish attempt at one of those pathetic self-help books.'

269

'Don't waste your lies on us, Josie. Get out of my house.'

Josie dipped her finger in Gregory's glass of wine and then licked the drops of wine from her finger. 'He even opened the good stuff.'

'You should leave, Josie,' Adela said, standing firm as Josie came up too close to her.

'You weren't happy with David, so you spread your legs for the waiter. But why did you have to stick your greedy claws into Gregory too? He was *mine*.'

'You can't make him love you but you can avoid humiliating yourself any further. Go home and sleep it off. There is no happily ever after for you here.'

'You conceited bitch.' Josie knocked over Gregory's glass of wine, pushing against Gregory as she walked past him, before storming out the door.

'I'm sorry about that,' Gregory said, immediately organising to clean up the red wine. 'She told me this morning that she recognised you. I didn't want to worry you, so I didn't say anything. She was just lying to cause problems between us. I always knew she was a bit wild, but...'

'She's hurt, Gregory. She's in pain because she loves you and she can't have you.'

'We're all in pain. And like the rest of us, she'll have to learn to deal with it.' He felt a sudden storm of anger towards David. 'This was not how I wanted tonight to go.'

'Things don't always turn out as planned,' she said, gazing at him.

'Are you sure about going back to David? If you need more time, you can stay here. We could talk some more about your plans for the barn, pretend I'm not a hermit. We could drive out to the beach again, bring a picnic...'

'Please, don't...'

'Do you love him?'

She held out her hand. 'I let him put this ring on my finger, didn't I?'

'Do you hand out your heart to every man you meet?'

'Don't be so cruel.'

'I'm sorry, I shouldn't have said that.' He cursed himself for his weakness. 'Yes, you probably do need to leave. This won't work; you and me, living here together. I don't know what I wanted but this isn't it.'

But she refused to let him walk away. 'Gregory, we both know I can't stay here with you. I have a life to sort out. I never thought coming here would turn out like this. I wish things were simple and I could have everything I wanted. I can't hurt him a second time.'

She wrapped her arms around him. Part of him wanted to thrust her away, but she would soon be gone, so instead he held her tightly, resting his cheek against the top of her head and wishing for the pain in his heart to vanish.

Chapter 47

DAY 14 - Sunday

'How's it going so far, Daisy?'

'Not bad at all,' Daisy said, throwing on her lime green jacket. 'Although all this cleaning up is making me look twice at my own pub. It's a bit of a dive, really.'

Adela shrugged. 'A makeover wouldn't hurt.'

'I knew it was bad, I just never noticed how bad.'

'When you're so close to something, it's easy to stop seeing it.' Adela pulled out Daisy's hood which was stuck down the back of her jacket.

'Have you seen John yet?'

'Not this morning, but you tell Gregory to make sure John doesn't overstretch himself today. John may look agile but he can't afford to wear himself out.'

'Concerned for his welfare, are you?'

'Not like that!' Daisy laughed. 'He's not long over the chemo. His body isn't as strong as it used to be.'

'Chemo?'

Daisy banged herself on the forehead. 'Me and my big mouth. I presumed he would have told you.'

'When?'

'About five months ago.'

'Why didn't Gregory say?'

'He might not even know. John probably wasn't doing much gardening for Gregory around then. I get the impression they don't chat too often. They were never what you would call "friends".'

'Is John better?'

Daisy locked the door of the pub behind her. 'Hard to know with John. Before the cancer, I don't think I ever even saw him with a packet of paracetomol.'

Why hadn't he said? Yet, that was John all over. She'd been too busy discussing her dramas, but what about the difficulties of *his* life?

'Josie paid us a visit last night,' Adela said, not wanting to hear any more about John. 'The woman was juiced up to her eyeballs.'

'Oh, dear. She's like a lovesick puppy, young but with teeth that bite and nails that scrape.'

'Tell me about it. She called me a whore!'

'Did she?' Daisy let out a snigger. 'Well, you've stolen the heart of her prince. Ha! Gregory, a prince, I ask you!'

'I think we should move her off John's team for today. It's not a good idea to have her and Gregory working together. She'll probably be too hung-over to turn up anyway.'

Daisy stopped walking. 'Are you really leaving tomorrow?'

'I have to get back to my life.'

'Do you miss the limelight?'

'How long have you known about me?'

Daisy shrugged. 'A while. So what?'

'So what?'

'Would you prefer if I were to judge you?'

'No, but—'

'This David, does he deserve you?'

'He probably deserves better than me, after what I've done. He's never been partial to seconds.'

'Come back and see us, won't you?'

She gave Daisy a sideways hug. 'Of course. I'm not leaving the country!'

'Yeah, but it's never the same when someone goes away. Something goes with it.'

'I only took a sneaky peak into your lives. I was never even meant to be here.'

The look Daisy gave her was filled with love. 'Oh, darling, of course you were!'

'I only wish my mother could make me feel half of what you do, Daisy.'

'You're an easy person to love; just ask the hermit!'

'Hey.' Adela patted her on the edge of the arm. 'And just so you know, I'm working on getting our hermit to permanently retire. I've seen how you rallied the troops for this weekend. You have significant powers of persuasion, Daisy, so I'm going to let you in on the plans I foresee for this place. You can threaten him with Josie if he decides to hibernate once I'm gone.'

Daisy rubbed her hands together. 'I love a good plan. Tell me more.'

#

Gregory was relieved to note Josie's absence. He wasn't fit for another round of glaring and hissing. He was working closely with John all morning. John had a real gift; his energy was tireless, despite being almost thirty years Gregory's senior.

'Once you've sprinkled some bone meal, then you can place the shrub in the hole,' John instructed him.

They worked quietly for the next hour solid, before Gregory took a break to have a cup of water.

'You want some?' he offered the first cup to John.

'Thanks.' John gulped down the contents of the paper cup.

He poured his own. 'I was thinking…'

'A tricky kind of a pastime, thinking. Tends to have consequences.'

'I suppose it does, yes.' Gregory smiled. 'You know the empty field in front of the kitchen window?'

'I do.'

'Could you turn it into an orchard?'

'An orchard? Of course!'

He nodded to him. 'Thanks. One other thing, John?'

'Yep?'

'Would you let me help you?'

'I'd be more than delighted, Gregory.'

'There's one condition.'

'One condition? What?'

'You agree to have your lunch with me the odd day? I hear your cups of tea are something quite special.'

John picked back up his spade. 'I accept.'

Returning to his work, Gregory was glad about his decision to plant the orchard. He would waste no more time letting the past consume his present. He wanted freedom to be more than a static word on the wall of his office.

He dug a hole for his next shrub. The sun was shining down on the back of his head. The feel of the air, the noise of people working around him, and the sweat on his skin, all felt calming to the blisters in his mind. Adela's proposal to him was half crazy, half sentimental. Susan would have been the type of person to make a masterpiece out of Adela's mindful of madness.

But Susan was gone, and no matter how hard Adela wanted it, he was not the person to kick-start her plan. Gregory knew that once Adela left, these people would slowly drift away from each other and all that would remain was the memory of that beautiful woman and the fun weekend, where old mixed with young, fat mixed with thin, and the look and feel of their village was improved beyond recognition.

#

By Sunday lunchtime, the crowd was getting tired, but pleased at the work it had so far achieved. Munching into more of Mary and Margaret's sandwiches and buns, the chatter was happy and positive in the barn.

Adela dedicated her lunchtime to ensuring she thanked all the different pockets of people taking part in the weekend's event. She had a good memory for small details and did her best to make each one of them feel special.

But there was one man Adela desperately needed to speak to.

'Hello, stranger,' John said. 'I hear you're spending the last chunk of the working day on our team.'

'I am, indeed.' She offered him a sandwich, which he refused. 'I thought it was only fitting to spend it with my favourite two men.'

'You smooth talker, you.' His eyes twinkled at her. 'This has been such a success, Adela. Look at the energy in these people today. Tonight will be a grand hoolie. We have never deserved a night out more, eh!'

'Why are you not eating?' she asked. 'You must be hungry.'

'I'm grand with this cup of tea. Mary Mary QC sneaked me a couple of the really fresh sambos earlier on. Spoiled, I am.'

'Why didn't you tell me?'

'About the sandwiches?'

She moved in closer so she could whisper to him. 'About the *cancer*.'

'What cancer?' he said, waving his hand dismissively.

'John, I've been moaning and groaning to you for two full weeks and you never thought to mention you'd had cancer?'

'No.'

Her cup banged down on the counter a little too hard. 'I swear, I don't think I'll ever figure you out. You should have told me.'

'Why? Tell me exactly why I should have told you?'

276

'Because friends tell each other stuff like that. They let one another in. But you never let me in at all, did you? You humoured me, like a parent humouring a child.'

He started to laugh at her.

'Stop!' she said. 'Be serious.'

The humour refusing to leave his face, he gently took her hand and held it in his. 'And that's exactly why I didn't tell you. I was not going to be one of those people who continued to pity myself because I was ill. I didn't want to suck sympathy out of everyone around me until we were nauseous. Two weeks ago, if I had told you I was recovering from cancer, the way you looked at me would have changed. You would never have called over all those times, wanting to dissect the essence of life itself. Instead, you would have tried to bring me pots of badly-made stew and lots of sticky, scared sympathy that I simply have no tolerance for.'

'But—'

'But, nothing, Adela! We both know it's true. I choose not to create myself as a victim of my cancer. That's my choice. I don't want to sit all day thinking about it or talking about it. Do you know what that gives it?'

'What?' she said, like a scolded school child.

'Energy. It gives it energy and I'm simply not prepared to give it any. I had cancer, so what? Yes, it was hard going and the treatment felt relentless and made me sick, but everything changes, so the outcome was to go either one way or the other. I'm back working in the gardens and I spent all weekend doing my bit, so I guess that means treatment was successful. So why would I want to become the official mascot for cancer? I'm not afraid of death, so I'm as sure as hell not going to be afraid of life.'

277

But you had cancer, John! Not some sore throat or sick stomach...cancer! 'Surely people have to talk about these things?'

'People can do whatever they want, that's the whole point of life, Adela. My choice was to have my cancer treated and move on. I don't want to use it as a topic of conversation. I was lucky. I want to enjoy today for today, not cling onto my cancer status of yesterday.'

'Why do you have a way of making everything you say sound right?'

'I don't want you to think I'm judging others who make different choices to me. It's just the way I feel about it. Think about your life; if you were to put a stone into your pocket every time you had a bad experience, and you carried these with you, day after day, year after year, soon you would be exhausted. Your back would ache and you would constantly need to lie down. Many of us do that same thing, only we carry those stones in our minds, and then we wonder why life feels like we're climbing up a steep mountain, unable to see a way forward. I have chosen not to carry all those stones. It's a waste of my time; it is distracting and unnecessary.'

'But what if you stop paying attention and the cancer comes back?'

'Another stone, my dear! "What ifs" are some of the heaviest stones we can carry.'

Unable to believe his attitude was real, she couldn't stop shaking her head. 'John, you're mad!'

'I changed my diet, I take more exercise. I listened to the doctor's suggestions as to how to help myself. Ignorance does not make for light pockets. But as long as I'm doing all I can to keep myself healthy, I let the rest go, the unnecessary detail that will only serve to hinder me...all those stones.'

'So, you'll not miss me when I'm gone, because that would only be another stone in your pocket?' she said, playfully.

'Do you want the truth? Think you can handle it?' he asked in his best Hollywood voice.

'Not sure, but give it to me anyway.'

'Of course I'll miss you. I'm not a machine, sweetheart. You've been a wonderful piece of my life. But I will find the positive in the loss; for example, when I walk around the village and see what you helped achieve, I will think of you and smile. Or when I make myself a cup of tea and remember some of our conversations, I will think of you and laugh. And when I think of you continuing to live your life in all its beauty, ups and downs included, I will grin from ear to ear. What a gift you have given me.'

With a lump in her throat, she wrapped her arms around this dear man and squeezed him gently, hoping he understood the depths to which he had touched her.

Chapter 48

That afternoon Adela worked side by side with Gregory and John. Very little was exchanged between them, a few questions about the task at hand and the passing around of cups of water. Any passer-by would never notice that these people meant any more to one another than co-workers or neighbours.

Adela enjoyed this quiet time with them. Digging through the soil and pulling up weeds was soothing to her. Her body needed the release of this hard work after the emotions of the last couple of weeks. It felt good to be doing something physically rewarding yet simple. She liked having Gregory working next to her. After the drama of last night, and with Adela's departure almost upon them, they had no words left to speak to one another that wouldn't expose what lay inside their hearts and cause trouble. This way, they got to be together, physically close, without having to explain themselves or find suitable topics of conversation.

Every so often, she would allow herself a quick glance in his direction, a small luxury against the backdrop of her uncertain future. His body was so strong. The muscles in his arms bulged as he dug his spade hard into the ground. If he allowed himself back into the world, Josie would have to compete with more than just Adela for his affections. Adela had noticed the women watching him appreciatively during lunch. They were intrigued by him, the handsome, wealthy hermit who had so recently come out of his cave.

She would leave, return to David, and Gregory would find himself someone to occupy his days and nights. Men never stayed alone for long, and although Gregory had been the exception to that, she knew her entry into his life had changed that for him. He had already altered his view of the world. She understood with total clarity that he would never again be content to live in solitude, with only Norman for company and the occasional visit from JB. He was beginning to untie himself from the chains of his family. The life of a hermit was no longer an option for him.

These thoughts gave her great comfort and pain all at once. In that moment, she understood she was in love with him.

#

At last, the work was finished. Daisy had given everyone an hourly countdown from lunchtime. The crowd now came together outside the barn and everyone cheered and clapped, for themselves and for one another. Even the teenagers, normally so grumpy and distant, had joined in.

Adela climbed up on the wall outside of the barn. She thanked them all for their time and effort, told them how grateful she was to be part of such an event. More cheers. The group took an appreciative walk through the village, surveying the results. A car drove by and beeped its horn. The crowd erupted again. Nigel and Daisy did some céilí dancing in the middle of the street. The sun shone down on them and the village lit up.

When all the fuss finally died down, Adela, Daisy, Mad Margaret, Toni, John, JB, Nancy and Gregory returned to the barn to clean up and prepare it for the party. Gregory attached his IPod to the speakers so they could have some music and John and Daisy did another little dance together in the middle of the room to one of Greg's favourite female pop singers.

They chatted about who had done what and how well the gardens and the freshly-painted buildings looked, about how clean the streets were and how happy everyone felt. They were high on life that Sunday afternoon. It was a time Adela would never forget.

When the barn was prepared and the dancing and singing finished, they all headed home to get ready for the party, except for Nancy who John had invited back to his house for an extra sweet cup of coffee.

Adela listened to her party mix as she showered and dressed. She danced around the room between every application of makeup, ignoring the packed suitcase lying at the side of her bed, deliberately attempting to remove the stones from her pockets.

Norman came scratching at the door. She opened it and let him in. He sat next to her as she applied her eye shadow and eyeliner. He didn't move as she blotted her lipstick. She gave him a hug. 'You're not as allergic to women as your owner may have once believed, eh, Norman?'

He nudged his large head into her leg, making her laugh. 'Let's go find your daddy.'

Waiting for her in the kitchen, Gregory turned around when he heard the door open.

'We're ready,' she said, lightly, doing a curtsey.

'I don't think I should let you out,' he said, taking all of her in. 'Dirty Mickey will never be able to resist you looking like that!'

How easy it was to laugh with him now. 'You don't look too unappealing yourself.'

They should have looked away.

'The public will never want to turn their backs on you, Adela. Stay brave.'

Reading his mind, her translucent skin shaded red. 'Who ever knew such a face was behind that caveman beard.'

'It's been one hell of a ride,' he said. 'Or *not*, but you know what I mean!'

'I know exactly what you mean,' she said.

His white shirt fit smoothly against his toned upper body, the top button still open at the neck. That firm jaw and those intelligent eyes sucked her right in. Not an ounce of hermit was left in the well-dressed, handsome man before her. Had she really ever hated him? Two weeks could change a world. Hers would never again be the same. She stepped closer to him. Or was he moving closer to her?

They stood, inches apart.

'I'd better get you out of this house soon or I'll not be responsible for my actions,' he said.

She touched his cheek, wishing she could lock all the doors and leave the party behind. 'We really need to leave.'

Bang…bang.

'Uh, what now?' Gregory cried. 'I'm beginning to resent that door!'

Adela watched him swing the door open.

'*David!* What are you doing here?'

David walked into the house, ignoring Gregory altogether. 'I've just had the heads up from my mate in the paper. They've discovered where you've been. The press are on their way, Adela. We've got to get you out of here.'

'How did they…?' She stopped. 'Josie obviously recovered from her hangover.'

'If *I* found you, they can too. We don't have any time,' David said, checking his phone. 'They'll eat you alive if they find you here. Are you packed? Where's your suitcase?'

It was not David's advice she sought. She glanced at Gregory, waiting for him to say something.

'You'd better go. You need to face them in your own time, not like this.'

'I'll get my things.' She left the kitchen and went down the corridor, still in shock at David's sudden

283

arrival. No last night with her friends, with Gregory, John, Daisy and the others. Her makeup bag and pyjamas got squashed violently into her suitcase. Gregory appeared behind her.

'I'll carry that out for you,' he said, taking it from her.

A couple of tears dripped down her face, splashing through her perfectly applied makeup.

He let the suitcase go and took hold of her. 'Schh, now. Don't cry. Please, don't cry.'

'Come on, Adela. Hurry up.' David's voice shouted from the kitchen.

She pulled away from Gregory, wiping the tears from her cheeks with the back of her hand. 'Thank you, for everything.'

'Thank you too.' He kissed her gently on the cheek.

They broke their embrace and he carried out her suitcase. Norman got one last wet-fingered rub on the way past.

David picked up her handbag from the counter and took the suitcase from Gregory without looking at him. 'Is that everything?'

Her eyes connected to Gregory's, an invisible force still trying to pull them together. 'Yes, that's it.'

'Okay, let's get the hell out of here.'

Turning away from him, she lifted her coat from the chair and walked out through his kitchen door for the very last time.

Chapter 49

Gregory waited for her to return. He waited and waited, hardly believing she was gone. But she did not return and half an hour later, he gave Norman some fresh water, picked up his coat and went to the party alone.

A cheer rose up when he walked through the door. But the cheer turned to silence when he closed the door behind him.

'Where's Adela?' Daisy said, dipping a straw into her lime-green cocktail.

Facing these people was the last thing he wanted to do. But they deserved his company for a little while tonight. A small part of him knew he had come here because he couldn't bear to be alone in that big, empty house. It had happened so fast.

'She won't be coming,' he said, walking across to where they'd set up a makeshift bar for the evening. 'I need a drink.'

John appeared at his side. 'What can I get you?'

'Anything. A beer. Thanks, John.'

Daisy placed her drink on the table. 'Why? I thought she wasn't leaving until tomorrow?'

He told them about David's arrival. 'From what I gather, the media are likely to arrive here any minute.'

'Are you sure that's not a bit over the top?' JB pulled at his tie. 'Sounds a tad dramatic, even for *me*.'

Gregory shrugged. 'David whisked her away like she was on fire. She was so beautiful, all ready to come here to celebrate with you.'

Toni appeared over Daisy's shoulder. 'What's going on? Where's Adela?'

And so it was explained to them that Adela was unable to make it.'

Josie came strutting across the floor, all bells and whistles. 'She left you then?'

'Don't, Josie.' Daisy pointed her thick finger at the young girl. 'You've said quite enough already.'

'She's from a different world. You don't need her, Greg.'

He jumped off the chair, his face like thunder.

John pulled him back. 'No, Gregory. That is not the way…'

'You selfish little bitch,' he said with a growl. 'You called them, didn't you?'

'Called who?'

Gregory stopped. Her body language was all wrong.

'Did you tell the journalists that Adela was here?'

'Hardly. I was vomiting my guts up until an hour ago.'

He stared hard at her. No signs of deception. Josie was still hateful, but it was obvious she hadn't called anybody.

'Sorry, I'm sorry, Josie. Sorry, everyone,' he said, raising his hands in defeat.

The crowd remained silent for a few more seconds, before the murmur of conversation could once again be heard.

'I should go.' A pint with the village folk would not change what had happened.

'You're not leaving here, Mr Sheridan, even if that means I have to chain you to my gammy knee,' Daisy said, pushing in to get close to him. 'We lost Adela, no way are we going to lose you too.'

#

The journey home was quiet, Adela thinking only of the people she'd left behind. How was the party going? Were they celebrating the success of the weekend in the style she had envisaged? Who was the next woman already trying to convince the hermit he wasn't so lonely after all? She glanced across at David. Everything about him was familiar, yet everything about the two of them together different.

'I made up the spare room for you.'

She should have been disappointed with his decision to continue the frosty behaviour now that he had her back, but instead she felt relieved. Space and silence might help to make sense of the feelings tumbling around inside her, not for David but for Gregory. She missed her room in his home, John's cosy little cups of tea, Daisy's friendship, even the challenges she faced with Toni. She missed it all. Yet the time had come for all that to end, like a holiday amongst cobbled Italian streets. She had reluctantly sneaked into their lives and now here she was sneaking back out.

'I'll pick up a pizza on the way home,' David said, not taking his eyes off the road.

'Sure.' She closed her eyes and swallowed the lump in her throat. Her engagement ring was hot and heavy against the skin on her finger. The way she felt right now, she simply could not marry the man sitting beside her.

Chapter 50

The Next Day

Had Gregory imagined he would spend Monday alone, wallowing in self-pity, he was wrong. His mother woke him up at ten o'clock that morning with a cup of tea and a plateful of toast. John rang the doorbell at half eleven and poured him his second cup of tea. Cup number three was mulled over with Daisy who appeared with ham and rolls for lunch and now JB had his face nudged up against the kitchen window, his expression one of desolation.

Gregory unlocked the door. 'You're only allowed in if you promise not to look at me like I'm a six-year-old kid whose dog just got run over.'

JB's face relaxed. 'You've had a few visitors already then?'

'They're trying to cheer me up, hoping the perfect cup of tea will do it. Tea with buns, tea with rolls, tea with toast.'

'I can't believe David came and took her.' JB's eyes narrowed. 'What's she doing with him anyway?'

'The house feels strange without her.'

'She really got under your skin.'

'I blame *you*.'

'Yeah, sorry.' JB flicked the switch on the kettle. 'The village looks great after all the work. Do you want to get out of here and go for a walk or something?'

'No, thanks. I've a few things to do today. Don't be fretting about me. I'm a big boy, friend; I've been through worse and survived. You can't have already forgotten that I'm used to being alone.'

'No more of the hermit rubbish, okay? That phase of your life is over. I'm not listening if you even mention it.'

'Well, do you want some juicy gossip instead then?'

JB stopped stirring his tea. 'Go on?'

'Guess who I caught having a sneaky kiss behind the wall last night?'

'Who, who?'

'My mother and John!'

'You are *kidding* me! Well, well…there must be something in the air. Do you reckon kissing at their age is pretty ugly? Does age turn stallions like us into "old men" kissers? You know how it happens with driving? See an outline of a man in a hat behind the wheel of a car and you know you ain't going nowhere fast!'

'Considering it's my gardener and my mother we're talking about, I'd rather not overthink that one, if you don't mind!'

'Ah, good on them! It's cute. As long as they don't use *tongues*.'

'JB!'

'Sorry! Here's your tea, I know you could do with another cup. I certainly could now.'

Gregory moved the cup of black tea in front of him and sighed.

'Maybe she'll leave him?' JB lifted the milk out of the fridge. 'She doesn't *have* to stay with him. She can still walk away.'

If only it were that simple. 'She already did.'

#

Adela wandered about their apartment, feeling the warmth of the floorboards on her feet, the sun shining in through the large windows. David had left her a note to say he was meeting his buddy for a game of golf. She tried to calm her feelings of resentment. Did he really think allowing her this time alone was a punishment? She picked up her mobile, still ignoring the full inbox and fifty seven unread text messages. Instead she rang her sister who had arrived home the previous day. Within thirty seconds, Adela was in floods of tears and although Lizzie couldn't understand a word she was saying, her sister vowed to break several sets of lights in order to be with her as soon as possible.

Adela, feeling better already at knowing she would soon see a friendly face, turned on her laptop and ventured into her favourite social media website. Her mobile rang. She grabbed it, checked the number before throwing it back onto the couch. First she would have time with Lizzie and then she would begin facing her messages. Ninety-three messages later and scrolling down quickly to get a flavour of the challenges that lay ahead, she was unprepared for one standing out from the rest.

A message from the waiter.

#

Gregory sat down at his desk and turned on his laptop. He'd had to almost push JB out the door. Now it was just him and Norman, like old times. He looked at his picture of the orchard on his wall and thought about those summers spent, away from everything except the smell of freshly cut grass and the feel of the sun on their faces as they lay in the long grass of the field beside the orchard. Their mother had an aunt who had invited him and Susan to stay in her farmhouse for the month of July.

Four whole summers of eating apples for breakfast, marvelling at the readily available stash. Susan was like a different child amongst those apple trees, singing and dancing, climbing dangerously to try to reach the highest apple and then perching on a lower branch to crunch into the sweetest piece of fruit ever born. They would talk about being rich and owning their own trees so they could pick apples for breakfast every day.

He knew no orchard could be like the one inside his head; this was why the field outside lay empty. Childish talk and fairy-tale dreams sometimes lingered in a way that made them impossible to completely outgrow. Gregory's orchard was such a dream. Sitting at his desk, he understood that part of letting Susan go would be through the process of planting that field. John had already agreed to show him how. The time to wither was passing and in its place a time to grow.

Norman scratched open the door, padded over to him and lay down beside his chair. The room was quiet except for the gentle hum of the fan in his laptop and the heaviness of Norman's breathing. Gregory found himself waiting to hear Adela clanking pots or humming to herself, but like Susan sitting in her apple tree, the memory could only come to life in his mind. Adela was gone and now the silence seemed incomplete in a way it hadn't before. He could no longer remain hermitted to this house, refusing to acknowledge the life around him.

#

Adela sat in the chair facing the window, watching random people walk down the street in all their shapes and sizes, moods and outfits. She peeled herself the mandarin orange she'd left sitting on the arm of the chair earlier, before her sister had arrived. They'd had quite the morning, catching up on all the other had missed. Adela was lucky to have her as a confidante. Of course there had been more tears and regaling of drama, but now Adela was once again alone. An hour of nothing but her thoughts, she realised she was feeling too calm, that sort of calm people feel before they crack wide open, like a bottle of gushing red wine…damaging and messy.

David's key turned in the door. He had stayed out all day, as he'd threatened. Subtle methods of punishment were where his talents lay, wooing her back here just to make her feel alone.

'Hello,' she said, opening her mandarin down the middle. 'Good game of golf?'

'Great, actually. Cleared out the cobwebs.' His set of clubs had their place in the corner. 'What have you been up to all day?'

'Oh, this and that,' she said, biting into a segment. 'Lizzie came over.'

'I can imagine the conversations between the pair of you. Glad I didn't have to suffer through those.'

'I hope your ears weren't burning too badly.'

'Are you trying to annoy me?'

She laid the pieces of orange down. 'Are you ever going to forgive me?'

'Give me a break, Adela. These things take time.'

Her right leg lounged across the arm of the chair, the way she knew it irritated him. 'Do you even *want* to forgive me? Seems to me you still hate me. Do you even want me here? You sure as hell don't want me in your bed.'

'Of course I want you…but what you did with that man…I can't seem to get past it…'

'And what exactly did I do, David? Care to draw me a picture?'

His glare was sharp. 'Don't be such a bitch.'

'You think I'm being a bitch?' This time she stood up, so she was facing him. 'You think that I trampled all over your poor ego and now I have to suffer until you say *when*. Well guess what David…WHEN.'

'What are you talking about?'

She removed a folded up piece of paper from her jeans pocket and handed it to him. 'It's an email sent to your mailbox six days ago. Read who it's from…'

His eyes bulged at what he read. 'How did you get this?'

292

'Not only did I chat with *my* sister today, but I also spoke with the sister of that dishy waiter who assisted me in my fall from grace. Except I didn't fall quite as far as I thought, now did I?'

'She could have been anyone. I don't take seriously every piece of junk mail I receive—' He flung the piece of paper to the floor.

'Except we both know it wasn't *junk*. You rang her. I know what she told you.'

This time he didn't try to speak. He stared at her.

'I also spoke to Carl. He admitted the truth to me.'

'You were drunk, Adela, and you went back to his apartment. Why should you get off the hook just because you didn't see it through to the bitter end? The intention was there. You *wanted* to sleep with him.'

She started to laugh hysterically. 'I can't believe you. I'd had a particularly bad day, you may remember. I wasn't looking for any complications. Yes, I should have come home after getting the bad news. Sure, I was foolish to keep drinking after Cheryl told me about my father making a show of himself.'

'Excuses were always your strong point.'

'I told you that I didn't remember the end of the night, but you didn't believe me, and all those pictures in the paper of Carl with his arm around me, bringing me into his house, what else were any of us to think? I left his place that next day still unable to see straight, having woken up in his bed, with someone else's t-shirt on. I presumed what any girl who got herself into such a position would. Carl was delighted to cash in on the drama, until his big sister got their Italian granny involved and convinced him to come clean.' Adela popped another piece of orange into her mouth. 'The newspaper will be printing a retraction.'

'Good,' he said, his attention fixed on the sitting room window.

'You came to Gregory's house…you soaked me in guilt and you never said a word.' Now that the revelation had been voiced, anger had replaced her shock. 'You wanted the upper hand, David, admit it. You enjoyed being righteous. You were supposed to be on my side…'

'Don't you dare pretend to be the victim here,' he shouted. 'You're not the victim. *I* was the one people were whispering about…"what was wrong with David that she took up with some waiter"…so you're not the victim in all of this, Adela. You as good as slept with him.'

'No,' she shouted. 'Shall I tell you what that waiter admitted to me?'

'What?'

'That I fell asleep in my drunken state muttering one pathetic word…*David.*'

'Then why did you go home with him?'

'He knew I was drunk, so he intended on helping me into a taxi. But by the time he got me into a taxi, I was half unconscious. He didn't know where I lived and all I had in my purse was money and a key…no address, no phone. The best he could do was to bring me home. Unfortunately that photographer was keeping better track of me than I was.'

'Then why were you naked?'

'I wasn't actually naked. He removed my clothes because I'd thrown up all over them and he put me to bed in his room because he was damned if he was giving up his bed for a drunken stranger, but he didn't touch me.'

'How can you be so sure? How do you know he isn't lying?'

Adela closed her eyes for a moment. 'I'm sure.'

'You can't be.'

'Carl's gay, David. I'm sure.'

David walked towards the window, turning his back to her. 'Oh.'

Adela looked around the room with all its comforts, the large TV, the couch, the cream fluffy rug in front of the fire, the candles, and the bookshelf. She removed the engagement ring from her finger. 'Would you have told me? You had to know I'd find out eventually.'

He shrugged. 'You made a fool of me, ending up in all the papers like a cheap slag. Some tiny retraction on page thirty won't change what people think. They've had their fun with the story. The truth is never half as interesting to them.'

'Or to you, it seems.' Adela laid the ring on the coffee table. 'I'm going to stay with Lizzie.'

He swung around, his eyes targeting the engagement ring. 'You're going…just like that? No trying to sort it out? No second chances?'

She thought about how he'd rushed her away from Gregory and the celebrations with her new friends. 'You were supposed to be on my side.'

'I gave you a second chance.'

'No, you didn't. You came to me only after you knew the real truth. You wanted to hurt me, David. You lied to me.'

'Everyone lies.'

He had knocked on Gregory's door that night. 'The media didn't know where I was, did they? You lied about that too. You were so determined to get me back here, you said whatever you needed to say to tear me away.'

'To tear you away? Give me a break, Adela.'

But despite his taunts, Adela knew that was exactly how she'd felt. Torn away. She picked up her keys. Lizzie had already helped her pack most of her things into her boot. He could keep the big TV, the fancy gadgets, the designer curtains. She didn't want any of it. She just wanted to go. 'Goodbye, David.'

He picked up the ring, following her as she turned to walk away. 'Get back here, for Christ's sake. Don't be so stupid and stop all this. I'm sorry…okay? So it's your turn to be righteous, you win. I'm sorry.'

'You were supposed to be on my side,' she said. 'I can never marry you now.'

She heard the diamond ring crash to the floor behind her.

Chapter 51

Four Months Later

Adela couldn't believe her eyes as she drove into the village. Baskets filled with pretty flowers hung on the wall where Mad Margaret's "curse" sign once stood. The flowerbeds they had dug out all those months ago were now flush with colour. She turned onto the main street, surprised by the freshly-painted appearance of the buildings, as well as the window boxes adorning every second window with bursts of greens, reds, pinks and purples. She laughed out loud at how lovely it all looked, proud of having helped instigate such a change.

She drove towards John's house. His garden had been wonderful in the springtime but was even more magnificent in its full bloom. Had someone told her she could break off a piece of John's house and dip it into her tea, she would have happily believed Hanzel and Gretel to be stored away somewhere inside.

John had seen her from the window and was already standing at his front door, beaming from ear to ear.

'Well, hello stranger,' she said, not bothering to lock her car door, instead running over to him for a hug. 'I hope you have the tea ready.'

'I do, and an extra-large cup with your name on it. We've a lot to catch up on.'

Adela followed him inside, observing the little differences since she'd last been here. 'You got a new lamp and I like that painting.'

But it was when he opened the door to the kitchen that she noticed the biggest change. 'John, why is there a woman's scarf draped over the chair?'

He carried on about his business of pouring the tea. 'Oh, that's Nancy's. She forgot it the last time she was here.'

'Drinking plenty of tea with you, is she?'

His face was glowing. 'She is a pretty remarkable tea-drinker, I must admit.'

Adela accepted his mug of tea before lifting the tiny jug of milk from the middle of the table. 'How is everything else in the village? The place looks amazing. Who managed to convince Mad Margaret to take down her signs?'

'Only Mad Margaret could truly convince Mad Margaret of anything. Daisy came up with the idea of the hanging baskets. I make them up and Margaret now sells them in her shop. I bargained with her that if she replaced all her weird signs with baskets of flowers, then I'd maintain the ones outside her shop for her. The village has me working my butt off since you left!'

'Ah, that's great, John.' She took a large sip of tea. 'It's so good to see you. I have missed all this.'

'Well, what's going on with you? We heard about you and David. JB was keeping us updated but even he hasn't heard much from you in months. Did you find another house to hide out in? Another hermit to stalk?'

'No, actually, I stayed with my sister after I left David. Once the public realised there was no story with the waiter, the whole thing died down pretty quickly. I took your advice and decided to investigate my passions, not those of the male variety, might I add!'

He chuckled. 'What did you discover?'

'A pretty darn good novel, actually! I sent the first draft off to my publisher yesterday and now here I am.'

'What's the novel about? I'm presuming you wrote it yourself this time.'

'Hey, cheeky! Yes, all my own words.'

'And while you were writing this darned good novel, did you do any clever thinking?'

'I tried to! It was good to have time without all my previous distractions to contend with.'

He leaned back in his chair. 'On that first day I met you, we spoke about discovering one of life's greatest secrets.'

'Oh, yes, I remember,' she said, taking another sip of his glorious tea.

'And have you?'

She paused. 'I'm getting there.' *How she had missed tea with John!*

He patted her on the back. 'Well, that's a better answer than "no".'

'I guess after all our talks, as well as my own extended search for answers during these last few months, I've come to believe life is my chance to choose who I wish to be in every moment of every day. I have more control over my life than I ever before imagined, because no matter what the circumstances around me, I have the power to ask myself, "Who do I choose to be in relation to this?" in each and every situation. *I* get to choose.'

'Well, lady, finish up that cup of tea, because I'm taking you for a walk. I *choose* to enjoy that sunshine with my best student yet!'

#

John chatted to her the whole way from his house to the main street, arm-in-arm. Adela told him about her book and he gave her more details about his happiness with Nancy.

'Where are you taking me?' she said. 'Because I have to visit Daisy. And then there's somewhere else I need to go. How is he, John?'

John nodded. 'For a hermit, he's been doing pretty well.'

Adela didn't know what to say. Although longing to see him, part of her was afraid he had moved on from her or else left her behind.

They arrived at Daisy's.

'Wow.' Adela walked inside. 'Would you look at this? It's like a different place.'

'Hello, missus,' Elly shouted from the corner. 'We've run out of googleberry juice, you'll have to have some grapefruit juice instead. Tastes like shit though.'

'Hi, Elly,' Adela greeted her with a warm kiss and a hug. 'Tempting offer, thank you.'

'Well, well, look at what the cat dragged in,' Daisy exclaimed, coming out from around the other side of the counter. 'What a sight for sore eyes you are! I'd think of another couple of clichés only I'm still high from the paint fumes.'

They hugged and smiled at one another.

'Your pub's looking great. You've been busy!' Adela looked around. 'It's so much brighter and you even put some of your photos on the walls. They look fantastic down here, Daisy.'

'A few of the lads helped me with my little project. You gave me quite the appetite for change before you disappeared on us, young lady!'

'Sorry about that. I was so upset to miss the party. JB mentioned it went well when I spoke to him a while back.'

'It was a grand success for the village, all right. But a few of us didn't enjoy it so much without you. That hermit of yours was in no mood to party.'

'John says he's doing well now.'

300

Daisy sniffed. 'John would speak well of the devil himself, but yeah, I guess you could say that.'

John frowned at Daisy. 'I'm going to take Adela across the road. Want to come?'

'Mam, lift yourself up off that chair, we're getting some fresh air.' Daisy threw off her apron.

Their little group left Daisy's and walked further down the main street, towards the barn.

'The door's open!' Adela said, watching a couple saunter out into the street, giggling together over some private joke. 'He kept it open?'

They all chuckled, enjoying her reaction. She stopped and turned to them. 'Is he in here?'

'Should be,' said John. 'He likes to spend an hour or two most days pottering about inside helping Mary Mary.'

She felt like she was fourteen all over again. 'This feels weird,' she said, but Daisy nudged her forward.

'Get in there with you and see what it's like, girl.'

Adela walked into the room she hardly recognised from before. Now it was filled with little wooden tables and pretty lamps in the corners and fairy lights decorating the ceilings, with new paintings on the walls and noticeboards that were not there four months ago.

'Adela!' A girl jumped up from behind the counter.

'Toni!' Before she had time to even look at her, the girl had wrapped her arms around her.

'Let me see you,' Adela said, noticing the change in her hair colour. 'Are you actually working here?'

'In between torturing John,' she announced proudly. 'He's teaching me. I don't have to steal his plants or nothing now. We're planning a village allotment.'

'Yeah, she's lethal with a pair of pruners, that one,' added John, sticking out his tongue at Toni.

'Are you staying?' Toni asked, holding her cloth up in the air in a threatening manner. 'Think carefully about your answer!'

'Just visiting this time,' Adela said, so happy to be surrounded by this bunch of people.

'Unless you're a total moron, I'm guessing you'd be wanting to say hi to the hermit.' Toni pointed out through the patio door, into the courtyard. 'You'll find him out that way somewhere.'

'Okay, thanks. I'll catch up with you properly later.' Adela gave them all a nervous wave before opening the door and walking out into the sun-filled courtyard, which had John's green-fingered touch all over it.

She looked around her but could not see him. They were all watching from inside the barn.

'Gregory,' she called.

'Be with you in a minute,' she heard from the small shed to the right. She sat on the bench and waited, tipping her fingers against the soft, red rose petals. Had all traces of her hermit vanished? How involved with the villagers had he become? Would he be glad to see her?

'Adela…'

She lifted herself off the bench and turned to face him, glad in that moment for all her heart knew about this man. 'You still remember me, then!'

He glanced over to the patio door. She followed his line of vision and saw four eager faces squished up against the glass.

'Take a walk with me?' He led her out through the courtyard and down a gravelly path.

'You walk now?' she said, trying to keep up with his fast pace.

'What can I say, you started a trend.' He gave her a tight smile.

'How's Norman?'

'He stopped eating when you left. It took me and JB a lot of pampering to get him back interested in food.'

'And you thought he was allergic to women!' *It felt good being close to him again.* 'Still no beard…not becoming vain, I hope?'

He stopped, frowned, and then marched on once more. 'You've heard about the barn?'

She giggled. 'Slow down, I can't keep up.'

He slowed his pace.

'You gave Toni a job? I thought you all hated her?'

'Call it a moment of madness. We bonded over our loss of a mutual friend.'

'Sorry I missed the party.'

'I heard you and David broke up.'

They were approaching the grounds of his house. 'A while ago now. I got busy writing a proper book. I finished the first draft yesterday and here I am.'

'And here you are.'

'Would you like to know what my book is about?'

'What is your new book about?'

'Where are we going?' she said, spying the top of his house.

'This way, you crazy woman. Follow me and tell me about your book.'

She touched his arm. 'I know you weren't expecting me, but please can we walk a bit slower?'

There it was. The effect. That connection. He felt it too. She could see it in his eyes.

'Okay, my book is partly my way of telling the world about my grandmother being the one who really wrote my first book and partly about my own quest to figure out what my life is all about. It's about a crazy woman on the hunt for a powerful secret, in fact the grandest secret about life there ever was.'

'And is this crazy woman successful in her mission?' he said, helping her climb over a low wall.

303

She nodded. 'Of course. She has to be; she's a firm believer in happy endings.'

'And what is this grandest secret about life? What does she know that the rest of us don't? Does she make lots of lists, this woman?'

'Oh, she's a fruit-cake, let me tell you! But an organised one. You want to know the secret?'

'Damn but you're annoying,' he said, bringing her into his garden.

She looked across at the place, once a field, now covered in baby apple trees. 'You did it,' she said. 'You'll soon be eating apples of your own for breakfast.'

The apple trees brought a smile to his face. 'Poor John hasn't had a minute.'

She sat down on the back step. He seated himself beside her.

'This is beautiful, Gregory. Susan would be so proud of you.'

'What is this most amazing secret about life that your heroine has discovered?'

'There are a few more details to it than this, but it boils down to one word.'

'The grandest secret about life can be summed up in one word? The trail may have gone cold on that poor, deranged woman, I dare say.'

'Maybe,' Adela agreed. 'The publishers may decide to agree with you and kill it stone dead.'

'Or it will be a runaway success.'

'I have absolutely no doubt!'

'And what is this one word that is going to save the world once we realise its greatness?'

'Love,' she said quietly. 'Loving ourselves, loving each other, loving the whole shebang, every tree, every squirrel, every goddamn hermit.'

'You want to love *every* goddamn hermit?' he asked, turning to her.

'Why, do you know any?'

'I used to.'

She could feel his leg touching against hers. 'I became one myself these last few months. I quite enjoyed hiding away in my office, reading and typing and letting everything else fade away. I needed the break, but I've decided I'm ready to start climbing mountains again.'

'It's really good to see you.'

'You too.' She smiled. 'Have you ever thought of climbing a mountain, Gregory? It's surprisingly airy.'

'I believe I could give it some consideration.'

'You haven't swept some local girl off her feet since I left, have you?'

He shrugged, taking her hand in his. 'Only Daisy, but she doesn't count.'

'Good.'

'Why, were you thinking of staying?' he asked, standing up, still holding her hand and gently raising her up off the step. 'I know a great hotel.'

She could feel his arm wrap around her waist. He leaned down and kissed her, intensely and without hesitation.

'And you told me you didn't like kissing,' she said, their lips hardly parted.

'Did I say that?' He held her hand and led her towards his back door. 'Trust *you* to change my mind!'

About the author

Originally from Dublin, Paula Yourell now lives in Donegal, Ireland, with her musician husband and two children. She also has two step-children. She has no pets but shamelessly uses those of her extended family to entertain her kids. She may in the future acquire a turtle. She enjoys the idea of yoga more than the practicalities of it. She has been writing novels for over a decade.